I'LL BE

ESSENTIAL PROSE SERIES 155

Canada

Guernica Editions Inc. acknowledges the support of the Canada Council for the Arts and the Ontario Arts Council. The Ontario Arts Council is an agency of the Government of Ontario.

We acknowledge the financial support of the Government of Canada.

I'LL BE

CLAUDIO GAUDIO

GUERNICA
EDITIONS

TORONTO—CHICAGO—BUFFALO—LANCASTER (U.K.)
2023

Guernica Founder: Antonio D'Alfonso

Michael Mirolla, Susan Walker, editors
Cover design: Andre Jodoin
Interior design: Errol F. Richardson
Guernica Editions Inc.
287 Templemead Drive, Hamilton, ON L8W 2W4
2250 Military Road, Tonawanda, N.Y. 14150-6000 U.S.A.
www.guernicaeditions.com

Distributors:
Independent Publishers Group (IPG)
600 North Pulaski Road, Chicago IL 60624
University of Toronto Press Distribution (UTP)
5201 Dufferin Street, Toronto (ON), Canada M3H 5T8
Gazelle Book Services, White Cross Mills
High Town, Lancaster LA1 4XS U.K.

First edition.
Printed in Canada.

Legal Deposit—First Quarter
Library of Congress Catalog Card Number: 2022947899
Library and Archives Canada Cataloguing in Publication
Title: I'll be / Claudio Gaudio.
Names: Gaudio, Claudio, author.
Series: Essential prose series ; 155.
Description: 1st edition. | Series statement: Essential prose series ; 155
Identifiers: Canadiana (print) 20220442371 | Canadiana (ebook) 2022044238X | ISBN 9781771833028
(softcover) | ISBN 9781771833035 (EPUB)
Subjects: LCGFT: Novels.
Classification: LCC PS8613.A918 I45 2023 | DDC C813/.6—dc23

For my brother Rino,
who taught me how to dislodge my brain in a hurricane
and find it again on the windowsill.

203

I'm fond of life, but death is the mother lode. Decades ago I washed ashore, flew, or I was carried, in due course I learned to cook, or that's how I've chosen to tell it. A muddle, essentially, but remembering wouldn't clarify anything.

The best recipes, I've heard say, are from the continent, a little meat, and then there was no end to what we could do with potatoes. But that's probably the hunger talking, or what's left of it. It was worse in the winter, or so I imagine. These renderings have been revised countless times so they are neither accurate nor consecutive, and I don't differentiate between what did and didn't happen.

202

Life is impossible, weather permitting, and then I'll shoot myself in Idaho. The task, as I understand it, is to write the pauses, all the rage in Paris. The story, as always, will take care of itself. I've committed no crime so long as we agree on the wording. Boundless is how I'd describe the distance from the bed to this chair, from what I say to what ails me, from where I sit to the birds that fly past my window.

I position myself so as not to impede my prospects, poke and prod to better receive my instructions. It is not I, but someone, who shops for tomatoes, though I'd be hard pressed to explain who that is exactly. Sorry to introduce that fruit so abruptly, it will figure prominently in the upcoming narrative. More so than people.

I'm living the dream, the one with nobody in it, as Bixby or Bray so they'll know what to put on my tombstone. Names from a book that I must have written, or read, that difference too is not what it used to be. I blame the French, for everything really. That country, that continent, is less important now, cathedrals and a few aqueducts that still carry water, and only the occasional massacre. Europe bloated and choking on the old stories, while Washington circles the carcass.

Perhaps I'll go back there when I am done failing, spend my last years in a country that keeps its appointments. Berlin, I hear, is a good place to be punctual, but not Lithuania. The camps have been outlawed, or so I understand. All that real estate behind wire was simply unconscionable, but only after we ran the numbers. A strategy outside all proportion, beyond the rules of animal husbandry and inventory. Finally revised by men with ponderous brows because mustaches were no longer interesting.

I was born Roman, but that too is a fiction, so I have decided to die in some other language, French, perhaps, though English is bigger. The where doesn't matter. I'm here now, but that's also porous since my absence is gaining, not death exactly, perhaps what it isn't, so we can't discount it either.

I prefer to be where I'm not and other places as well, but mostly I wait in a jar, the one next to the cutlery drawer. It's easier that way to change the scenery, here and in Papua New Guinea. Italy, I've heard say, has the best tomatoes, but oceans, real ones, tend to slow me down, when I must get there by Tuesday, for instance. Happily that day is when and wherever I say it is. Then my luck continues.

Borders are less consequential nowadays, so the poor can follow the money. People without cash make the best shoppers, just not in the Hamptons. They can still shop in Manhattan seeing as the substantial people are all holed up in the sky in that city. Tokyo too would be unlivable if not for much smaller furniture. Thank god for Sweden.

I LIVE IN THE north where, forgive the repetition, I spend the winters hunting for a good tomato. Sometimes I pretend it's elsewhere, the north, of course, a tomato is just a tomato but we'll get to that later.

Nobody gets out alive from the places I mention, and what doesn't happen comes anyway. A door is a door, and sometimes it's a heart attack. Here, is the problem, the initial privation, here, regrettably, is not a destination, but we can still call it Paris. I'm there now, in a manner of speaking, cooking chicken and dicing carrots. That I have all I need is the mystery. Don't ask, is my motto, it could lead to thinking, be patient and you won't have to undergo anything. By the way, Paris is the same, chestnut trees and cafés.

I'm older now and my gathering demise is but one of many obsessions, as are the dishes. I wash them soon after each meal and before I go shopping. It's better than taking down the mayor or shooting up a hotel full of bankers. I worked in that field, a consultant to the middle because the real bosses wouldn't talk to me. Money, approximately, was all I had time for, and lunch, a real punch in the liver. Italian mostly, just like in New Jersey, and to flatter the clients I'd pronounce their names actually.

200

The world is a mixture of blood and shit, but I have heard rumours of a posthumous version, forever clean, because god loves those who round up the empties. Heaven is where the meek will be slaughtered again.

Soon I will introduce someone else to this story, the stillness eludes me so he, or she, can't be a Buddhist. A philosopher, perhaps, someone who will misconstrue things more deeply, for when I disagree with the things that I'm saying. The truth is I can distract myself with whatever is available, I'm lucky that way, the past participle or the morning shower, but not daily, when it comes to hygiene I'm still European.

Breeding ensures us a place at the table, helps us to see things in general. Culture, broadly, is why we envy the English and ambush the Iroquois. Then we wrote our story, and theirs, so we could settle in for the long haul. We cut down the trees to plant tomatoes, used the lumber to build schools, churches and museums, so indigenous peoples would know their status. We also built hotels, restaurants and golf courses, but they weren't for everyone.

Never the same war twice, as I see it. So we put all the tomahawks in those museums and took to selling guns to whoever wanted to take down the government. At West Point they still tell the story of how tomahawks became hellfire missiles, but enough about civilization. I'm out of oatmeal and it's too late to go shopping, so we'll just have to pick this up again later.

199

THIS MORNING WAS LIKE any other and so was the murmur. It sounds like drowning, if you can't hear it go jump in a river. The difference between the whirring and my erection is one will still be here when I am done flailing. After which I'll go get that oatmeal.

That grain has been around since before taxes were sheep or sacks of barley. It was here before money made everything simple, its absence specifically. Swipe and the world bends to your wishes, press *ok* and you own it. Remember, it is your index finger that drives the economy.

The injured will ferry the mighty and the rich will finally own everything, but that too is just an idea, and how they got it is nobody's business. They'll come for your house after the downsizing, when shopping finally gives way to austerity. When it's too late to take back that leaf blower.

Less is more, but we have since reversed that maxim because it's bad for Amazon, the company not the tropics. The strategy is still disputed, grist for those hardcover analyses that follow every recession. The correction, as they say in Lower Manhattan, and then it's damn near impossible to burn every copy.

Hunger in Bangladesh is what keeps New York humming, but I'll discuss that with Bob when he gets here. The war never happened is what I'll tell Kiki, she's a child sent by a squirrel or the universe to teach me everything. She looks like that little girl who ran faster than napalm and then won the Pulitzer. Bob is the philosopher I mentioned earlier but you can call him Bill if you want to. Kiki exists so we don't have that option, but I wish her name was Betsy, or Bo, in my world everything begins with a B, the names notwithstanding.

198

BRAINS, LIKE EGGS, ARE so much stronger after boiling, and before they are eaten. Speaking of sizzling, of music in general, Scriabin played the piano this morning while I made breakfast. God by another name is what I took from his phrasing except he, like me, was a real ace at not saying it. Clearly the composer wasn't here actually, he's been pushing up daisies for more than a century, and he was crazy. There never seems to be enough room for his immensity, Scriabin's, that is, whereas god, also dead, just isn't that complicated.

I didn't have eggs this morning, not after that paragraph. I opted for cold cereal and blueberries, with a dollop of yogurt. I have no issue with yogurt. After breakfast I washed the dishes, as always – note the consistency – purchased from various and sundry second-hand shops, vintage, if you live in the gallery district. Then I talked myself out of a shower while I made coffee.

What I do and don't do are the same thing exactly, so I'm never confused and it doubles my options. I am object and witness to my omission, I like how it accentuates my nonexistence. Bob has yet to admit his absences, I've never liked what the knowing does to his thinking. Friendships have been lost over less, but why fret while grocers are still bursting with produce. I polished off the cereal and downed my coffee, then I grabbed some cash so Chiquita Brands International couldn't track my purchases.

A lapse is a hole and the moment lived, then I string them together like popcorn. Each day I do something familiar, touch every cup and fork, and then again in the evening. This routine attenuates my immobility, before I am distracted by whatever is stirring. I'll say the same thing tomorrow because nothing succeeds like the plural. Some wiser than I have called this living, they are survived by the cutlery.

I was on a roll, in a manner of speaking, revelling in my forgetting and the day was finding its repetition. Half notes mostly, pranks from the pot drawer, puns in the pantry. I use them to turn statues into clay again, and talking out loud.

In speaking without knowing there is still the hint of form, the stench of a self. There are things I can't bury. I learned that in therapy, a blessed unravelling, or another take on the muddle. It's a good idea for the mind to find its body, that's how I know I'm not a hedgehog and why, for example, I prefer oatmeal to cabbage.

The soul is of no help at all, after the fall it hightailed it to China, now it's a butterfly, or an ox. In the west its absence is still gaining, as in Nevada, or from wherever we wage war remotely. Baghdad is burning again, and from the inside of twisted buildings people are reminded that steel is just flimsy. Death out of the blue because the empire must be seen to do nothing, sun steered, to close the distance between us.

YESTERDAY I PULLED DOWN a star, stuck it on the ceiling and painted it silver. Then I painted over it. After which I made myself a sandwich, chicken, better yet tuna, and ate it while watching television. Al Jazeera, though the government says it's un-American, unlike Murdoch's programming because he's Australian.

I swear that star is still there. Unlike the sandwich it need not be here to appear, and switching that chicken to fish will help me remember. As I walked up the stairs I knew all I had left to do was make sense of the stutter. Nothing is something and then fatal in the story I'm telling and soon, I hope, we'll know the point of my saying that.

I can still recall the night I took down Bin Laden. I did have chicken then, on rye with a side of store-bought tomatoes. A Tuesday, I think, or a Friday that goes by that name anyway. Early May so the pickings were slim and summer was all in the future.

The next day I finished what I started in accordance with Islamic tradition. The burial, at sea, but that may be hearsay because nobody saw the body on television. I also watched a program about truffles in Tuscany while eating ice cream. What better than food to mark both occasions, that's how I reason.

I err on the side of not knowing anything, variously indexed for scholastic endeavour. The world at the end of the world, and sometimes I call it the present. Empty is, because it's unbreakable. I have yet to hear anything that belies this delirium, a speaking in common, for instance. Though I hope it doesn't happen, it would take forever to unlearn what I won't know then.

I prefer eating to anything and anything to people. I'm doing all I can to delay their arrival, my friends in particular, but I may have said that already, or something similar. I don't answer the door, or the phone, in case they do or don't call respectively. I'm seven feet long in the story I'm telling, but that's just so I can see around corners.

Two of me is the condition I'm going for, one for the rack and the other to bring in the groceries. I was wrong to think there'll always be a there and a when. When there's no one left, say, to empty the trash and people our cemeteries. Who then will discharge the will of the tyrant. The victim is always guilty of not being guilty and what happens is not yet information. We are the governed, and therefore suspect.

196

SOMETIMES I TURN ON the TV and walk out of the room. There should be speech, I think, but no good will come of my listening. People are dying on all the wrong channels, so I've had to kill them again in this sentence. In a letter to the editor I spoke in praise of moguls, of madness, of power in general. Through you sir, madam, to your boss in Australia.

Mr. Murdoch, what isn't is still news to us, so please take your foot off our throats and show us the pieces on the cutting room floor. I'll rearrange them with just enough words leftover to write your obituary after you jump from the Trump tower. Then I'll go back to writing about ducks or tomatoes from the point of view of the squirrels outside my window.

The president is at it again. Muslims, he says, are infiltrating the homeland. But I think he's feeling a little nostalgic for those years in Hanoi. When the empire dispatched its black soldiers because homosexuals weren't allowed in the army. Luckily there are no lack of places in which Raytheon could empty its warehouses, freeing up space for more dazzling technology. After which Nestle will step up production of their bottled water, an unusual moment, or an age-long cycle. It takes a disaster to create a market.

The regular army will secure the perimeter so trucks can move freely. Filled to the brim with that water and corn syrup because the government does not subsidise spinach. But it doesn't matter now that corn is chicken, chocolate, everything really, therefore standard issue in our war against children. The chocolate is used to discern a child from a sack of potatoes. Potatoes, apparently, will not be persuaded.

A think tank in Yemen is a sleeper cell in Manhattan and in Salem it was a two-headed cleric, or a three-headed dragon. I can't say for sure because so little remains of our solutions. An early morning knock on the door, cattle cars, or Kabul in a Subaru, and when the smoke clears children still strut their anonymity, dragons their invisibility. Some things do better when we don't see them, but that doesn't mean they can't contribute new sounds to the language.

In Kiki's world there's no difference between pie and lasagna, and Grand Central is in the school yard adjacent to the fire station. A ticket will get you to Salem in ten seconds flat, but don't look for those clerics. They followed the burning to Mississippi, the place not the movie, and then to Kampala. When in Salem do look for those dragons, they're not there either but Kiki assures me their lack abounds.

Our kids are the future, said the first lady, my butcher, baker and gardener. Kiki is all of those things already and the engineer on the fastest train ever. I asked, but she has no interest in the presidency. On Friday we were in Moscow and home before seven, then I visited that city again, but this time on television.

The rich were driving Audis next to soldiers with automatic weapons. The poor still had their bundles. On the BBC experts argued the plight of Russian hostages, specifically and then generally, as per the rules of journalism. They were outraged over last week's, or was it this morning's massacre. The horror, one panelist said twice, and that's when I realized she was Francis Ford Coppola.

195

WHAT'S GOOD FOR HOLLYWOOD is good for the heartland, America and the world, said Reagan, my movies especially. I have it on good authority the Gipper is still making that speech on Jupiter. Soon we'll know for sure, said Kiki, after I finish my rocket ship.

There are secrets between this world and the next, but knowing them would only put out my eyes. Still, there's no reason to moan and who am I to say there's been too much killing. Presidents come, are soon gone, and then decades before we can know the body count.

From where I live, sit mostly, the world begins at the sidewalk, between two oceans and then Asia in every direction. Next to my chair is a large window with four panes and no shutters, they are sealed units. Double hung windows trap flies, it's where they stop to rest, and by rest I mean die. On the other side of the glass are three Norwegian spruce trees. All day long birds come to perch, and they are traversed by squirrels, rodents really. We do not speak, or the time of our speaking is passed.

On Thursday, approximately, a unicorn promised to tell me everything, unicorns can't talk, I said to him … they did in your last book … which one … how many have you written … that one, and Moby Dick … really … maybe more … I see … do you … no … did you read it … which one … either … don't be ridiculous … then how do you know about the unicorns … I was there … oh … as the whale … no you weren't … the mouse then … that was you … is there a problem … I no longer talk to rodents … since when … it's in the last paragraph … I see … and the mouse was very unpleasant … that's your opinion … also corrupt … that was the war.

Prowling is so much more productive in the heart of the city, though I have been known to revise where that is exactly. I like to step out with a long sharp object, as I wouldn't want to stumble on a death without redress. I live in Chinatown because I can't read the signs, and it's less likely America will go to war with its creditors. An enclave adjacent to all the main hospitals, and from where I said goodnight to my mother.

I am in good health, statistically speaking, half by half way there which by all calculations is here, with you, should I need an alibi. To the east is my favourite market, to the north is this town's great big university. My son attends classes there so I know what books to mention, or for some other reason. At all other times it's just me in this house, and no zebras.

There are rules, well and good for the living, but the dead have stopped listening. It's not an issue, they say, since this world is a place in between. But what in hell is so important they can't visit their grandkids. A few from each generation returned from the ether, that shining city on a hill, call it what you will for, despite our attestations, it belongs to no nation.

Personally I prefer the smaller eternities, the distance, say, between me and a cucumber. Then nothing can hurt me, except maybe a tumor. I could also cite trucks and buses, but I generally see those coming.

Speaking of cucumbers, yesterday I renewed my commitment to vegetables, soon after my chat with the unicorn. It was he who told me, before catching a flight back to Jupiter, that the Gipper was running for office again in the afterlife.

All of that happened, I explained to Kiki, but at first she didn't believe me. Jupiter is just too far for a unicorn, she said, and that ticket would be very expensive … he flew standby … I see … and he was tired … of flying … of talking.

194

AT THE END OF each day, in the palpable dark, I walk to the store for rapini, spinach on alternate Tuesdays. The night is a canopy, I built it to shield me from heaven while I forage for the things I just mentioned, and cheesecake. Routines to ensure my equilibrium, or not, which is much less disturbing. Before I make my way home I stop for coffee, and sort words or sugar granules that fall from my spoon before I hurl them to destinations unknown.

The places I've been, are not worth mentioning. Saskatchewan, but I didn't learn anything, all through the night I could hear the wolves howling. When in Rome, I still think

I'm in Saskatoon. In the eternal city they use scaffolding to climb down to the ruins, and then trowels to disentangle the bodies. Ever so carefully because once petrified there's no telling a stone from a femur. Whereas in Saskatchewan they don't know a column from a cannoli and, if they did, they wouldn't call it breakfast.

I was begotten, but it depends on who's asking, every stain has its genesis and soon we'll no longer need passports. In the future our arrivals will precede all our itineraries, we will already be where we're going. I'm there now, growing in bits and bytes across a million mainframes, in the cloud, on the ground in southwest Baltimore.

Fort Meade, said Edward Snowden, is bigger than a bread box and smaller than a mountain, so long as we don't mention the tiered twelve-acre bunker beneath it. Two buildings, glass cubes for the Gipper, targets come to mind, that's how it is with architecture but, whatever you do, don't buy your drones on the internet.

For a time these streets were my father, my mother a warm hypodermic and then any womb that would have me. I've worked hard to remain unemployable, below the radar but, to be fair, this country is safe. No one I know has fallen from a sniper's rifle, and not since 1970 have tanks roamed the streets. But that was in another language so it may not have happened. The French shouldn't kidnap the English, is all there was to learn from that, from anything really.

There are so few calamities that break the skin north of the forty-ninth parallel, not to suggest we don't support death in general. The government has our proxy, scalable, of course, god knows our partners to the south can deliver the numbers but, as with death anywhere, cost is a factor.

All morning long I've had a headache, I get them whenever I have a hankering to see my physician. This city is where death goes to sleep, doctors are free to hit and miss while the patient contemplates the knot in their hospital gown. In the north dying is easy, we're rich, you see, and we have the technology. Whereas in butt-fuck Florida you have to pay money to bury your kin, unless they get eaten by alligators.

Luck is just another word for proximity, like rings on a tree, so I'm fine with the warming because the earth will burn from the middle. That's why I'm moving to Nunavut, more on that later. I also bought a ranch in Texas in case the melting's an ice age, right next to my favourite wartime president. Now I'm set for the end and the infinite. The correction, as they say at the Chicago School of Economics.

192

I CAME HERE TO scatter these fragments, to see what there is when there's nothing. The play's the thing, said Hamlet, and some other stuff that has yet to be thought or is still being written. I know for he told me so on the telephone.

The stage is no place from which to take down a king, is the last thing I said to him … how do you know … I stormed the palace … when … in my last book … which one … Les Misérables … which palace … Buckingham … wrong country … are you sure … reasonably … the queen wasn't there … you mean the king … do I … yes … absent is a good look for a monarch … that's true … and the moneyed … the what … the rich … they're one and the same … not anymore.

Everything that prince said plus a dollar will get you a coffee, so long as you don't buy it at Starbucks. Civilization was invented in Pakistan, China and Ethiopia, but that was before Celtics and Saxons knew they were English. No matter, it has since been rethought in Seattle, the future already and to come, so say the good people at Amazon – the one that's not burning.

Speaking of Ethiopia, Starbucks is taking a bite out of poverty. Pennies per cup are more than enough now that their logo, that green longhaired woman, dots every city like birds on a wire. We'll check in later to see how they're doing.

My own plans for the poor and the maimed are all in a heap. I need a bit of time, a little help, a dose of therapy to air out my noodle. Until then I'll temper the blurring with a nod or a question, prick the air with my index finger. I am so tired of not knowing everything.

Like Starbucks, I too wish to pull a worldview from my anus, I am death, for example, and therefore indestructible. There's nothing like coffee to keep them big thoughts rolling, except maybe cocaine or methamphetamine. Blueberries too, but then the genius in me is more subtle, less noticeable. At any rate, all of my solutions are temporary, like the planet, say, or the sunset.

A flicker, or nearly, is the bulk of the visible, squeeze your head through that needle and you're bound to see something. The stars in Nunavut, say, but that's my idea so don't all of you think it. Besides, there are just as many stars in the city, except they're invisible. More sky to chew on, said Kiki.

After Einstein zero too is a multiple, though bankers have known that for centuries. That's why its permutations are still out of reach for most people. Nothing is the new plenty, all the rage at that school in Chicago, the one I mentioned earlier so I could bring it up again in this sentence. I like how Albert's math disappears, its expression, and what's good about that is the rich no longer have to make anything.

THERE'S A HOLE IN my head dear Liza, I put it there. What I don't know is like riding a bike for me now, and knowing is like riding a bike with a rhinoceros. The universe travels at twenty years per second exactly, or faster, that's a fact, but we'll still need the science to prove it. I'll leave those computations to some astrophysicist, I'm sure one will get here eventually, subject to editing. The evidence is due for a reckoning, or a ploughing.

Everyone is tired and poor, or rich and living longer than ever. We are perfectly situated to annihilate all other species. That's a fact too, with distinct ramifications. Soon I'll introduce my analyst, now, since there's no denying the thing I just mentioned. As for those disappearing species, they'll simply come back as commodities.

I have fought and lost the next war already, fired all of my weapons before I got here, so I may have mixed up the order. The experience was a little uneven, I took the word of a bird, a swallow specifically, he told me he had the ear of the president.

I used to sit in taverns, remained deaf to the voices around me, and to the violence in Asia. Frolicked instead in my quarantine, but that was years ago. Don't see things, I said, and don't listen either, damn near impossible after what that bird told me and now that I'm alone in this house. Here there are only answers unless I change the channel, but they just reel me back in with Family Guy.

You should try reading, said my analyst, or listening to music … I don't understand … instead of watching television … because they're more discreet … more calming … less traceable … I don't think we're talking about the same thing … intelligence … and what do you know of that … it is what I say it is … that's true … it doesn't exist … possibly … I could report on the Mexicans … what Mexicans … under Orange County …. you mean in Orange County … there too.

In the streets the parade goes on without me and the past never hesitates, does not ask my permission. I have wrestled both bears and alligators, advised a terrorist, he runs a food truck close to where I buy my tomatoes. Commerce, he thinks, is the great equalizer. I told him to just try and fit in until his children can take up the mantle.

When something is over it begins again, that's why I'm keeping my pantaloons and matching khakis. Blanche, my ex, more on her later, told me they'll never go out of style in New Zealand. Then she went to British Columbia to live with the redwoods, but I can't talk about that now. I have bigger fish to fry.

Amazon is not delivering books in eternity, said Herbert, he's a poet from Poland. No zip codes in heaven I guess, but I'm not bothered unless by books he meant television. At which point I'll trade in my khakis for jockeys and go to bed early. Then there'll be no time to read poetry.

The only good Mexican is a dead Mexican, is what we used to say about black people. There's dust on the farm and worshippers aplenty, the same old signs of the apocalypse pending. But I don't think the Huns, or was it the Romans, will come back this time to open our tracheas.

Monsanto is making a play for the breadbasket, soon it will have been theirs to begin with. Their patents will blow into competing acreage and bees will take one for the team or the queen. Bees, like people, don't know how to die for no reason.

Wall Street will assume the work of distribution, of hunger specifically. What they're peddling won't leave the silos, except through a chimney. From Cameroon they smell the wheat burning, and it sure is sweet when the wind comes right behind the rain.

Little by little is how I kill an hour. I smell smoke, said the pear to the apple, we should get word to the pineapple. I don't think we can, replied the apple, it can't hear us speaking and the narrator favours tomatoes.

There's money in garbage, in what we don't eat, I know for I used to be a gangster on television. Tony was my name then, a big house in Jersey, two kids and a wife, a nurse, strung out on opiates, though I may be conflating dramas. Still, had I known I would have gotten her the help that she needed. I died suddenly, approximately, twice actually, though the first time was more of a suggestion, a cut to black, as they say in the movie business.

Today I'm called Isaac, like in the bible, before the onset of mechanized killing, round about the time the Egyptians invented silos. Death then was no more than a flutter, a twitch in the grass, and Abraham was still living inside that thing that he did.

189

I've had to go back a long way to come back correctly. As a child I pulled on the wings of a butterfly, they stopped flapping so I reattached them immediately, but all I could restore was their symmetry. I guess some things weren't meant to be after I killed them. The universe is vast and throws nothing away, but it is I who will decide what is trivial.

I turned on some music to silence the pear but by then I couldn't hear myself listening. I see things differently now that I'm older, but I'm within spitting distance of not seeing anything. What soldiers have been regarding for centuries and what we learned again in Southeast Asia. That bodies burn brighter on a pyre of magnesium, but seeing that will singe your cornea. No matter, I put on my cap in fair and foul weather, it keeps my brains in my head while I'm shopping, and while I watch the news.

My neighbour could be a terrorist, the first lady is losing the war on obesity, and whatever became of Barbara Eden from I Dream of Jeannie. A question for the Vietnam generation, or what's left of it. Those crazy decades before nine-eleven, when it was possible to lose a war, lose a war, lose a war, and put it on television.

Nowadays we just watch each other thanks to YouTube, or is it the metaverse. But I can still remember when phones were phones, laptops were typewriters and mainframes were mostly for killing. As for Jeannie, you can still check her out on the internet.

188

I HARDLY SHAKE EXCEPT after people, so why the itch for the two-legged critter, for Bob, in particular. Everything is so much more interesting when I talk to my television, or a sandwich. That's me and my robe, now we're a threesome. Still, I'm always ready to do the town, from my little oasis, my Costa Concordia. There are heroes behind every catastrophe but sometimes they row to shore early.

I watched while that fated liner ran aground. Munched, in real time, as the last passengers jumped or climbed down from that oversized tub. Except for the thirty-two who were still sunning themselves by their ankles. I don't mind the upside-down or the horizontal, here it's the dancing that kills you. Or so said that German philosopher who thought his pen was a hammer. Wrongfully, in my view, since intellectuals rarely do their own carpentry and if that sophist could build we'd all be in cages.

Sunday mornings I watch nature shows, hunting and fishing in the Deep South, where accountants in battle fatigues have been lying in wait since the mid fifties. They review, recommend and sell gear to like-minded compatriots.

There's nothing better than the promise of carrion to bolster the love men feel for each other. Wildlife populations have been declining in recent decades, hence the double barrel to shoot down a quail. Excessive in my view, but feel free to think otherwise. Opinion is never opinion enough when discussing a takedown, even if that quail is from Costco.

There's the kill, the thrill, but the skill is in the tracking, the carving, though perhaps I'm confusing the wetlands in Florida with the Sudan. There's no denying the similarities, no mistaking a killer's enthusiasm, except to say those birds have wings to fly, while the Sudanese are always in season.

LATELY IT'S BEEN GETTING dark before dinner. Winter is coming but I don't speak for New Zealand. It's just me now, and the experts on television. They're discussing school shootings and the second amendment. They can't agree on anything, but that is the new format. Clearly, I like faking it as much as the next gal, but there are ways and ways to say nothing. Or what producers call the first, second and third rule of broadcasting, not talking is the thing they can't manage.

Murder just wouldn't be the same without its pundits. But the people who work for Ted Turner have never been waterboarded, they have no reason to lie. America is not killing or locking up journalists, at least not yet, or not in Atlanta. As for the victims, the kids who don't make the cut, be it in Kabul or Chicago, the earth will preserve their innocence in granite or carbon, as in oil or a diamond. The people we kill are not ready for primetime.

Incidentally, I'm also a stringer, a hack and a Stanford graduate, unless and until I say otherwise. We had different masters at the academy, professors instead of editors, and all the same sponsors. We were young and ready to mobilize, it was just easier then to blow smoke up our asses.

Nowadays I prefer the meaningless bustle, but it should have some bounce. The news will only prolong disaster and it's corrupt. Talking is how everything slips through my fingers, how I empty a room. I need that which never was and so I will never have done with conjecture, this swill of hilarity and terror.

A story is what happens to what's happened already and the worst is always to come. The people are just details on which to hang a hat, a cat, or the weather. Should anyone here walk like a duck, talk like a duck, they're probably Mexican.

DUCKS WILL NEVER SAY what they're thinking, but that's not why we eat them. We roast them because they go well with cabbage. As to their opinion on the matter, translations from those quacks to English have not been reliable. Again, I blame the academy.

Kiki and I are working on the problem. She's mastered the phonology, the cackling, whereas I have yet to form those syllables, that quack in particular. Its meaning we've allocated it to inscription in general, since neither exist but they function. At least that's how I'll explain it to Bob when he gets here. Philosophers do not yet have an ear for the garbled so, until then, it is we who must carry them.

During Bush's war, the one we're still fighting, I was a hostage in Babylon, and later that morning Blanche and I went for coffee and pastry. A little out of the way café for the compulsively hip, the decor seemingly random to subvert its own pretext.

I digress. My desert captors were stubbornly silent, me too, until they mentioned my genitals. That's when I started talking, without pause, giving scope to the cavalry. They arrived just in time to show me, and them, the past that comes later. Not to suggest history is provisional, since what we do, what we did, lives in the body of others.

Nations rise from behind a little smoke and a banner, that's also how they fall, making room for new stakeholders. That's why the old wars don't matter, unless you're an Algonquian still stuck in Manhattan. In the Congo they're hunting women, the Security Council has agreed to be outraged, provided all delegates understand, said Angela Merkel, the Congo is not Berlin.

I don't see things as they are. Where there are airfields I see birds sucked into even bigger birds weighed down by hellfire missiles. Projectiles fast enough to be motionless, to reverse the earth's spinning. How fucking poetic, said Blanche, but there was a time when that line would have led straight to her thighs.

From my window I follow a cobble footpath to the road, the stones are from India because Italian granite is much too expensive. How those rocks got here is nobody's business, but I'd assume the worst. Suffice to say it took months to find a compliant supplier.

The gardener - I'm rich you see - planted two miniature pine trees where that path meets the sidewalk. They're indigenous to the region, though the dominant species were more likely deciduous. It's hard to say because most trees were cut down when they built this city, concurrent with the genocide that was happening already.

The remainder of the grounds are variously adorned, and in the back we planted cedars. But those little pines at the foot of the walkway are a brilliant green and today, like most days, a child stopped to touch them, but this time I cried.

These are the same words I spoke yesterday, I place them in rows like potatoes, but it's the spaces in between that grow bigger. The same thing happened in Northern Ireland, to the words I mean, the spuds simply rotted.

Blanche likes potatoes. It was she who told me to bandy pizza for tubers, over a plate of tofu and spinach. She waited for dessert to announce she was leaving me. She's not here anymore, so I cannot abide by her counsel.

London rising, in Belfast this time, since Boston is no longer British. Governments plan, but it is we who must finish things, by force, by consensus. One walks the other and then we get to talking, it's a kind of leapfrogging about the weather and the absence of money. Your name too was right up our alley, swing a dead cat and you're bound to hit somebody. Join us, or we will take a bat to your absence.

Everything disappears before it reaches my noodle but, like the Irish, I can really draw out a minus. Oxygen is all it takes to prolong a syllable, bone and tissue to these orphaned sounds. I won't mention Beckett because it might upset Brian. He's from

British Columbia, a cultural analyst, says Wikipedia, so a critic approximately. Something, is the worst thing that can happen to literature.

Moving on. In Belfast there's no light between a saint and a killer, and they like you even less if you're neither. While there I waited, not to say I did nothing, it's not the same thing. I split the room and played it, rolled the dice and spared my larynx, until everyone was seeing double.

That was a long time ago, post Finnegan - but I didn't catch his meaning - before we tried everything. Roundabout the first ceasefire, a Tuesday in 1994, a Wednesday actually, but I don't see the difference. After which a legion of BBC shutterbugs and a few independents set up in Paris to take down a princess. I was in a Volkswagen, approximately, but I can't tell you where I was the day they shot Kennedy because I didn't yet speak the language.

184

In the eighties I received an all round education in those taverns I spoke about earlier, and in the nineties I outgrew higher learning. In coffee houses and in darkened lecture halls we ate, spat and shat the mosaic, unless it was the sprouts we were eating. Tolerance our mantra and the new tyranny

Soon the earth would love us all equally, so I bought houses from the meagre, immigrants, because they never could afford this city. To ease their transition I showed them pictures of what people like me did to Brooklyn. I gutted and sold those boxes to low hanging coconuts. To progressives and hipsters, because a liberal will always pay more than the liberal adjacent.

There are things, Horatio, I can't say in this language. So I'll say them as a giraffe. There is madness and sanity in my genealogy, though the latter has not been diagnosed. The subjunctive is how I stay nimble, and blueberries, though I may have said that already. They're good for the brain, them synapses, and that's the only other thing I learned in the eighties.

Yesterday I had lunch in the kitchen and dessert in the study. Outside my window I watched the clouds gather. A spider entombed a fly while another fly waited, loosely stitched elsewhere in its web. Both flies twitched and succumbed, or so it seemed. Defeat is not a word flies understand, nor will the spider report a victory. At sunrise all three were dead in its web. The arthropod should have eaten one of the flies, I reasoned. But I'm not a spider, for I woke up that morning with a name next to everything.

Nothing lasts forever, that's why we switched to a faith-based economy, or what we call money. What's important is those flies knew what to do, no fuss, no muss. Whereas the spider worked all night to secure the food supply for the upcoming weather, and then collapsed from exhaustion.

Such scenes were choreographed in the blood, before god, when death was still permanent. Nowadays you have to swear allegiance to something, the clan or Jesus, why not both, before catching that little black train to nowhere. Your wife will still be here, statistically speaking, even if she is a Chevy. Then don't worry, that heap is now vintage so it too will do better without you.

183

EVENTUALLY I WILL LOSE the murmur, the one I came in with. After that spiders will still spin, but not the one I just told you about. I take my mornings slow, hesitate before leaving my room. Soon this night table will be my home, and then the bed at the end of a spoon. Before I go I'll thank my wife because she divorced me, but the doctor just tracks in more dirt. It's true he's good with a knife but I doubt he can steady a pistol. It's best I tell him now how it ends.

Kill me, I said … that's what I'm doing … I see … slowly … is that necessary … so you can get close to everything … I'm close enough … quietly … why … so we don't hear you speaking … I have things to say … you don't … I see … do you … what should I do … wait … like a monk … like a scar … I wouldn't know about that.

Others will get here eventually. My friends, in particular, are the glue, the horsemeat in this hamburger. Luckily what they do or say is at my discretion entirely. They won't love me either, but I'm not bothered since I couldn't be happier. My friends are happy too, though I'd hoped, by now, they'd be over it.

The trouble in Syria does help mitigate their bliss a little, that's why I never stop talking about it. Those wailing women are a real kick in the kidney, elsewhere, is how I'd characterize their predicament. That country is a hotbed of archeology but here, in the West, we don't mourn the ancients. Syria is just another place that needs fixing, before we dispatch the next busload of Norwegian tourists.

182

Recently I've taken to watching the news in Korean. It makes no difference to my understanding, all speaking is foreign. From the bedchamber to my desk and then to the television, though occasionally I walk to the corner. With Shakespeare, but please don't tell Brian – that critic I told you about earlier – I wouldn't want him to think me pretentious.

Thinking is the problem, what they call coding in Palo Alto, the nomenclature of our collective stupidity. Twitter is how the goose took down the gander, and Hillary was her name-o. Technology runs wild, brazen, as in the names that I'm dropping, and will again, so you know what's coming.

I blame Starbucks for rousing the competition, a scribbler will convene on a meme, or a latte, faster than a Texan on

Jonestown. Coffeehouses are what Brian and I have in common, the evolution, the expansion of the Parisian salon. Of culture, broadly, and you can use it to bludgeon your old uncle Charlie.

I'm talking about civilization, the light as it escapes a sarcophagus. Or the fixture above my dining room table, without which I couldn't count my tomatoes. I wrote those lines while waiting for Blanche at Starbucks, next to a blue-haired film student critiquing an episode of Family Guy. People like that don't see people like me, and I feel no compulsion to mitigate my genocidal orthodoxy. I go there because they can't see me, and for the pumpkin spice latte.

God goes there too, and one day we got to talking. What's going on here, he asked … tweeting … what's that … what we used to call speaking … to who … no one … about what … everything … I understand … I thought you might … in heaven we call that string theory … makes sense … it doesn't actually … I see … you don't.

Deities don't like change, so I waited until he was hopped up on coffee to give him the lowdown. You could still win this thing, I said … what thing … there's been a spike in your key demographic … the poor … that's right … the wretched … they're one and the same now … what do you need from me … the word … how much time have I got … all of it … one word … fewer if possible … you might be confusing me with the Buddha … well … well what … what's the word … no … no what … that's the word … makes sense … it doesn't actually … even better.

I'm for and against consciousness, at one and averse to the classics. But I didn't have to read them because I believed what the critics were saying. I would like to know more of what came before god started loving us. The rituals, the dancing, those maddened festivals. What the Greeks could do with a goat was simply marvelous, apparently, though, to be clear, none were harmed in my saying that.

Onward, said Beckett, but he didn't mean it, gravity is the thing he knew perfectly, nothing but the nothing apart from the wandering. The future generally, the nineties precisely, a theatrical blunder or Didi's level best to fix the approaching. He simply needed to know whether or not there'd be others.

The future again, so I changed the dates on all my devices. When the universe loses my address I'll plant a garden. With tomatoes and string beans aplenty I'll double, nay triple, my chances for a prize that will not be given.

When I go out I'll leave the door wide open and tell someone, a woman, for instance, I'll be back by eleven. She'll acquaint me with what I wanted to say and then she'll stick around for the bluster. I'll stop after she tickles my ear and after the government allocutes to the body count. How clear this life when there's no one to talk to.

THIS CITY IS ENORMOUS, bigger still by the light of the moon, but I can't say for sure because the brink keeps on moving. Luckily there are plenty of skyscrapers to guide me, and the windows are sealed so there are no falling capitalists.

I once followed my shadow all the way to the Rockies. When the skies were overcast I walked the rails, interrupted by silos next to endless fencing. My plans were to talk to Blanche about everything, to get me some more of that ear tickling. She had become obsessed with water and avocados from Mexico but, from her emails, I already knew not to eat them.

The time we spent together in those mountains was a dream, but that counts now that I'm in therapy. It all disappeared in the morning and then I reinvented it after two cups of coffee. Then again on the couch in my analyst's office, where finally I had to decide, then edit, what Blanche and I talked about.

I'm in the kitchen counting the coins I keep in a tin behind similar tins, in case there's a robbery. After I determine what to do with that money I'll pin a note to my ear, so as not to spoil the surprise that comes later. I won't see it, is the short of it, but it would have been even shorter had I not said it. It's hard not to sneak a peek at that memo, now that there'll be a hole in my ear to remind me.

I live in one room at a time. To sleep I count sheep and I don't wear a nightshirt. Sometimes I let in the wolf and we eat in the kitchen. Over coffee he asks if I think he's sexy, or better yet edgy, but I keep all answers to myself, and the phrasing I get from Hank Williams.

I have nothing but respect for the man and nothing to report. The distance between us is perfect, that's how it is with dead people. Music is the celebration of departure itself, unless it's something different. Hank and I meet in his songs, lonesome symmetries clamouring for love, here and in infinity. Still, it's best not to get too close to those who have a stake in forever, the icecaps are melting and who knows what other talent lies buried.

180

THE SMALLER THE SPACE the brighter the light, Kafka said, or should have said. Now imagine how bright his afterlife condo. That's why I'm moving to an igloo in Nunavut, unless I live there already. I see no reason to speak consecutively but, if we're to believe the preceding, there will be plenty of light in my little ice house. From there I'll quote the Czech master precisely, follow his path to the end. Death under cover of writing, or a hypnotised beetle, but Kafka is Kafka, said Brian, that's how I know I'm not him.

Brian is this city's chronicler, umpire to the avenues, a legend of at least one defunct patio. A fellow of some order in British Columbia, he's climbed the pinnacle to café culture. I forgot to duck, to roll, when last he turned on his faucet, that's how he got into this story.

One thousand years ago this morning I, like most people, wrote a book no one would publish. I was the narrator and the protagonist, that is to say I did all the talking because I didn't like what the other characters were saying. *Progress, From the Pliocene to the Present*, but a book is not a pamphlet ostensibly.

I'm sure Brian would have come a-calling had I and that folio become famous. But the arbiters, the keepers of truth and its heaping refused to acknowledge its greatness. So I went in search of that fortune I spoke about earlier and, by then, I needed more money for therapy.

Your thinking is a little fragmented, said my analyst, after I had lucre to pay him … really … too many voices … how many … two, so far … that's all … I don't understand … I thought there'd be more … really … how much for a third … what … a fourth … that's not how this works … can we get rid of both … both what … voices … and then … something better … how would we know … is that important … is what important … our knowing … probably not … let's do that then.

Back to what matters. Between me and my Asian commodities are four billion poor people. The frontlines, the grease in the combine, that's why they're indispensable and why we can't see them. When towers rise, or fall, it is they who will be made to erect the scaffolding and install the new windows. They are the economy stupid, but given strides in technology and capital mobility we no longer need to promise them anything.

There is a time to work and a time to learn, and then there's that time I stared down a racoon for a pizza. My big brother told me there were no racoons in Mussolini's Calabria, just rolling blackouts and rats that tasted like chicken. He told me other things too, which we'll get to eventually.

Sooner or later the insane will join the indigent and together they'll march on the gallery district, the village, the clientele, as we say in the property business. The meagre are rethinking high school civics, the agreements they made with the rest of us. They're attending meetings in church basements, while lunatics keep vigil from ATM vestibules. Used clothing is not vintage, is but one of many concessions they're seeking, and heaven help anyone caught speaking with an upward inflection.

Whimsy is mostly for white people, since nobody else understands it. We wield the stick and the carrot, especially in so called public spaces. We put lighted pathways where there used to be shadows, planters next to benches with multiple armrests so no one will fall asleep accidentally.

The canopy too must be protected, those magnificent oaks, maples above a growing number of one way streets. Followed by the inevitable uptick in austere cafés and boutiques filled to the brim with your grandmother's satins.

Be the one, is the idiot's mantra, and thanks to real time connectivity it's so much easier to garner a following. If you don't do it right the first time I suggest you try again as a Joe Rogan. There's money in it too, pennies, or part thereof, per click, subject to copyright and community standards. The people who make the news and they who watch it are the same, finally, so anybody can be a real world vigilante.

178

VIOLENCE COMES NATURALLY TO smart people, to expression in general. The media's job is to deliver the story as product, otherwise known as the people. This is a theory that's not studied at Stanford, it's assumed. I was there as a teacher, or a janitor, I wish I could be more specific.

Let's agree I too am a journalist and that this is my story you're hearing. Reasonable, handily, since the government now meets in my living room. Ergo I'm perfectly situated to attend every briefing, with a little something for when I get peckish.

Every day is Tuesday but not all Tuesdays are equal, or Tuesday, for that matter. There are days when I do and days when I don't buy tomatoes. Again, I wish I could be more clear on the subject. The details are not important, the details are all there is, the heart wants what it wants, tomatoes, is the story I'm sticking to. I step out after I check the forecast, grab an umbrella and my sunglasses regardless. Should I return with a little cake or ice cream, we'll call that Tuesday Sunday.

Speaking of ice cream, there's a McDonald's a few blocks from my house because people like a little meat with their soya, a little milk with their corn syrup. It must be a thrill to be an American after the proliferation of those golden arches. True here as it is in Paris, so it's only a matter of time before I see the Eiffel Tower on the way to my local library.

Incidentally, the French have their own way of disappearing, with great eloquence or beneath falling buildings. I hail from whatever country I speak of, the sound not the patria, the label, the logo, the illusion that binds us. Kiki likes alliteration when she's not contemplating her next trip to Saturn. Accordingly, all of our naming, our borders, are already within striking range of her experiments.

THE WORLD WAS MADE in my mouth, though I have yet to find the link to my cerebellum. Nations may or may not exist and cities, landscapes, are engineered to drain with the first rain after a massacre. There's nothing left by the time film crews arrive, though it is possible the camera sees but will not reveal our intentions.

I am of a mind, several, if we're to believe my analyst. Versant in many languages, perhaps all of them, but I don't speak to pigeons. I do talk to ducks, when I have a hankering to disagree with their politics and Kiki is there to assist with the translation.

We were in Italy last week and then Ethiopia, but there was no need to changeup our palaver. Thanks to Mussolini almost everyone in that country speaks Italian, whereas no one in Milan speaks Oromo. As to my altercations with ducks, they're well annotated on the advice of my doctor, though the birds themselves have yet to make his acquaintance.

Soon I'll say all this again from Bob's point of view, then Blanche will know that I'm smarter. This is not without risk, everything that happens here has not happened yet. As from a rope, I said to a flock of Roman ducks swimming in some famous fountain, knowing full well the pigeons were listening. Neither had any idea what I was talking about, whereas African birds understood perfectly.

There is a time to love and a time to love no one, then we'll take the guns and bury them next to the river. When all else fails think of me as French, I told Blanche, and then ride me like a buffalo. That was the day before the day after she left me. I know because she didn't turn up for our scheduled rendezvous at the café I talked about earlier.

176

THIS IS A LONG story, but I'm telling it in a way so you too can go fishing. I'm more into movies anyway. Clint Eastwood, for instance, especially the films in which he takes his directives from Washington. Still, I wouldn't mind if from time to time he'd try reversing the narrative, the ending specifically. All the good guys die in the movies I'm thinking of, the locations too would be authentic, Honduras, say, or present-day Kandahar.

I've never been to the Middle East, but I did write a book about it. America's current, premier destination for death and madness, and yet somehow more balanced than the Florida

Panhandle. The deserts surrounding Baghdad are a perfect setting for my first motion picture, since I've written that story already. That's how I know that city is in Texas. Write what you don't know, is what I tell young people, how in hell did that one get by the academy.

Let's resume. For twenty odd years I provided bankers and money managers the documentation to leverage a Subaru and the bungalow adjacent. Together we showed people who couldn't afford dinner how to buy houses.

Equity makes converts of us all, especially when you don't have any. I got in to get out, so I could stay home with my money. Work is an exit strategy, though many think otherwise, what's true in Manhattan won't fly in Kentucky. Neither will the colonel's chickens and they won't fry themselves, that's why the good people of the Bluegrass State go to work daily.

When I was a journalist, a claim that will not be substantiated, I fixed the body count, and then I lied about situations in general. I practiced the art of omitting the where, what, and whyfores, as a service to they who already owned everything.

I did the same thing as a consultant, property evaluations were my speciality. Nothing but blue skies and golf thereafter, except I called it tennis. Money is how I steered clear of the world and its misery, before I forgot it completely. It works, I'm reminded of that each time I put on an Armani jacket, especially when I pretend not to know the designer is Italian. My father was both of those things, except in his day designers were tailors. More on him later, now, technically, unless I mean literally.

The suit makes the man, said papa. Why then, I ask, are billionaires still rocking denim. I explained all of this to that gaggle of screamers and misfits, my brand spankin new friends on the corner. We meet regularly over coffee and sandwiches, cookies when I want their attention, and then I tell them all there is to know about real estate.

Now back to that movie, my desert opus. My life in Hollywood is but one thought away from the life that I'm living. When the script is complete I'll redo it in Swedish so there'll be no telling what is meant from what is written, finally. Then I'll instruct the actors to adlib the dialogue while staying true to the text in the subtitles.

I hope the director doesn't mind my meddling and that his name is Bergman. He too preferred life to eternity, the interruption to knowing but, just so we're clear, I've not seen his movies. Though I have been known to say otherwise about books, films, paintings, about everything really.

Ingmar would be perfect for the Swedish rendition of what will undoubtedly change the course of cinematic history. You do realize I'm dead, he said when I phoned him, no longer a card carrying human. But I think that's just something famous people say when they're busy.

175

Down the block from where I live is my only friend and colleague. I'm talking about Bob, obviously, but let's not rush into anything. He taught philosophy, of the kind that fits in a book or an hourglass. At least that's how I explained it to Kiki, she's nine so she understood immediately. Then we agreed that glass was more useful before some fool thought to put sand in it.

When sophists retire they move to France, or around the corner, someplace they've already been. That's why Bob can neither fly nor plummet, unlike me, when I have to get someplace quickly. Bob is all about constancy, being, he calls it, but not the kind you have to pay for monthly.

I take instructions from my cocktail napkins. Every drink and occasion to revisit the injury, a hitlist, essentially, redress for the accident that is my existence. This knife, for example, is not real, but if it were it would still be invisible. Most things do better when we can't see them. Unicorns is the example I cited earlier, and dragons. Kiki assures me both are doing fine in absentia and, she winked, they're big in Japan.

I'm describing the future, or my upcoming trip to Kyoto. Truth is I'm set for every contingency. Last week I decided my outfit for the warming and the ice age that will inevitably follow. Look for me in upstate New York though, by then, it may look more like the Arctic or Bogota, and don't be surprised if the road signs are in Mandarin. Beijing is taking a bite out of all the right places, with more stealth than a Manhattan broker or a Vietnamese communist. I'm not worried, all empires are deserts in waiting.

Alligator shoes and a seal skin hat, gloves to match, in case you're wondering about my brisk weather getup. Feathers, are what I wore to the crucifixion. The birds were dead already, as was that alligator, the seals too, but Blanche still couldn't condone my choice of adornments.

There will be a reckoning when all species come together again in Jerusalem. In the time of time over the subject will become the accessory and raccoons, say the squirrels in my neighbourhood, will all be driving Mercedes.

174

NOT YET AND NOT at all are the same thing exactly in the Pelican State. In the bayou everything is surmountable so long as the bank does not have your address. The windows need caulking and the back door is off its hinges, but say nothing of that when you go to deposit your supplemental.

Sell whatever is rusting or rotting in the yard to fix those deficiencies. They go crazy for the stuff in the city, those barn boards especially. The same planks that make up the rafters you couldn't help but notice when the ceiling fell into your cereal. When they're all trucked and paid for you'll still need potatoes, so dig a hole to stay warm. You knew when they handed you those papers you've been meaning to read for twenty odd years this would be home for eternity.

Nothing happened when I worked in finance, but some nothings are bigger than others. We could make whole neighbourhoods disappear behind the red lines we were drawing. People will believe and sign anything to keep eating, and though we knew those loans weren't collectible the rates were magnificent. Good enough to bundle and sell to Iceland or German pension funds.

In Louisiana they know what to do in a cyclone, how to wait on the roof for a cheque or a pizza. The people no longer have a stake in what happens, because of the electoral college, their skin colour or that cybernated chicanery. To complicate matters, nobody will receive the cheques they were promised unless they have state sanctioned documents to coincide with their face and an address.

Everybody row, because the empire is collapsing. I know it's true because I saw it on television and then on the internet. It's the weather, apparently, but it might be the Mexicans. That's why I buy tuna by the case and oatmeal by the barrel.

Produce is the problem, plant matter, be it blueberries or roses. Orchids, if you live in the bayou. There god goes about his business like a rat in a snarl. He doesn't like frogs because they're amphibian. Critters that don't need oxygen make flooding superfluous, he said the last time I saw him at Starbucks.

In Arizona the Virgin of Guadalupe hangs from the rear view mirror of every van and pickup truck. There's nothing Latin men won't do for a good looking icon. To the east Muslims are buying condos within striking distance of Lady Liberty. In New Jersey, because Manhattan real estate is much too expensive, but that could change in an instant.

In the hills of Appalachia people are being born and not much besides. They wait for the call or that cheque like their daddies before them, but mostly they wait to go fishing. Believing is everything in those hills and the heartland. Faith for breakfast, lunch and dinner, apart from the occasional jackrabbit with potatoes and turnips. Still, I'd like to think there's a story there, or here, somewhere, and every possibility it will be bursting with detail.

I suggest we wait for Ingmar, unless Fox sees a series. He must be working on something in that place where directors go for always. I hear it's no different than a Swedish winter so I'm sure, by now, he's gotten used to it. I like to think he's working on a script without words or people, the one I'll write when I get there.

As for my current project, we'll start shooting the moment he gets here. Then the good people of Louisiana will know how many Syrians are on a rowboat to Boston, who's digging the tunnels under El Paso, and who had whom in the shower.

WHEN I BEGAN THIS work my analyst put a knife to my ear and set a course for the nursery. A room is just a room, he said, and that was the first time he lied to me. The breast is how I succumbed to my mother's tyranny, but that was before I'd tasted chicken. Meat gave me strength to keep killing, ants mostly, but from there I extrapolated.

Seeing and not believing is how I came to love Jesus, Big Bird too. It takes a village to confound an infant, or a smattering, a smidgen, of hellfire missiles. They're more circumspect, said Rumsfeld, and therefore more humane than yesterday's ordnance, what befell on Berlin or Calabria.

Those earlier sorties were later re-enacted in Hollywood, followed by lunch and Scotch whiskey for Bogart. I couldn't help but notice there were no roles for my brother, for petrified toddlers, forsaken too in St. Peter's Basilica.

I explained all of this to Bob but, being a philosopher, he managed to maintain his impartiality. I wish he was a psychologist instead, for them at least the immediate comes later. Things are so much easier when Bob and I don't understand things together. In Paris they call that postmodern, but I don't subscribe to such precepts, to precept in general.

It was Blanche who recommended I begin therapy, followed by everybody who knew me. Her last ditch ultimatum, so I agreed immediately and I could think of no better way to stitch up my family. After several excruciating sessions I became obsessed with the door, its imminently reasonable proximity. But by then my brains were scattered to all corners of the talking room floor subverting all hope of a sprint.

I'm there now, or then, depending on your point of reference. We are in fact here and this is now, says my analyst … really … naturally … what about later … later is later … I thought so … we agree then … what are my options … we can disagree … you decide … it doesn't work like that … it might … nope … give me an example … now … now what … it's not working now … you mean then … do I … I think so.

Moving on, yesterday a raccoon ate my zucchini because the tomatoes were still too green for his liking. Raccoons are like those slum tots in that movie from India, for whom scavenging is a lifelong fixation. With this difference however, the kids could be made to realize it's my zucchini they're eating.

By the time I left Stanford I was practised in the art of madness, the chatter. I never could master the stillness. All I ever wanted was a diagnosis and the requisite pension, a stipend so I could keep scribbling. There is no crazy without that designation and, after Freud, they don't hand those out easily.

An ache and its epithet are the same size exactly, said Sigmund. But he forgot to write it down so I just did it for him. At any rate no self respecting lunatic would stoop to such parity, except perhaps in the presence of that doctor's brain-busting disciples. Bob sides with those theorists, with Skinner, especially, since he too was sane to breaking. Whereas I only read those thinkers phonetically.

172

When I was at Stanford Reagan was in the Whitehouse, Nancy too, on a promise to reform the indigent. I was young and needed so much to fit in, so I said yes to drugs and no to the government. During the Gipper's second term I took to thieving, like Robin Hood, or nearly. I took money from the rich and kept it. When I'd banked enough I commenced to operating in plain view because then it's called business.

I want to know everything about everything, said Kiki. We were in Shanghai, if I remember correctly, she was an aerospace engineer and I was Jimmy Cagney. But I didn't reveal anything of my checkered story because her wonder exceeds my rattle and I'd like to keep it that way for as long as possible. When she's an adult I will disclose to her the whole enchilada. I'll tell her who wins and who dies and then, as is our habit, I'll spring for the pie and ice cream.

171

Bob had little to impart after a lifetime of study. The fog, I suspect, had lifted too early, but he kept his appointments. He found all things interesting. Sealing wax and the New York Times, the mighty oak that protected his mother's tombstone, and us, from inclement weather while he planted another. I wonder what life would be like if she were here still, Bob thought aloud so I could write it down.

Death wasn't enough to revive his astonishment, measured syntax and regular grooming would secure his longevity. Love this fucking branch Bob, or we won't be forgiven. As we left the cemetery I could hear the trees whispering. You'll be fine here, said the oak to the seedling, and every day they bring in more corpses.

While walking Bob did his best to hold back his tears and I didn't ask for fear he might tell me what he was feeling. Besides, there's every possibility I wouldn't have understood what he was describing.

Thank you Jesus for obituaries and funeral directors, and thanks anyway for the stone markers. In the future forget the hieroglyphics, forego the ceremony, the burial when and wherever possible. Point us instead to our final howl, or at least a violin, back to the way things were before your suffering became the first rule of rejoicing.

Gods lie, gather us in their loving absence. Now that you're up there distract him Jesus, don't tell him there was music before you, before him even. Keep pappy happy or he'll come for the rest of us. Everything was easier before he started killing us. Sacrament, the pulsing chest of a deer in the crosshairs, followed by the thud of making ends meet.

170

I'M HUGE WITH MY eyes closed, frozen amid the sunflowers in Holland and Idaho. I can't see a thing when they're open, everything gets in the way, and I don't like what the looking does to my thinking. Clearly, it's not fastened to anything and I'm good at forgetting the thing I just mentioned. Idaho, in case you weren't listening.

After so many words I plan to live off my death like Vallejo. I'm sure by now he's come to love the disaster, and I'm not deterred by his absence. We still have the shards, the words, through which to see the house where he put on his trousers. That's how I know who he was, and other supposings. The ditty's the thing, said the poet, or he would have eventually, but Bob and I can't sing so we just went for coffee and cheesecake.

Don't go, I said, as my own mother lay dying, wait for the sweetness of spring. This petrified calm shall be your inheritance, returned the old woman, then she laughed and slipped away. That's how I know this is funny. Home then was a hospital room next to a nursing station, to the right and down the hall from the elevator. At the helm was an old nurse who would soon need her own gurney. My mother slept, thanks to the morphine, a few more drops and she'd be ready to bury.

The days got longer, and shorter somehow. Finally, the whole bloody mess was just a chair in the hallway, the contiguous deprived of all substance. Eventually god too set up shop in that corridor. A woman this time, which would have been a revelation to some, but it made no difference to my understanding.

This was years ago, or the day after the day before I last ate a cannoli. I could hear the oceans, all shores at once and what must have been mermaids calling from behind steel and masonry. My mother had lived long enough, but there's treatment for that too, apparently. The doctors probed every orifice to confirm their diagnosis, and then simply killed her.

Meet the new priests, said the old nurse. Then she told me to go count the tiles between the door and the elevator. The walls were lime green and they stayed that way too while I counted. It's good to know I wasn't hallucinating. Neither a name nor a body be, said the god in the hallway, which did help a little. It was easy for me to assume those absences given my experience with time travel, but it just wasn't the same without Kiki.

Murder is the clarity I aspire to now. I wish I may I wish I might when confronting a crack team of medicos, but circumstance has yet to align with my purpose. My mother would have lived a little longer had she been the president's daughter. Whereas I couldn't even obstruct the flow and then a torrent of oral probings. As many as it takes, explained the old nurse, until she stops eating completely. A doctor's best work is post-mortem anyway, so I just packed up my dead and left the building.

What follows death is a story about a mouse or a bird, but after a shower, preferably. A shower is just a shower in most instances, but run if at one end there's a loading door. I was visited by god a few pages back and then again in the hallway. You may be conflating god with Eichmann, said the mouse in this paragraph, more likely the bird. No right-thinking rodent would scale the exterior of a twelve-storey building, so let us not speak ill of the mouse we will not speak of.

A bird then, perched on the windowsill of that hospital room for hours, days, before talking to me directly. An incident I should have predicted. This was not the first time a member of the avian persuasion attempted to gain my attention.

We were at war then, in Mesopotamia, I was a diplomat and that bird was a CIA operative. Kiki is fine with the bird's status but she's having trouble believing I was ever a diplomat. In my defence, I was not there and so I had no choice but to invent what was happening.

The last president, like most squirrels and billionaires, slept with his trove and gadgets, while press secretaries fell to his tweets like dominoes. He couldn't keep his thumbs in his pants, but it's hard to do seeing as he preferred to rule in his bathrobe. What he let slip was all newscasters could talk about from Jacksonville to Seattle. There was no oxygen left for what the people were saying in Homs or Aleppo.

Putin is in Syria too. He and the president talk occasionally about the blood and the bluster. Not often enough for our commander in chief, though he's been told it's un-American to love a Russian. You can't see the Kremlin unless you live in Alaska, said the President to Steve Bannon. That's why, Steve explained, we didn't send Sarah Palin to Washington.

Let's get back to that war in Babylon. As I intimated, the feathered were not excluded from service. That bird was sent by the Pentagon to find me in my prison room, before I started blabbing. But I can't be sure what that bird came to tell me given our lack of commitment to interspecies communication, that under resourced field of translation. Kiki is working on the problem but her focus is ducks mostly, and it's unlikely to change anytime soon. It takes time, research and plenty of ice cream to crack those monosyllables.

We'll fight them over there, said Bush the tadpole, and then he asked Cheney where there is exactly. We plundered with god on our side, while other deities were cleared of all meaning. Except maybe the Buddha who preferred the gist anyway.

China meditated, simply waited to bankroll the winner. While post adolescents from Mississippi and Arkansas brought democracy to a people, as they say on television, whose names they would soon learn to pronounce. Birds were essential to the enemy too, as lunch, with a side of them French fried potatoes. Birds then rats, was the consensus, because that's what makes us human.

The feathered, contrary to what they'd have us believe, are not good at recognisance. They don't always report back and those smartphones are too big for their pockets. What they see cannot be substantiated. To further complicate matters the average bird takes days, weeks to traverse oceans and continents, so all they could report on were yesterday's massacres.

I am who I was before that bird came to visit, but my analyst doesn't believe me. These days, I explain, when sparrows speak, I know not to listen … what if that bird were here now … is he … maybe … can I get that in writing … no … he's got some explaining to do … it's better if you do the talking … see if he'll pick up the tab … for what … this session for starters … he won't … why not … he says he doesn't have any money.

168

There are physicians for every crisis and ailment, a diagnosis for each anus and anima. I make no distinction since I can't see either and did I mention my other doctor is a woman.

She swears I'm fine but I find her diagnosis too personal, untenable, inconceivable, I said, though I may have mixed up those syllables. When she tells me to stick out my tongue I wiggle my toes, but that still doesn't stop her from asking. As for my condition in general, she can't stop that either.

My philosophy is dance with whoever is talking and who can resist a female, a doctor no less, with one glove showing. More on that later. Educated women, men too, take me back to those heady days when I was neck deep in the canons, they never did reach my ears. A good book is like a tire iron, I said to my students at Stanford, unless I was there as a parking meter. They didn't understand so I brought in Kiki the musketeer to stab them in the ass with a computer.

It's just me in this house, and my predicament. No Bob, so I called Blanche on the telephone. She and I are close, distant, is how she put it. We have just enough history to fill a thimble. Less, say the squirrels outside my window.

Incidentally, a thimble is bigger than my anus and smaller than Uranus, the perfect size for a finger all decked out in latex. The plan now is to change Uranus to Jupiter because that rhyme is even more ridiculous than comingling diagnostic probings with fornication.

A woman needs a scalpel, a cleaver, said Jesus, Confucius or Shakespeare. Across the street from where I live is this city's Chinese Women's Association, a small house and a sign comprise the meeting place. I've yet to see anyone come or go, but the lights do come on in the evening.

I prefer clubs that discourage membership, it shows restraint and an address is a good way to keep out the rest of us. Commiseration is the point of such gatherings, since god does not speak to women, or Chinese for that matter. I think of that little place as a safe house, where a mother might decapitate a pig or a chicken until such time as she can pass the axe to her infant daughter.

Every Tuesday a woman comes and cleans my house, but before she gets here I hide the utensils. Anything with weight or a blade. She's from South America, which is far but not far enough to be nowhere at all, unless this is nowhere as well, suffice to say this could be Brazil.

Whereas Bob comes and goes with the weather. I'm working day and night with The Centre for Atmospheric Research to pin down his schedule. Though his visits are a good thing because I'm allergic to cats and I can't have a dog - I just can't be counted on to leave the house daily. My son has two cats, Crunch and Lunch. For them it is we who are strange, he explained, and then I heard the same thing from a passing zebra.

Let's move towards the situation we're in, the hole and its crevices. Mornings I review my list from the night before, but I don't leave the house before exhausting all other options. I choose a route and go down another, because you can't be too careful. When I return I put away the groceries, but not before I review that list again to make sure it concurs with what I think happened.

I am the third person, that's why I can't be annihilated. Though sometimes he and I pass one another in the hall. He's the cock of the walk, all thought and no action. Remember to eat that last tomato, he said yesterday, I'm buying more tomorrow. An awkward moment for it is I who decide the menu and his agenda.

When I graduated from Stanford dolphins waited in the wings. I was first and last in my class, but that could not be substantiated. The experience was deleterious to my equanimity and my reputation, so I spent the next several years correcting, draining the swamp that was my education.

At convocation an old general flanked by two crisp cadets, one black one white, spoke to us of the future. Of opportunity within and beyond our borders and inside the concrete beneath some as yet undisclosed desert. But I knew from my brother he was talking about the bunkers under Nevada, and Afghanistan would know it too in a couple of decades.

Officer material, boasted the general, looking at me and Bob adjacent. Except Bill was Bob's name then, or Bartholomew. War is not what it used to be, explained the commander. Then he showed us footage of far and not so faraway places, in which the corpses had all been pixilated. Soon, I thought, we'll all die on television.

After the speechifying they rolled out pizza and hamburgers because nothing sets kids to dreaming like what they've eaten already. In England, I said to Bartholomew, Bart, for short, they'd have served us tea and crumpets. Or fish and chips, he said. Then I told Bart the story of how the queen got her sugar, her spices and about other royal shenanigans.

Eventually those two toy soldiers set up a desk next to the food trays and signed up a caboodle of debt-infested ragamuffins. Leaders all, said the general, since there were so few black students at Stanford but, he winked, why fix what's not broken.

166

People are assets too, like petroleum, say, or a jeep. Not always, says Bob. Context is everything, is how I'd summarize his position. But I don't know that now, merrily, merrily unto death. It's what Bob and I argued about the first time we met, and every hour thereafter. Without a framework, a language in common, he says, there could be no understanding. But what, I ask, does that have to do with the price of tomatoes.

A tomato is a tomato in so far as we agree, said Bob … really … obviously … do bears understand context … of course … I thought so … it's how things are made coherent … for bears … possibly … they learn … obviously … what's it like

… coherence … learning … it's like a toothache … bears have toothaches … they do … except they can't talk about it … not to us … other bears then … possibly … how … they just do … that's remarkable.

While Bob and I talk I dream of cornfields from Saskatchewan to the Mexican border, ears attached. Mine were severed in college so listening is a problem, even when I don't do it. Bob doesn't believe any of what I just said, but an ear is an ear and a homonym so it cannot be reduced to the plant or the skull it belonged to.

Fire and forget is my approach to discourse, to intellection in general. That's also what they do from those bunkers under Nevada, while they wait for burgers to grill, chicken to fry or a cob salad. At night they drink because there's nothing like a good punch-up to stir them homicidal leanings.

This is not your grandmother's war, said the general finally. Our specialists, our brothers and sisters in arms and in concrete are worth more than all the limbs in Kabul, and less than the missiles they're launching.

165

I PREFER THE PICKLE to knowing. I go through what and whyfors like kids go through sneakers, and did I mention I also like mangos. To know is to die a little, or so said a poet from Afghanistan, unless it was that monk from Assisi. They've been dead for centuries so there's no way to say who said what exactly. And given what's happened since we'd need a jackhammer to cut through their speaking. Besides, not talking, mostly waiting, is how poets and monks become legendary, though sometimes they did talk to birds, bears too, but less often.

Here in the provinces the consequent still matters, but in Paris they're making sense of the fragmentary. A word used to be a word, a chirp or a grunt. Now it's a riddle wrapped in a conduit, snakes underfoot. The story for your eyes only, the exosphere all up in our business, the cloud, as the kids say, so Amazon can see what they're thinking.

I'm talking about satellites, or satellites, as they say in France. Who needs the Algerians when they're not laying cable. Technology is fleeting, more circuitous than linear, so resistance is futile and inevitable, the difference in negligible. In Gaza the pointless and the imminent fused decades ago. Nothing and then more nothing after an Israeli incursion, but we'll know more once the good people of Jabalia rejoin the conversation.

In August, or this morning - why not both - I found a sketch next to the oatmeal adjacent to the mangos, to the left of the lentils I was soaking for dinner. A beach, and on that shore was a branch from some tree or other. It must have floated in from Africa since there was nothing growing in that composition. I know Bob didn't draw it because he's not an artist. Kiki signs all of her pieces, so I must have done it. I examined that outline again over coffee, in the clear light of day or the garden, and that's when the squirrels caught sight of it.

They were critical of the endeavour, disparaging of my technique, balance and content. Draw the shore from the other side, they suggested, from the point of view of a tuna, and the trees will be trees again in the blink of your drowning. Clearly, they'd not grasped the breadth of my illustration. A line is a line, the shore in this instance, but it takes more than a change in perspective to hear those squirrels talking.

164

OUR FIRST DRAWINGS WERE but the beginning of a long illness. Blood red and later charcoal black, though both were state of the art for homo erectus. Those sketches depicted other species mostly, the slow ones, the menu, specifically. Squirrels still speak of how their legs trembled on seeing wood burn, splinter into an eye or an ear. That's how it is with new technology, I know for there are books on the subject, at least that's what it said in the documentary.

The preponderant were killing artists long before there were governments, and after Pinochet many took up ceramics and some moved to Hollywood. There they continued to workshop their skills, in focus groups and in those cafés I spoke about earlier. Security, community especially, will render artists irrelevant faster than you could snatch and cook a pigeon in Syria. So please, for their sake, support your local terrorist association.

There was art before art, before Gutenberg, before Oxford even. Evidenced by those chiseled messages next to the half skull of the artist and her cousins, presumably. Heirlooms, say archeologists, a bowl, a cup to wash in the river. A gift, perhaps, from our African grandmothers after they decapitated their lovers, and before the Chinese invented porcelain giving rise to the English. Kitchenware is largely plastic now, or styrofoam, petroleum basically, so we're still drinking from the skulls of our ancestors.

In the beginning men wore loincloths, women too, made from the skin of whatever hubby brought home for dinner. That's no longer a thing in Milan or Paris. I have yet to find an outfit to match my sealskin hat and alligator shoes, what I have assembled of my afterlife getup. Not even at Walmart, though I can't say enough about their matching throw pillows. Still, I don't think today's purchases will be tomorrows collectibles.

Speaking of what they're wearing in heaven, yesterday the president said the Taliban is still lopping off heads in Afghanistan - that's a place on the internet. I can't confirm or deny it because the Federal Communications Commission won't allow decapitations on television.

When something is over it begins again, I said previously, except this time I'm saying it as Edward Albee. As one speaks to toilet paper or a mirror, his most trusted companions, but after he realized the universe had no need of his commentary. Why else would he bring a knife to the theatre, unless a stabbing on Broadway is more consequential than murder elsewhere.

Still, we must not rest on our laurels, our ability to eradicate life as we know it. Dolphins are consorting with Malibu liberals and those west coast mammals can be very litigious. They're complaining about rising carbon and melting glaciers. But there's no precedent for what they say is coming, so long as there are experts to refute the inevitable.

Climatologists, unlike philosophers and politicians, don't traffic in absence and too much of what those dolphins are grumbling about remains invisible. They'll have to wait until the worst happens because in America, as in all civil societies, you can't go to court without evidence.

When I'm not watching television I sit atop my roost with binoculars because I don't own a rifle, and sometimes I scan the atlas I keep on the coffee table. From Philadelphia I head to Spain and then south through the strait of Gibraltar. Veer right at Sicily, past Libya and Egypt to the outskirts of Gaza where children smash barricades with their bodies. So I'm told, I can't see through concrete and from this distance I can't hear them either.

I'm Italian by birth but that ended immediately, though not before I used Nero's fiddle as kindling. I think best with my shoes on, especially when I'm with people, Bob in particular. With a finger in each ear is how I hold the interval, how I wreck what I make. Things as they are, as they were, as I see them, are all ablaze in the world I'm thinking of.

Speaking of fiddling, Beethoven had a secret steadily growing between his dying ears. As does the mighty oak that has insinuated itself between my front door and the sidewalk. A tree is a tree and an injunction, death deferred and then a piano.

Music then is a stay of execution, whereas a table is merely a reshuffling of what's dead already. That's why squirrels don't live at IKEA.

Forgive the digression, Swedish conglomerates will do that apparently. Yesterday god called me on the phone. I acquiesced to everything he said because it was the only way to extricate myself from the conversation and I don't argue content.

It's not me who's annihilating the living, he said … really … not anymore … good to know … but should you get to heaven don't mention the body count … no problem … especially around Abraham … ok … he's still sore about that kerfuffle with Isaac … I see … I'd have had him go through with it had I known that kid would be my last well nigh cadaver … what about your son … what about him … he died after … that had nothing to do with me … how so … it's complicated … I bet … I did talk to his killers … wow … theirs is the version that matters … really … trust me, nothing is what it seems in that story.

I'm compiling these words by the pound. Feel free to pilfer, the lot for a spent cartridge, a soiled bed, anything that sets us to dreaming. Notes played to breaking, said Ludwig, or I said it for him because he couldn't hear them. I like to think we're in this together, two slugs in the chamber, except I'm not bleeding from anywhere, from my ears in particular.

This afternoon I was in Moscow with Kiki, that's a city between my backdoor and the kitchen. Bob was there too, but I'll know for sure after I count the kiwis. There's also a half-eaten chicken that needs explaining.

Where would I be without these investigations, my searching within these four walls, six if you count the floor and the ceiling. The alternative would be to name the town, the places and the situations that made me. Unthinkable except perhaps in a footnote but then my readers – who, said Blanche – Brian couldn't peg the genre.

Blathering on. In the twelfth century the Pied Piper was at the top of his game, exterminator extraordinaire. When the town's people wouldn't pay he baited the children. What happened next is ambiguous, but we know from his songs he may have eaten them.

These were dark times. Rumi, that poet from Afghanistan, was building his name in the provinces, so he could abandon it later. Not to suggest a poet is his work, but I wouldn't discount it either. I'll know for sure after I read him.

A hit is a miss in the story I'm telling and the only train out of here. In my defence, in defence of hardening heads everywhere then, as now, nobody read poetry and only Christians knew what was coming. It's dangerous to compare a bard to a deity, only one is all knowing and the other's not saying. That's how it is with immortals.

Centuries later Murdoch and Time Warner scrambled to build a better mousetrap, so the masses could get in step with their programming. Not a death march exactly, mock rescue from real catastrophe because they can't tell which is what in Kentucky. The lowdown, the skinny, we'd gotten decades ago from Jimmy Cagney, roundabout the time the scribblers on Madison Avenue stepped up to secure our stupidity.

The future is in China, finally, and their secret is in the canning, said Marshall McLuhan, but why did he have to chose this book to say it in. Tomorrow is just a theory anyway, like it was in the sixties. It seems Lady Liberty has had enough of sunny days in September. Never again in Manhattan as they say in the Hamptons, but there's plenty of other places to hit which, as it happens, does make us feel better.

America runs on oil and methamphetamine, heroin on alternate weekends. Whereas Iraq is the birthplace and Afghanistan the aftermath of civilization, though Kathryn Bigelow scripted it differently. She's also rethinking Yemen, Libya and Guatemala as they are now and in the eighties, when the CIA went there to save them. Those were the best of times, said Clint Eastwood, yesteryear's Bigelow, so don't nobody tell him he peaked in the seventies.

THE AGGREGATE IS HOW we flush out the missing, behind which are centuries of endless brutality. It was easier when those tolls were official, before death went digital. Forgetting is crucial, but not having known is divine, said Freud, or find somebody who did. He was talking about the blots behind the thoughts. The truth, as they say in the news business, to muddy up our time of dying.

YouTube has agreed to receive my postings, the words not the pictures, of summary executions from Homs to Manila. Followed by reviews, after extensive testing, of reliable can openers. Riot gear too, but they don't allow those evaluations, citing community standards and because democracy does better without all that information. Some postings do get through occasionally, and then what is said must be unsaid of our great multinationals, our governments and their crowd busting posses.

Bob is pining for a time when after every massacre we could still believe in the tally. But I can't say for sure because he's not here. It's just me, finally, and that half-eaten chicken, so this must be later, later now, or you wouldn't be reading it. Bob thinks my brain is unravelling, my reasoning obtuse. Ridiculous, if I were to quote him directly. Apparently it is me and not the world that's in pieces but how, I ask, is that different.

In darkness there is vision still, light marks the limit, is a line that should have died in the gullet, so Bob must have said it. Moving forward, all such phrases will be attributed to him, but I will need to see them before Blanche reads them in case he lets slip something clever.

I used to be all-knowing. From the cradle to the moment I realized critics roam the academy and Brian the coffee houses. I said all I had to say about that to my analyst, though sometimes I'd confide in a salad. More on that later.

My therapist says I'm lying accidentally, on purpose and by definition. It's comforting to know I have that part covered. A few plot twists, I figure, a climax and finally a denouement. It's only a matter of time before Kathryn or Clint come a-knocking.

160

A BOOK IS A PIPE, a birthday card for the species, or a sunhat for Kiki, but feel free to say otherwise. Hieroglyphics are, after all, mostly for tinkers and pharaohs. I came here to explain the dispersal, via the referent – it – briefly, like a knife in the larynx.

To be is to be better gone, the light only, said Milosz, the light preposterous. Faith was an afterthought, ancillary, a way of repeating the unrepeatable. A shot across the bow and the ages, said the Nobel committee, even though he was only talking to his neighbour Alice and her dog Charlie.

I was like that dog once, unencumbered, before my mother talked some priest into running my name up the flagpole. If only she'd left well enough alone, then there'd be room for the pain only. Dogs continue to die without knowing, though Blanche says that's presumptive. No matter, the boneheap welcomes all comers but, if there is a do-over, I'd like to come back as a superpower.

Incidentally, that other guy, the one who told me to eat the last tomato sits just behind my eye. Over there, roughly, which is always where I am going. Intentionally, coincidentally, somehow he always manages to slip into the spaces I live in before me.

Let's assume for the moment I am who I say, him, in this instance. In Baghdad he's wanted for murder, but that's true of most people. Whereas my dead were dead already and I have no memory of torturing prisoners. He's also wanted in Oxford, but I can't say much about that because the investigation is ongoing.

They have nothing on me, I told my lawyer … who … the academy … I see … and the government … you don't say … I do … you did … you believe me, right … about what … murder … what about it … the Pentagon has the exclusive … I thought so … on murder and atrocity … really … both and neither is the pill we must swallow … clever … thank you … you should write that down … I did … of course … Ingmar is coming … who … Bergman … the director .. that's right … he's dead … your point … never mind.

STEEPLES ARE HOW GOD first got word to black people in the fields and the bayou. His was the smoke, the speaking, behind the burnings that were happening already. He talked to white people too, in which case he'd say something different. These days his spirit is transmitted via a string of radio TV towers where there used to be windows and timbers.

In Manhattan a church is a skyscraper subject to permits and financing. High-rises are how notables steer clear of the rabble, but I know from experience those municipal processes will have you eating your fingers. I suggest New Yorkers take a page from their southern brethren, seeing as until recently you didn't need a permit to burn or to build south of the Mason Dixon.

In Palestine too demolition precedes the planning, like how it was in the bible. Progress is all about what happened previously. Luckily there are many such tales, recent and ancient, for New York and the Knesset to emulate. This then is just a reminder in a heap of remembrances. Don't run with scissors is another.

The words penetrate these walls from every corner of the universe. They're scrubbed before they enter my living room so

I don't mistake this place for Somalia. Women there pray for rain because that's when killers and rapists stay home to catch up on their reading.

The victim will learn her stalker's secrets and there's nothing more terrifying than a band of women wielding machetes, save and except the hour before their arrival. At which time they will address his every itch and craving.

The problem is the solution, said Marshall McLuhan, but feel free to insert your own guru. English politicians on television try and fail to pronounce the names of those women and villages. Let's help them over there, say their constituents, seeing as there are already not enough cucumbers for all the Somalis in London. But why, they ask, must they ride the tube with my sister.

A box in a box on a cul-de-sac is what I know of British television, that is until Westinghouse brought us the flatscreen. They haven't had to think about anything since, except Kate, Kate and the Kates who have not yet been vetted. By the way, all the houses on those cul-de-sacs all come with a waffle maker, if I'm not mistaken.

In West Sussex they're storing cucumber seeds in a bomb-proof facility to protect them from the coming apocalypse and Somalis respectively. At least that's what it said on the evening news after that bit about rape and migrants. The queen is pleased because without her cucumber sandwiches she'd be Ukrainian.

158

LET'S GET BACK TO Blanche now that she's back from the Rockies, so I can decide directly what to say when I see her. The sound of her name reminds me of Willie Nelson's Texas, not the place, his lyrics, his twang in particular. Something felt, something real, whereas the state is just a concept.

I'm there now, rustling horses and mending fences, while my honey bakes pies in a Stetson. We met on a train to Istanbul and later watched a sunset in Cairo, but I'll let Blanche tell the rest of that story. I have a tendency, a hankering really, to invent the details, but I swear on all the tomatoes in Italy I'm the guy who was there with her.

Incidentally, my Texas home, the one in the last paragraph, is just a short gallop from Prairie Chapel Ranch. It's where George lives, W for short, a fixture of wars recent, now more elusive than six hundred thousand Iraqi cadavers. Blanche is attempting to entice the president with those pies she's baking, but I can't tell you what she plans after that because it's illegal.

I prefer the unrevealed, be it my shrinking liver or the world as I see it. Bob and I talking trash while children wither. Like Omar, the lone Taliban in Brampton Ontario, you might know him as that Afghan teenager who was once on American television. While in Kabul he'll always be the kid who spent ten years in Guantanamo.

That place may soon know the pitter patter of children and teenagers again. It's only logical, said Donald Trump, since Cuba is so much closer to Honduras than the cages in Texas. Crating people, children especially, is unconscionable, said Bob. Then I said something, then him, now me, and so on.

Like chickens, I said finally … what are we talking about … kids in cages …. they're not like chickens … yes they are … how's that … the cage makes the animal … it doesn't … the shoes … no … the suit then … stop … bears live in cages … sometimes … chickens are bears … they're not … it stands to reason … why are we talking about bears again … so we don't leave them hanging.

157

Yours is a most insignificant nation, said Kofi Annan to General Dallaire, your warnings of genocide are a dog that won't hunt in Washington or the United Nations. It's true, thought the Canadian commander, eagles do grow powerless as they fly into Manitoba, but we're no more insignificant than the Dutch, he protested. Wheat and timber are your only levers, replied Kofi, and a few stubborn cod off the coast of Newfoundland.

God loves Americans, and when they run out of water he'll move them to Canada. Hence I've instructed my realtor to buy up land around Winnipeg. The lake, not the city, that metropolis is worth less than a Manhattan condo. My plan is to register those acquisitions in Damascus, so Americans-cum-Manitobans will know what's it's like to be Syrian. Better yet I'll log those deeds in Beijing, and on receiving my Chinese passport I'll slip down to Washington to collect on the trillions they'll owe me.

There's no bad time to annex your neighbour. Canadians are Bolshevists anyway, worse than the Mexicans by Floridian standards. But effective, and accommodating, explained Dallaire in a letter to Washington by way of the Canadian Broadcasting Corporation. But the general should have written to News Corp instead, as I'm sure congress coordinates with Murdoch directly on matters of annexations and carnage.

Don't abandon us Rupert, we need to know when to spend, where to bend and what they're wearing in Malibu. Democracy is just something we say, what's ours is yours and what's yours is yours too, every drop and barrel. Ink, blood, from where we sit the difference is negligible. We are but adjunct, the conquered absent the clobbering, our knowing has been greatly exaggerated, it's a bald-faced lie. The gist is so much more important.

Say the name and kill a sunflower, choke the life right out of it. Vincent favoured canvases, he wanted to touch the leaves without seeing them, so his best works never happened. When I'm done rambling I plan to catalogue them precisely, an addendum to the things I'm not saying, but I still won't see what he saw in those flowers.

Soon everyone will think I'm like Van Gogh, so I've asked Kiki, Bob too, to tell no one I'm happy. Vincent suffered for his work, or for some other reason, whereas I'm just jangling my keys. Sound before art, is my motto, at least until I can grow me some wings. The sun shines all day in the places where I say these things and my problems, far as I know, are all in New Zealand.

156

BOB AND I HAVE been arguing, without pause, since the eighties. We follow one word with the next to steer clear of the spaces between them and, more importantly, the dishes. Sometimes I pretend our talking days are over, and that I have finally learned to play the piano.

Evening threatens and Bob and I have been yakking since noon, though not all of my appliances agree. The oven is refusing to cohere with the microwave and both are at odds with the coffeemaker. Still I see no reason to align those displays, since I'd only have to do it again in November.

There's no accounting for time, or the muddle. If I'm not careful Bob will be here till dinner and the stores close at seven, eight, if I side with the coffeemaker. I'm out of oatmeal as I said earlier, roundabout the beginning of my disquisition. All I can say for sure is whatever the hour approaching, it would be so much more productive if there were one less philosopher.

I've ushered Bob to the door, to the stoop even, where he remembers his bladder is not what it used to be. That's how it is with ontology, with our tinkling in general, and each time he goes to the loo he comes out swinging. I guess it's just easier to philosophise on an empty bladder.

Excrement is the great equalizer, plumbing our one true kick at democracy, invented in Egypt, appropriated by Rome and abandoned by Saxons. Later restored because of the plague, more so the dying. A river of shit beneath London town, sifted and scrubbed, finally, before making its way back to the channel.

In Gaza and Bangladesh they have only their kidneys to turn water into water again. Bob says it's due to their economic and social instability, but I think it's because both of those places used to be English.

He's out of the lavatory. Don't you have somewhere to be, I ask … this is somewhere … somewhere else … is there any more of that chicken … no … what do you suggest … you just ate … I mean where should I go … Finland … I see … or a movie.

155

I WISH PHILOSOPHERS WERE more like Kiki, though secretly I envy Bob's lack, his incessant probing in the same old barrel. If only I too had a question, then I and my asking could leave here together. Why not just pretend, said Kiki, but that's hard to do when she's not with me.

My friendship with Bob would be so much more gratifying if he were the squirrel who runs along the hydro lines outside my window. Or that zebra who passes by and says howdy occasionally, and sometimes I see her on television.

I keep the remote at the ready in case the people on screen are too good-looking for my taste and temperament. Sometimes I forget and then I take to the alleyways to restore my equilibrium, or wherever old Chinese women compete with first peoples for discarded beer cans. Nothing is something, returnable, in those attending arteries. Secondary markets is what we called garbage at Stanford because we've known all along the real money is in poverty.

I studied economics there, or whatever I said previously. I was the empty chair next to some terrific note taker, in case you were there too and didn't see me. Marx came up occasionally, enough to forget, if I remember correctly. On graduating I considered various employment opportunities before saying no to all of them. Being in between jobs is a job too in California.

My brother taught me to play cards and whistle, how to dislodge my brain in a cyclone and find it again on the windowsill. In Calabria we ate pan fried potatoes for breakfast and lunch, but in the evening those potatoes were chicken. From wild dogs he learned to pick clean a bone and from stray cats how to dislodge his eyes. Here in our adopted city the cats all have valets so my brother took up residence on another galaxy, but not one we'd been to together.

Come back, I pleaded … I can't … why not … because of my situation … what about it … I can't find it … like a scarf … that too … have you tried retracing your steps … what I did … that's right … where I've been … exactly … it's not there … your scarf … my predicament … really … though it might be there now … that's good … but I can't know that from here.

We're just a kiss now, but I hear from my sister he's been working on another speaking, far from the heaping, these rectangular proxies. The surprise only, is how she describe it. Pieces too are a worldview, fragments, poetry worthy of the name concrete. But honey, said Adolph to his intended, nothing beats a bunker.

My brother phoned me last week because we no longer meet. I'm going west, he said, the world needs to know about what's going on in Nevada. As for the Reich's first couple, their subterranean condo would just be too costly for the people we're bombing. Not to mention ineffective, given what we now know about busting concrete.

There are holes in the sky, said my brother, that are making the children fidgety. In Yemen they no longer look to the blue, but cloud cover for inspiration, because that's what keeps the shops open. Every week there are fewer buildings to die in, and fewer Toyota Tacomas for them slapdash altercations.

At Annapolis they're teaching cadets how to make the world safe for correspondents and contractors. This morning's heroes are this evening's talking points, while their targets grow cold in the rubble. This story is about slaughter, and Annapolis is like West Point but then the word point would have appeared twice in this passage.

I'm nothing if not economical, first one then the other. In my world death and its absence are the same thing exactly and both fly out of Nevada. After which the pilots all go to McDonald's because their asses are too big for them new fangled flying machines. Their victims do surface eventually, look and look for a jackboot to kiss but the bosses are all wearing loafers.

153

IN MY BROTHER'S GALAXY every shoe is a different size, shape and colour. Out there, in the universe, we're all wearing clown shoes. In the sixties the state strapped his arms to his ribcage, a wet sponge to his temples, while my mother and I smuggled in cooked eggplant in discreet packaging. It's dangerous, she explained, on the bus ride down to see him, to draw undue attention.

After Reagan blew up Keynesian economics we manoeuvred lunatics out of captivity. Crazy people were us too in the eighties, so long as we didn't have to maintain all those buildings. Throwing open those doors is the compassionate thing to do, said the propertied, and then politicos reallocated the surplus. Boomers don't know doing nothing is expensive.

Eggplant was cool in the eighties, finally, as were all manner of anecdotal therapies. My mother tried to get the doctors to swap those watts for more aubergine, but they would have none of it. She reversed her position immediately, with great humility for fear her attestations would affect the voltage.

A pendulum, is how Foucault describes our dance with the insane. The philosopher, not the physicist, though I'd be hard pressed to explain how they're different. In centuries previous the righteous would have put holes in my brother's head and hung him by his ankles to release the demons. They also burned people, but mostly they just roasted chickens.

152

The city I live in is a knockoff of the very best environs and the best people. As in New York, so it's only a matter of time before Frank Sinatra writes a song about it. Junior, that is, since his father sleeps with the fishes.

In my neighbourhood coffee is more than a commodity, it's a statement, a hipster's first and last stand, downright tribal, if you want my opinion. Starbucks, say, is a place where one might come together with like minded aesthetes. Prospects, pigeons, as we say in the property business. With every cup they save a child elsewhere and, on the wall, are the pictures to prove it. How much, I ask, is that little boy in the window.

Blanche and I would meet there occasionally, and then go elsewhere for coffee. A small café in the market, the Guatemala in our minds, two doors down from our favourite vegetarian restaurant. Beans ethically picked, burlapped and shipped so the good people of Central America could buy back their bananas. I would often buy a bag to take with me, perfectly roasted for my Italian espresso machine.

It was there Blanche and I hatched a plan to take down the Dole Food Company, Proctor and Gamble, Kraft, Nestle, and Sara Lee, for starters. History will record the revolution was waged from such addresses, since what happens actually is decidedly not our kind of violence. The point is we fell in love, who wouldn't, but that could lead to spilling and what is said cannot be unsaid - but I'm working on it.

151

THERE ARE MANY SIDES to this story, and then there's the one I'm hoping to blow past the editor. Sometimes I like to pretend I'm an actuary and in my pocket is a list of schools hit and the names of children still asleep in the ruins. It's been done, says my redactor, and you wouldn't want Ai Weiwei to think you stole his idea.

A book is not a list, I said … that's true … but it could be a pipe, or a sunhat … you don't say … I did … you know nothing about the deaths of those kids … I see … do you … no … stick to your own story … when … now … where … wherever … here too then … of course … what about if I imagine myself as not here … when you are here … what do you mean … you can't imagine yourself as not here unless you're here … why not … because then you're not here already … I thought so.

I digress, it cannot be otherwise. The question then from Seattle to Boston is just how many coffee revolutionaries it will take to save the children. Still, I agree with the editor, a list is a list, a consolidation, whereas a book is a rephrasing, a scattering of those selfsame numbers. Only engineers, and those subterraneans in Nevada can keep schools from falling. Presidents too, but that's complicated.

150

WAR IS A STORY best told at a safe distance from falling buildings. When I was a field correspondent I filed all of my pieces from a hotel in Manhattan, say, or Paris. Room service proved indispensable in my attempts, my strategies, to steer clear of the carnage.

Just me then, and my traveller's guidebook, what we would later call smartphones. Thus I may have evaded those warzones as a tourist rather than a journalist. Either way dead people, be they correspondents or globetrotters, write lousy copy, is a line that should really be in a movie.

A threat isn't a threat unless we agree, and then it's like shooting kids in a barrel. From ten thousand feet the Tigris looks like barbed wire, so said Time Warner, but there's no way to confirm that because everybody drowned in that story. Still, there's nothing better than a moat when fixing a target, because those below can't cut their way out of it.

Nepal is where Gautama first said yes to the river, the one that now feeds my tomatoes. By way of an African wind, I checked, the same wind that brought in those black people. Jesus, by contrast, spends all of his time on the Mexican border. In El Paso and in Juarez they still do a fast trade in awaited deities.

To recap, the Buddha got onto the continent, the country, my garden and finally into my kitchen via a southeasterly breeze and the water supply respectively. But for indoor plumbing we may never have met. There he sits crazy as a loon or a bat on the ceiling. He does come down occasionally for coffee and bagels, but only after he checks for zebras.

I could write a book on what I don't know about Buddhism, but it would be no different than the book you're reading. Neither motion nor stasis, is all I know of his teachings, like a prisoner on receiving his death sentence, or a child caught in an air raid. It's possible Siddhartha talked to my big brother, since neither of them are fastened to anything. Still, I doubt they'd agree on the subject of happiness seeing as, unlike gods, not all crazy people are crazy.

Onward, though all of our incursions die on arrival. Everywhere the media holes up and trucks out information. It's a trick they do with technology and an army of correspondents. Dispatches from the Marriott is how I described my work to the Times of New York or London. The coffee was free, but one had to have an assignment to expense the liquor. Luckily, there was time and content enough between the bed and the shitter to invent what was happening, and any pilot worth his salt knows not to bomb the hotels.

I'm more productive with a few countries or at least a parking lot between me and the enemy. As in Paris, or Baghdad but before we lit up that city. All writing is jazz, as we say in the news business, and then a documentary that cycles from the BBC to the History Channel. I know for I subscribe to both, bundled and discounted, thinking made easy by an ever-diminishing list of conglomerates.

IN THE SUMMER I have coffee in the garden and leave the front door unlocked. There's nothing more unsettling than finding Bob in the kitchen, nothing more disturbing than his assessment of what's what before breakfast. He's here now, contemplating the dried figs I keep in a jar on the counter.

I'm not for these latitudes, he says … would you like a tomato instead … once again you fail to grasp my meaning … from the garden, very fresh … just a tomato … that's what I said … a tomato is not an apple … that's true … embellish a little … yesterday I had coffee and bagels with the Buddha … think garnishes … I am … a drop of oil, a sprig of oregano, is that so difficult … no … and you should only buy figs when they're in season … sure, but if it's fresh figs you're wanting, might I suggest Syria.

Figs are fragile, subject to local conditions. Their lack is ubiquitous in Nunavut. They don't travel well, unlike whiskey, toasters or money. Oregano too, dried obviously, though the fresh stuff grows wild in my garden. But let's keep that under our hat because what Bob doesn't know is a godsend.

Kings, governments will tolerate scarcity, hunger, slaughter even. For the greater good, says Bob, for the citizenry who, in turn, will forgive those transgressions, as in Leopold's Congo.

Or Obama's Yemen, the spoils to the moguls he worked for, the butchers, the bakers and deal makers, and none of them gone to the fair.

Our leaders no longer send priests to baptize the victims. Those early Jesuits who, after services, would chase schoolboys up a rubber tree to minister sausage and sacrament. To this day Antwerp continues to bring home the bacon, and some of those lucky rascals now study in Brussels. Though many stayed home with a paper bag of inhalants and what was left of those Belgian Gatling guns.

Bacon is an interchangeable unit of production, of value, when pigs fly there'll be less of it. Supply is key. Extortion plain and simple, for oil, pigs or rubber, said Blanche over cannoli and coffee. The greenback underpins the global economy, especially in places where they don't have any, and then it's shipped by the boatload to China.

Buy real estate, I once told a boatload of Congolese youth as they spilled into Sicily. Kidnap the Flemish or just sell them heroin to amass the down payment. Better yet pharmaceuticals, because there's nothing like the warmth, the glow, of peer-reviewed product. If you're not a people person, and I could not be more sympathetic, think smart phones, mainframes, bank codes. But when they come for your keyboard, remember to tell them you heard it from a fictional character

148

NOW COMES TOO LATE, said Freud, his words my sequence. Unless it was Einstein who said it, in which case it would have meant something different. Roundabout the time Mr. Nobel awarded his prize to the guy who weaponized mustard gas. Fritz Haber, best known as the father of chemical warfare, though all men looked the same then, sharing but one mustache among them. Luckily, ideas still came easily to the whiskered in those days.

Extraneous, tangential, Bob says of my equating genius with bristles. Blanche would say the same thing if she were here also. I hope she shows up soon and agrees to be me while Bob is still talking. But if she starts talking too they'll have consensus. The same conversation until I turn purple.

Regal was the colour to die for before Fritz killed an entire generation of monarchists. Sovereigns were the first to put the un in livable and then things got worse, as they say in the Punjab. The industrial revolution was in full swing by 1918, that's how Europe was able to produce all that mustard gas. But after that terrible war there weren't enough white people to work those factories and that, sweet Kiki, is how all that good curry got into Hounslow.

147

Every night I pray for sleep, settle for a little toast and marmalade. The jelly is local and the jar comes from China, but I'm sure that's temporary. China, that is. A jar is forever and then a diamond, a girl's best friend, said Marilyn, but it took a few million years for those stones to adorn her clavicles. A crystallized hippo with a speckling of Jackal, or so I imagine. Hot diggity we're back in the Congo. The bowels, as they say in Antwerp, where those jewels were cut and polished to a shine befitting the superstar.

I'm steadying myself for a world beyond honey, hence the marmalade. Without bees, after which we'll need to adapt to a life without oxygen and, what I like about that, is I won't have to do anything.

There's really no difference between a bee, a dodo and us, eventually. By the way, Kiki and I googled that bird and it's doing fine in absentia. Then we went to Chicago, circa 1920, and danced the Charleston. There are days when toast and marmalade are not enough and that, Kiki announced, is why we dance and eat ice cream.

Bob is in the pantry looking for olive oil and oregano. He's got me cutting up that tomato we talked about earlier. When something is over it begins again, he says … that's my line … it's not … it could be … it isn't … what are my instructions … sliced, not diced, and definitely not random.

I do what I'm told. It wouldn't take much to start the sparks flying and it's not my tomato we're contemplating. Besides, a tomato in one hand and a knife in the other is a good way to stop the brain churning. I have always been a fan of self-directed lobotomies, popular in the seventies. They're even more common nowadays but YouTube, unlike smack, won't stop the buzzing.

Everything is better when Bob and I don't speak, so long as we don't do it together. He hands me the oil and oregano and walks to the window. Fixates on a squirrel looking back at him, the same squirrel who had the audacity to critique my doodling. I've pinned a response to his favourite tree in the garden, but he's refusing to read my disputations. Bob says there are no words between me and that squirrel, except for the ones I'm inventing. But I don't see the distinction he's making.

146

THE PHILOSOPHER'S GIFTS ARE not for us, they're for the language. The sophists themselves are expendable, we learned in Germany, unless they first caught a train to Vienna. Never again, is what we said after, but again is not the same as the same, explained Netanyahu to the American congress. The desert to Tel Aviv and the spoils to y'all. That's us, said Lindsey Graham, but we will need to throw a bone to the British.

Dispensation is the first rule of democracy. Acquittals all around now that we're pulling from a much smaller atlas. Seizure is fine but forfeiture is legal, thought the German chancellor as she watched Bibi on television. Go now, she instructed her diplomats, her winged monkeys, and tell the world it's nobody's business how we came to own Athens.

You can't storm the Deutschmark and you can't bomb an injunction. Soon everyone will know what they're teaching at the Frankfurt School of Economics. As for Crete, just tap your heels three times and swallow, said Mutti to those good island people and then she made the same speech in Portugal.

I know, for the Bible tells me so, it was different in the beginning, when we first started killing Hebrews within our then capacity. I read that book cover to cover except for the pages inside it. There were no trains to aid in the flow, the flood, and no reason to burn the bodies. But that was before we tacked up Jesus, also a sophist, though his predilection for the profession has been greatly exaggerated. To think, perchance to dream, but for a few spikes Iraq would still have its libraries.

The story again, but from the inside of a cucumber this time. I scour the block and the city, a grid really, tagged and apportioned a few centuries prior, so I could find that oversized pickle. The surveyor, like the one in Kafka's book, was also dispatched from the castle, except this city's monarch was English. Still, the job is the job, the dream come to roost in the tracing.

The stars too have been earmarked, patent pending, I can't wait till they come to Walmart. I like the shiny things for they will be with us forever. That's why I put every bead and trinket in my last will and testament. We're all go-betweens, down-market hucksters. I've bequeathed all I have to the fishes, in the hope they'll welcome me in, or back. I'll hitch a ride on a raindrop on its way to the ocean and then, like the Buddha, I'll ride those tides back into my kitchen.

In the forties Jersey boys went back to Italy to make love in fields and bombed out buildings. It was a very good war. They returned to a New York parade, more sex, we have the numbers, before taking the party all the way to Korea. Their kids went back too, eventually, as the musical or to visit their half-siblings in Sicily, but it was no longer romantic to die an American in one's country of origin.

In the fifties intellect had all but deserted the American experience, but for a few poets who hightailed it to Paris. In a decade they'd return with a vengeance, Berkeley marched, Virginia watched, while Montgomery burned.

In the sixties we were the numbers and we had the songs, the coffee houses from which to topple atrocity. Imagine the pentagon's surprise when Walter Cronkite put us opposite that war on television. But it was nothing like the campaign in Europe, in Southeast Asia our boys had to pay for their women.

We can't look at clouds from both sides anymore and mainlining is rarely practised in polite society. Apart from these rants, my ever-expanding discourse on the perfect tomato, I forbid myself all other excesses. If pressed, I'd include my conversations with Bob because they too don't go anywhere. As for my travels with Kiki, I'm merely a foil to her brilliance.

In the seventies we waited for the eighties. Then we leveraged all the houses we used to play in, only to lose them again in the nineties. Except for those immigrant families who stashed coins and small bills in lupini cans. Their industry rewarded in a wartime bungalow, a palace really, next to some factory neighbourhood.

Thank god for spam and backyard zucchini. Banks didn't like lending money to foreigners anyway, they didn't understand leveraging or consolidation. It's as though a house was just a house to those people.

Juicing spinach was all the rage for us movers and shakers, agitators-cum-longevity-addicts. Sweaters too, and don't even get me started on cocaine and Elvis Costello. Social justice was us in the eighties. Thus parents no longer shuddered when they discharged their daughters, now that they were part and parcel, morsels, in the general economy.

An ocean of debt is better than a mountain of money, but don't tell the poor or they'll ruin everything. They're still waiting, praying for Manhattan to fall into the ocean, what's wrong with the world is right with that city.

I too looted and supped with the elephants, different borough same pachyderms. I was despot and saviour, though I preferred the former, without ever knowing whose bread I was buttering. The cannoli was better and eventually we did find a way to encumber those outsiders.

Life is all about shopping, at least until we run out of everything. It shouldn't take long now that the Chinese have got wind of it. But what I really adore is treks to the third floor, from there I pretend I can't hear the door. I do what I do for a song but I'm working my way up to no reason at all. I will die at eighty-four because it rhymes with war and ninety-four would just be ridiculous.

144

DEATH IS FINAL AND then a thicket, there's no need to grieve for a seedling or a burnt sparrow's wing. When I am done talking I'll go and shoot ducks in Kentucky. There the second amendment is deaf to the statistics coming out of Chicago, they will defend to the death my right to drop bodies. By night I'll make moonshine, so should I take to scribbling again I'll be blind already.

When Kiki visits we'll listen to the birds cackle, and then we'll decode those quacks, log the process and publish our findings. We had to put that research on hold because where we live the ducks don't say anything. They adorn hooks in the windows of Chinese restaurants, so are reluctant to state what they're thinking.

Ridiculous, says Bob of our lingual investigations … you mean important … you can't decipher a quack … why not …

it's not a word … what about when we say it … say what … quack … we mimic a duck … in English … in any language … all languages then … I suppose … beyond language … hardly … so if it quacks like a duck it could still be Hungarian … what … or a chicken … you're insane … you mean funny.

Bob and I talk less when I'm cooking, he respects the process. I'm making spaghetti, aglio e olio, as they say in Connecticut. It's not what I want but yesterday I refused to go shopping. We'll eat that pasta with a bucket of sauce and a mountain of parmesan, like they do in Kentucky because nobody does that in Napoli.

The days are long and the years short, phrasing is everything but it should have some bounce. A spark will level a forest, napalm too. That we were here once will be true eventually, but once is not in my vocabulary, it has never been my situation. I have this surplus, a black and hardy sound. Speech, if you must, before I beat it back with a shovel.

Bob is leaving, says he'll be back later. He knows I don't like surprises, or knowing, there's simply no upside to what he just told me. While he's gone I'll kill my brother or bury my mother, and then I'll touch myself inappropriately. Fuck the story and the horse I rode in on. When it's all done and gone I'll fall asleep to cello, the sound and that's all.

When I woke up Bob was back. I never left, he said … so you say … try not to go down every rabbit hole … why not … because it's a hole … your point … there's nothing there … what about when there is … I'm tired of this soup you call a conversation … so we've done this before … yesterday … I see … and in the nineties … with the Irishman … that's right … the tall one … yup … was he dead … not quite … but he was here … absolutely … what was his name … can't say … why not … it might upset Brian.

TAKE A NOUN LEAVE a noun, is how I read Augustine, so that book is the same size I found it. I read the last word first so as not to delay my understanding, then breakfast, oatmeal with yogurt, walnuts and blueberries. Later that afternoon I translated the Iliad from Greek into Mandarin. I don't speak those languages so the process was more or less instantaneous. I'm not an intelligent man, all meat and no luster, so I spent the rest of the day baking muffins.

Empty carbs, is what Blanche would say about the spaghetti I cooked yesterday. When in fact pasta was established long before we pronounced carbohydrates. We also ship noodles to Africa. People there are the beneficiaries, after his shareholders, of what Bill Gates sets in motion. But that landmass, those dominions are the story of two Bills, now that I think of it. The other is William Jefferson Clinton. Willy, for short. Africa is where presidents and billionaires go to rehabilitate themselves and, before that, it was a continent.

Neither rain nor gloom of night will keep a billionaire from planting his money, a democrat from his willy, except maybe a daiquiri or gutting Glass-Steagall. The hungry just can't resist Will and Bill's pearly ivories, whiter than a Minnesota cue ball, aka an elephant's trunk. They're building a future in which the poor won't have to do their own ploughing, sowing or shopping, and Toms of Santa Monica will supply shoes via China. Benefaction comes in all styles and sizes, from the left, the right, on planes, trains and trucks. Tanks too.

The first rule of philanthropy is take a dollar leave a penny, but a penny costs more than a penny to make so the people we give it to will just have to owe us the difference. Endless poverty is the rich man's garden, mothers with children in tow for the clinic, the cauldron. One door opens to close all the others, and where there are no roads we kill by proxy, so not all of the graves will have markings.

There's no such thing as a wasted catastrophe, and after we privatize the grid and the railroads every vote will be a vote for the army. After soldiering old generals are rewarded with careers in munitions. Still god's work, but with contracts this time. Soon the whole world will be choking on democracy's promise.

In Detroit there's no difference between a roof and a ruling. It's getting so only the weather can mitigate that disaster. Sleeping under the stars is a real kick in spring and summer and the winters are getting shorter in Motown. Everywhere cities are collapsing, and there's barely enough money to rehabilitate the boulevards of Santa Monica.

When the landlord finally kicks you to the curb, do take his refrigerator and then hitch a ride with a scrap guy. In his head are a list of all the forsaken places and they know soup, so you can still pull a last meal from the load you've been hauling.

Let's get back to the story of Bill and Willy. The children they're saving have begun tracking Nasdaq to learn the worth of their lithosphere. Soon they'll come through hell and high water to collect their inheritance. Out of mind out of earshot, so Florida, I figure. And when they spill into the lower east side, we'll bury them on Sesame Street.

Bob is arguing for and against Bill's largess … which one … I don't understand … which Bill … how many are there … two … really … Bill and Bill … interesting … but I call the president Willy … I see … because of his willy … I get it … he's doing good work … is he … with malaria … that's the other one … is it … or Bono … the nets right … the nets … for mosquitoes … exactly … indoor plumbing would be better … we're leaving that to the Chinese.

I'M FINE WITH WHAT I don't know already. What I don't know yet is the problem. Do something is the first, the last and the only thing Blanche said to me while she was still in this city. Otherwise she'd send a note to that effect every year on my birthday.

To be clear, I am and have always been perfectly situated to receive my instructions. But what I've heard so far doesn't interest me and it's unrelated to the things that need fixing. Time, the past and the future, the present, by definition. My foot to the floor, I am still driving to catch up with Blanche's leaving. The not yet of her boarding, the lies, the truth in particular. For the record, I take back the promises I made to god as she left the tarmac.

Her poem, finally, about a man who lives in a box or a shoe and only comes out to buy groceries. In the days to come, Blanche wrote, you will have never made it out of this airport. She claims it was the blubbering, but I think it was my grit, my irrepressible temperament that inspired that lyric. I will not comment on the ode's suppositions or its aesthetic merit, but I could drive a truck through what she calls living.

I asked, but god waited until I got home to give his opinion, and I know it was him because he did it on television. A National Geographic documentary of our incursions into his blueprint. It delighted him to hear we're still stumped by his cock-ups.

He said he'd just crossed the tundra, or was it the galaxy – gods are no good at geography, they simply do not understand our physicality. We got to talking, it's a way of delaying the inexplicable, not talking is another. He laughed when I showed him what we thought was his likeness.

Time is a bitch, I said, what in hell were you thinking ... it doesn't exist where I live ... where is that ... here and there ... I see ... why is nothing familiar ... the world isn't yours anymore ... really ... except maybe Texas ... oh ... they're still waiting for the end you promised them ... I didn't mean it literally ... you should tell them that ... I was never there ... really ... or here ... what about now ... nope ... what should we do ... wait ... anything else ... watch out for falling anvils.

There's no bad time to shop, but the sun is going down and I'm still in my jockeys. I review the list, on the agenda are yogurt, rapini and my brand new tuxedo. Different than Obama's docket, plus my tailor is not vetted so he could be an assassin. Suffice to say there'd be more Afghans if that president had to buy his own groceries.

My haberdasher leaves at six, so I'll need to plan carefully, but the guy who does that is not me apparently. The clothier told me to call one day before my fitting, but between what he said and what I heard there was a dog barking. A Wednesday, ostensibly, two weeks from tomorrow. As I said or will say, in my world every day is Tuesday, so I've had to call daily since we agreed on the fabric.

A few fashion tips were all I needed from our lord and saviour, for I already knew where angels gather. Which cravat will complete my ensemble, a seal skin hat and alligator shoes, in case you've forgotten. An orange tuxedo is hard to accessorize. The fabric was popular in the seventies, during the Vietnam generation, my tailor explained, so you won't be the only one wearing it.

From my teachers I learned what not to think and from my father I gleaned the difference between suitable and flamboyant apparel. Nowadays we have the metaverse for that, more effective than singsongs or Mao's calisthenics. Herding children is so last century anyway.

All those adolescent tremors, the communal twitches and tics are a godsend for parents. Especially since dad starting working two jobs and mom took the evening shift at the food terminal to keep those screens flickering. Luckily, we don't have to worry about food because here, in the first world, there's no end of bruised fruit and vegetables.

Soon all armies will be voluntary. War is more fits than starts regardless, a series of random and not so random sightings. Best we wait till it's over to grasp the objective, for the media to put lipstick on that pig and name a few heroes. It's also important to edit out those who've been detonated. Humane even, seeing as their friends and families will soon be working shoulder to shoulder with the army corps of engineers to rid the water supply of rats and cadavers.

140

Customers are made not born. Christmas is best for warm thoughts and trinkets, updos and new boots for walking. Shoppers are patriots not stakeholders, fashion as the first rule of coercion. Different is the new conformity and debt is money for they who don't have any.

Between a citizen and his creditors there's no need for airs and arithmetic. Acquisition is its own reward, so say the people on television, and me while I was in the real estate business. Nothing is better than something, better than Jesus, a Buddhist once told me. But that was before I helped him calculate the payments and made plain the terms of his mortgage. Your lack, I explained, is the bank's plenty.

It's been hours since Bob and I ate that pasta. The current crisis is tuna, the state of solid white in my pantry. The philosopher surveys the situation, quietly, smug as a bug in the last millennia. Knowledge waits to the right of my kitchen table, ready and able to execute the inevitable. It knows every can and cranny and where I keep the mayonnaise.

Give me no more tins to open, said Aristotle circa 1962, if I'm not mistaken, roundabout the time we invented the pull tab. Glory be, said the beer-drinking English. I did too, not knowing that technology would soon be transferable to puddings and tuna. Gone are the days when I could divert Bob's attentions by concealing the can opener.

I'm glad it's fish Bob is contemplating, I'm simply not in the mood to watch him tear through a chicken. The resistance in those tiny ligaments is nothing short of a miracle. Organic, because of the tumors, in the chickens I mean, mine are still pending. Dismemberment has always been our best plan – dragonflies, frogs, deer, before we get round to people.

Bob struggles to remember the name of a song while he forages for black pepper and scallions. How does it go, I ask … the ocean, it is said, never gives up her dead … that tuna you'll be eating might disagree … well … well what … who wrote it … Gordon Lightfoot, and it's the lake … what is … the lake never gives up her dead … such fury from a pool so tepid … what pool … he's Canadian … what's wrong with Canada … Winnipeg … I see … have you been … I never left.

139

EVERY DAY I GO someplace familiar, in search of truth or rapini with a long expiration date. The people I meet don't know what to think, so I do it for them. The guy who goes shopping is me and not me, but I may have said that already, adaptable, open to all manner of dissimulation.

When I get home I put on a little music and match what I bought to the list in my pocket. If things don't align I append or delete as the situation requires, and sometimes I plead ignorance. I've also been known to bring back a cake in such instances, but I'm sure that's coincidence.

Where I live and spend – forgive the redundancy – hens come with a calling card, so I'm assuming they're from Virginia. Cows have their story too, but I'm simply not interested. Well bred animals are expensive. It's the cost of roaming, says Blanche, before they are quartered and seasoned. She also said a chicken is a chicken, but that could mean anything. Luckily those costs are offset by bananas and mangos from Latin America or Haiti, now that their farmers are pickers.

I buy tuna because Bob won't eat luncheon meat. It's expensive but still a fraction of the cost to keep Bob from those exalted capons. He thinks my cockerels are the kind that live and die for Tyson or the Koch brothers. The kind that need buildings, not fields, just cages to die in.

Fish rear their own and chickens don't surf, said Kiki … that's true … that might explain the different prices … I never thought of that … their personalities are different too … obviously … that's why we didn't see hens sunbathing in the Barbados … not a one.

Kiki and I were in California last week, for a meeting on the rights of migrants working in the poultry business, agriculture more broadly. In times of drought grow guns, was all I could think to contribute to that assembly. Then I told them that in Alexandria, Virginia they're patenting chickens, 600 Dulany Street, in case they had a mind to begin the dismantling without me. The birds themselves live in Arkansas or Oklahoma, I informed, so there's zero probability of collateral damage.

There's too little space left in the open. Blanche says we needed it for airports and open-pit mining … what about cows … what about them … they take up a lot of space … they do … and the methane … ah yes, the methane.

138

WELCOME EVERYONE TO A world without people, without me in particular. I hope I didn't get hit by a torpedo. I was here and did nothing, unless Google says otherwise. Nowadays you don't have to be famous, or here, for the government, or anyone, to look up your anus. They can do what they will with my having been but, until then, they shouldn't try to contact me. I promise to say all after digitization.

I have been meditating on the enormity of one and multiples of zero, and then I think about something different.

Tumors, perhaps, or money, each cell and integer, the numbers behind our every prognosis. A billion is the new million, as they say on Wall Street, but why quibble with the things we can't fathom. I'm comfortable with all manner of malignancy, but those laissez-faire towers are just a facelift on Virginia's cotton plantations.

The universe is infinite and yet somehow smaller than a ladybug between my thumb and forefinger. I'll leave those computations to some other genius, an astrophysicist perhaps, the one that's not here yet. Or Kiki, because what this story needs is more spacewomen. The stars are a daytrip away when I'm with her, and when I'm not, now that I think of it.

Allow me to explain. Each morning I settle on a phrase, I can't find my socks, for example, and then I repeat it to the four winds. Sound travels at three-hundred and thirty-two meters per second exactly, so by my calculation those words are now rounding Jupiter. By way of Fort Meade, Maryland, so the government knows it's socks and not a bazooka I'm looking for. Coincidentally, that compound is twenty-one miles south from where they're rethinking chickens, so both facilities can be hit before lunch, traffic permitting.

I prefer a saw to a scalpel, either to no cuts at all. For a time a cell will still crave the air without the heart's pounding. Without me, without me, because the little things are worth repeating. There will be time after toast and marmalade, to move toward the thing that is killing me. I don't have a point here but motion is mandatory.

A cell absent its host is immaterial, Bob counters … what about the dead fish you just ate … what about it … dead stuff matters … it's in no way animate … that's what dead means … thus inconsequential … are you full … not quite … fuller … I suppose … therefore consequential … do you have any cake … no.

The first rule of matter states that nothing can be added or subtracted. What falls from space is roughly equivalent to what we fly to the moon. That's how I know we're living within our means. Petroleum is simply the reconstitution of a hundred-million-year-old tiger with a mountain on top of it. Give or take the few centuries it took to invent and then mobilize the technology to access it.

Here's how it happened. In 1858 John Henry Fairbank, of the Fairbank Oil Company, lowered a straw into the Mesozoic strata, below what was soon to be Ontario Canada. The other end he put into the tank of my Subaru. Sometime later we did the research on just how many of those sabertooths could fit in a Volkswagen Beetle. The answer was all of them, to the last drop and whisker.

137

I AM MY BROTHER's keeper, and so I must learn to differentiate between the dead and the living. The war to end all wars will be for the last fish in the ocean and when that time comes Google maps will show us where it is exactly. Should that fish prove too fast for the navy, any cook will tell you, cleaved and garlicked we all taste like chicken.

The queen will eat first and last so one fish is plenty. What of my generals, she'll ask, my trusted advisors … they died in their beds your grace … and what of my subjects … they died in compounds.

In the time of time to come we will not need fish, fowl or their factory cousins because we won't be here. Self immolation has always been the objective, so said my therapist, except he was talking about me specifically. But those compulsions are fundamental, part and parcel of the collective. Our suicidal urges are what keep the world churning. Why we built and took down those Manhattan towers. The pyramids too, still standing, but that's only because the people who live in them are dead already.

My analyst knows this, people with his skills are the architects of inquiry, of torture if need be, as in Abu Ghraib or

Pinochet's Chile. Protocols too nuanced and too stark for prime time, and we wouldn't want the public's knowing to prejudice the confessions they're logging.

Lickety-split is how cockroaches will describe our trajectory when they rule the planet. God's speed, since it will have taken them three hundred million years to reach their apex. After which insect scholars, or whatever the schema, will unearth and alphabetize our tenure. People before pigs, and after parrots, but it may be presumptuous of me to infer a bug's syllabary.

I'll be fine. On Wednesday I picked up my tuxedo, that no-weather getup. Finally, Wednesday is Tuesday once more. As for the world without me, without me, I live there already, not here, not now, not ever. But, said Kiki, we will always have always.

I hope someone then reinvents archaeology and they pull my corpse out of the Atlantic. The west coast lacks discipline and with the warming it's unlikely I'll be preserved in a glacier. Besides, I prefer the sophistication of the eastern seaboard, its hardboiled cities, how people of means outlive their children.

Should I drift or continents collide I will shake hands with Calabria again, reunite with my fossilized kin. I have returned, I'll say then, like Osiris and not Jesus because he'll still be in South Texas. Did I mention I still speak the dialect, a gift from my mother, and from my father the language proper.

136

Speaking of Tuesday, my analyst is suggesting a reckoning now that pappy's been mentioned. All I can say for sure is he's my analyst not my accountant. Still, I agreed with him because he's an expert and it's easier than listening. Traitor, saboteur, said my ghostly other, the one who slides cakes into my grocery cart while I grub for tomatoes.

The doc's on a roll. He's talking about turning a flood into a trickle of confusion and misery. Ends can be beginnings, he says, but I may be paraphrasing. Something about family, had I listened correctly. A story told from the inside of a mirror, about mirrors, about findings, ostensibly.

Leaving matters, I said on the subject of kin. That's your solution to everything, he countered, unless he was praising my unwavering consistency. I'm partial to statements that don't explain anything. Besides, I'd already heard that stuff about ends and beginnings, in Katmandu roundabout the fifth century, if I remember correctly, but then I didn't have to pay money for it.

As a child my father exposed me to the rigor of diction, there is power in nullity, but after I converted it all into English. Regrettably my analyst had concocted another piling of language to find the kid I dragged kicking and screaming into the talking room. He's doing his best to sort out the what-what of my rambling. He's good, but from watching Tony Soprano undergo therapy I know what not to tell him in case he talks to the government.

Moving on. After gassing Ethiopia we strung up Mussolini and then hopped a plane for Ontario. Early December, since a few weeks later I met Santa Claus. A demonic figure and chimney plunger, a delivery boy for Sears Roebuck. He's responsible for the implacable nothing languishing in every garage and basement.

Santa is benign, a fable we tell our children, says my inquisitor. But I smell collusion. A doctor is a doctor, emissary unto death for the state and the pharmaceuticals. Careful, said my cake-eating alternate, talk about yogurt instead.

I was in university when I first tasted yogurt, I said … really … in the cafeteria … I see … I got excited about the microbes … surely you'd had yogurt before … maybe, but I didn't know what it was … there was none in Italy … not in my town … where was that again … Calabria … sorry, I meant which school … Stanford …. that's in California … yes … you've never lived in California … your point … you didn't go to Stanford … some other school then … what was it called … Stanford … except it wasn't … that's right.

Empires come and go but cherry blossoms will outlast the sun by an hour or so. Levelling Japan was a good idea and a real boost for the scientific community. Truman reached out to the victims eventually, or nearly. He wanted to give the world time to understand the science, for us to savour his accomplishment. After bulldozing the rubble, corpses too in this instance, Harry knew the Japanese would get distracted by the more technical side of his enterprise.

When in Nagasaki don't eat the mushrooms, a carrot once told me. Each time Kiki and I set a course for that city we end up in San Francisco. Our intention, but after the fact, since to be lost one must first have a destination. Besides, that city has more sushi than Tokyo and both of those places are behind the fire station next to the playground where Kiki parks her train and rocket ship. So hold on to your hat if you're coming, lest it end up in Portugal.

Nowadays the Japanese know more than Detroit about Motown and Frank Sinatra, more than New Yorkers about hotdogs and cheesecake. That's why hang-ups and bang-ups don't happen to them, at least not while they're making trucks in Texas and cars in Kentucky. Those fabled blossoms can also be seen on screens beneath the Nevada desert because you can't be too careful with friends and allies.

We are what we were, armies are just a throwback to our crooked primates. When fear was a calling from no place in particular, unless there was a mammoth in the general vicinity. Fear better, said Beckett, or something similar. One four-letter word was the same as another for that Irish writer, much like an old soldier waiting for god or the VA to clean up their backlog.

My analyst, like most gurus, says one must go below to break through. I think of it as the place below under, though I admit neither then both, as I count the leaves outside his window. Below is cited twice in the preceding sentences from a total of four similar references, fully half of what has been represented, if we don't count the below I just mentioned.

Counting anything is never simple and subject to scrutiny a junkie once told me. Numbers aren't real, he continued, but they do keep me busy. They were invented in Mesopotamia, or China, to tally the days in perpetuity. A place I know well, perpetuity, that is, China won't return my calls and conferring with Mesopotamia nowadays would require a different plan altogether.

134

THERE ARE PLACES WHERE it rains but a few times per annum, except when it doesn't, and then women cart water for their children and rapists. Life in Niger is a documentary in Maine and conjecture in Fairfax Virginia. At the Washington Post fonts are adjustable.

Every downpour a sprinkling and the other way too, when flesh collides with our need for petroleum or bauxite. Bananas in Guatemala, pork bellies, if we're talking Chicago, though the pigs themselves live in Iowa.

We have the machinery, the incentive to grow, or short, every disaster while Africa chokes on the numbers. The poor will support the rich without ever laying eyes on each other. When the time is right it just happens. The banks will send representation, cocks bare and the money spent, and then the president will explain it on television.

A sweatshop in Bangladesh is a laboratory in Palo Alto, carbon negative, neutral, or at least tentative. Silicon Valley is a magical place of ping-pong and light. Everything that happens there and in Dhaka now fits in my pocket, thanks to a few adolescents who had the wisdom to drop out of college.

Asia rising, in the wake, the promise of mass urbanization. The proletariat is itinerant in the new economy, a little quicker than death and slower than money. Rice with a hint of pork will keep workers humming. Gone are the days when the master had to shoulder the cost of feed and transport.

I'm reminded of those nomads who once roamed the prairies and died in the slaughter house that was Missouri. They dogged the bison, judiciously, but sustainability proved inimical to nation building. Hence there was no need and no provisions were made for that beast's continued existence, and for the people who hunted them. Those communities wreaked havoc on property values, still do. As for the bison, now we only shoot them on television. Their pain is our pain after Maybelline.

Rice is the great equalizer, be it steamed or a lobster risotto in Tuscany. This ship rights itself and goes wherever the tax code is friendly to commerce. Borders aren't for everyone, but who needs an address when you have everyone else's. Not to mention a rocket fueled penis for those weekend trips to Uranus. Zip codes pinging, slithering, like worms inside thousands of mainframes, except there's no eating your way out of those Macintoshes.

As a journalist I'd have cut through bone and through ligament to get to the Pulitzer. I once filed a story from a catamaran on the Mediterranean and another from a canoe on the Gulf of Mexico. In both cases I exaggerated the threat and the numbers. I put Muslims and Montana, Latinos and Laredo, as often as possible in the same sentence. I chose the best words and asked all the wrong questions, so I could stay true to what the president was saying.

In the eighties I reported on the exodus that was quietly forming in Honduras and Guatemala. The story wasn't picked up, or not until recently. Our readers didn't have the attention span for slow moving caravans, and it would be decades before those refugees reached San Antonio.

In Vietnam American soldiers moved from failure to failure, and I along with them. Recognisance was the issue, in that you had to see people to kill them. That has since been corrected and pilots, while still an option, are no longer required. Our enemies are identified and exploded in the same instant, more often than not to the songs of Bruce Springsteen.

There was screaming in the preceding. A howl is not a word but it could be a book, or a song, was my thinking. You'll never blow that past the academy, said Bob. Don't abandon either, said my brother, you know what the naming has done to our species.

I believe all things are possible since Brian played Jesus in celluloid … who, said Bob … circa 1970, back when a commoner could still buy a dead parrot in Greenwich … that was a skit … about Brian … that was a movie … about Jesus … that's right … in Palestine … why are you obsessed with Nevada … I'm not … and drones … who told you that … you were just talking about them … I wasn't … and you think of nothing else … I think about tomatoes … that's true … and zucchini … I see … yogurt … I get it … and drones.

132

THE MAN FLEES, THE horse falls down, wrote Éluard. He didn't need a reason to start the man running. Surely by now we've come to understand such provisos. Not I, not now, not here, all language is prayer, as one speaks to stone or the weather.

After I'm done talking Bob and I will only meet in libraries. There someone will have already written the distance between us, and they don't allow food on the premises. It takes a philosopher to stop a philosopher, or a hunch, innumerable in those repositories, a stamp for each gap and banner. More seers than pigs in Iowa, than corn even, except the plants know not to say anything.

I used to live on the moon with my brother, twelve kilometres northwest from where I buy my tomatoes. And though we could never agree on where that was exactly, a tomato then was still a tomato.

Each morning we'd try again to fix those coordinates, as though we had never spoken. Every thought was hatched in its druthers so the talking itself didn't matter. Since then I've relived his every gasp and fragment. His was a speech like no other, thus I needed a theory to keep him from becoming invisible. But hypotheses were too expensive for the son of a tailor trying to stay one step ahead of Armani. So I took a job as teamster in a mayonnaise factory before applying to Stanford.

I WILL PUT AN end to art, but I may not be here when it happens so I'm telling you now it was me who done it. Should I come to know then, when I am dead and dead, that a word is a word and a bird, I'll report back immediately. We'll meet in Hollywood so we'll already be where we've been and where we're going. Starbucks, say, or wherever scribes go to jingle, twinkle and die before lifting their heads.

Until then the movie business will continue to thrive since those keyboard zealots, those one page a day addicts, will still want their lattes and Teslas. It's the fictional characters I worry about, when LA finally slips into the ocean. Digital refugees, those figments in search of a story should look to Ontario's burgeoning film industry. That Precambrian slab ain't going anywhere.

Engineers are working on the transition already, charting dams and tracking glaciers. Canadians – they're such good friends – have been clear-cutting for decades. Eminent domain cites the farm not the farmer, that's why sovereignty is such good business. Annexing one's neighbour is less expensive than George's – not the smart one – blitzkrieg in the desert.

Canada is not Iraq, but it could be, and for a ten-gallon hat they'll throw in the arctic. The deed at the ready, from the hip, as they say in Laredo, to this cherished dominion, but we will need more Walmarts for farmers to work in.

Who needs jurisdiction, acreage, when you have just-in-time merchandising. With increased scale and mechanization it will be easy to keep the warehouses full in North Carolina and the New Golden State of Ontario. That's why in Honduras they have no bananas, they have no bananas today.

130

Bob and I finally stepped out for some air and I needed to get him out of my hair, rhyme notwithstanding. The difference between a poem and a piss is the orifices. Poetry happens, on tiny stages, in bars and better cafés all over this city, but there's always a way out, two if you go through the kitchen.

Keep moving. Be it in the pouch of a kangaroo or on the Kon-Tiki with Kiki. The cockeyed is my preferred mode of travel. Last week, while on a junket through Kazakhstan, Krakow and Kandahar, Kiki reminded me she had homework to do for the morning. We abandoned our plans to see the kites in Kabul. They're to die for, literally, the last several decades have not been good to those runners.

We set a course home through Ukraine by way of Helsinki, with a quick stop in Kiev. Kiki was at her desk in a shake where she explained her assignment. An adventure around a single character but, try as I might, I couldn't guess that letter. It's K, she said, where on earth have you been for the last couple of paragraphs.

That was two months ago Tuesday, the day after the day before Kiki finished her rocket ship. I remember it like I don't remember it. I had drinks with Blanche later that evening, at eight eastern, five pacific, because she was in Vancouver. We talked under that star, the one I painted over so I could see it better and I didn't have to wear pants for the occasion as that city was now in my living room.

Bob and I move steadily toward his apartment. We walk and talk like priests at the Vatican and, in the tradition of those fabled clerics, we repeatedly pause for emphasis. Though I couldn't help but notice Bob preferred to stop while he talked and walk while I babbled, so I made it a point to interrupt as often as possible.

He's becoming animated, peppering his speech with embedded clauses. A few more insertions and he'll close the circle, but I could easily turn that round into a triangle. The perfect aspect, a kite runner once told me, to catch the wind. The plan is to grow tired after Bob has gone too far to turn back. That's how I end most evenings, with or without the philosopher, and in the morning I tell myself they didn't happen.

Bob continues to speak, or not, but that's talking too. He's saying something about culture, its functionaries. I chime in with tales of an attaché whose name is not Rita, because that would be actionable. Bureaucrats are forever, keepers of the general and the particular, the downgraded present. Her adherents, poets mostly, came and went talking of beans and some guy named Angelo.

I fell into that gaggle after a long absence, a two decade stint in the real estate business, and for a minute this city was Paris. Writers, or they who go by that name anyway, look to each other to confirm afflictions. The smaller the fall the bigger the aria, that's how it is with poetry, so here's to the few who stayed home with their keyboards.

The venue, the gathering place was a mess of my own making, a building I'd bought in the nineties, the real ones. Now a watering hole for middling authors and their attendant barnacles. It's where I met her who is not she, I with my dick and she with her standing. Luckily I didn't need what she was peddling.

Talking exists because thinking doesn't, said Adorno, approximately. I think therefore I'm not, said the Buddha, ostensibly. Who'd a thunk it, said Descartes, allegedly. None of which matters because the revolution has now been appropriated. Before that I was Rimbaud, the crumbs and Kafka's deformity, in the eighties, before the culture industry went to work on my genitals. May Brian, and she who is not her, forgive the audacity.

129

CULTURE IS THE PLACE where nobody dies, or everybody, I can't decide. It exists so we don't have to, so people can visit. We just can't get enough of them masterpieces. Art as breeding or the past that wasn't, be it Marx in Manhattan or Che in Honduras. To every failing a name, to every gravesite a number, except for all those people we killed in the desert.

In Jerusalem they're unearthing god's plan, and before that it was a stopover on the way to Damascus or Baghdad. I'm talking about civilization, war's binary cousin, before the advent of quantum mechanics. Those theories are rarely translated into Swahili, for all the known reasons. Science is what happens to other people, history too. The Japanese, for example, but I may have said that already or I will in a minute.

I quicken the pace, while Bob makes a point of halting more frequently. I feel a cold coming on, to expedite my departure and then I'll ride that virus till Christmas. All my life I have been building these exits, arrive late is my praxis, then squirm like a worm and run like an ostrich.

Speaking of stasis, of progress, the modern prison is rooted in the great transformation, on the heels of the nation state. Incarceration amended so our jailers could make a few dollars. The soul is the body, said the convict to his custodian. We agree, said the children working the mills in Manchester city. But their masters knew that already from squeezing those same kids down soot-filled chimneys and from strapping brown people to the mouths of cannons.

Discreet deaths thereafter, more idea than factual, practically blameless since they no longer torture in the tower of London. Thank god, whispered the queen to her son Charlie, for Romanian contractors.

Nowadays Alabama is the best place to found a compound, because in Portland there aren't enough black people to drive the per diem. I'm not from there, or here, though I've been walking these streets for decades. I came for the dream and stayed for no reason. A good thing too since my house is worth more than a mansion in Yemen. Value is inversely proportionate to the distance of whatever they're seeing on those screens in Nevada. I should know for I was a guesstimator before I was a parking meter in Africa.

Bob has yet to discern my plan to ditch him and we're standing beneath the streetlamp at the foot of his building. We've reached that point in the evening when people are holed up or sleeping, and my favourite time to drive a truck through his cogitating.

He fiddles with his keys while an alley cat stops, looks and pretends not to listen. There's no light above the door, Bob explains, as he tries each key individually. I'm sure it's a tactic to delay my departure. I pivot, he mentions Blanche, and the cat snickers.

Has she confirmed her departure, Bob asks … not exactly … so no news of her arrival … next week Tuesday … why not say that … you asked about her departure … you're an idiot … good to know … did she say anything else … she's tired … of what … the mountains … what did she say exactly … I'm tired of the mountains … anything else … people … really … finally … don't start … is that an option … I'm going to bed … goodnight Bob.

128

I LIED ABOUT CATCHING a cold and then I lied about everything, except maybe some stuff about Jesus. Heaven is closer than where it used to be, on television, I think, or Texas. I hope I can still talk to the woman who brings in my peaches.

Yesterday I pumped up the tires and greased the chain on my bicycle for my upcoming ride to El Paso, after a quick stopover in Fort Worth and Dallas. When god opens the books I plan to be there already, though lately he's been making himself more available. I need only Google his name to receive his message and each time I masturbate he kills a kitten.

Life is a dream or a memory, it is what it would have been anyway. Tofu is steak and kale is potatoes in the Lone Star State, whereas I always buy broccoli when I'm thinking strip loin. The point is the food in Texas will be spectacular, and imagine my surprise when I bite into it. Steak is steak and broccoli is broccoli, says my analyst. But there's no way to confirm that without knowing the places he shops in.

I reported all of this to my brother. I agree with you, he said, tofu does have one more syllable, but steak makes a better stir-fry. That's how we reason, so the state gave him a bed, three squares a day and someone besides me to talk to.

Madness will eclipse the sun and every summer thereafter. So will a bullet except then you can't talk about it. The government is all but out of that business now, as are the insurance conglomerates. There's no upside, no place for the insane in a market economy.

127

THE EMPIRE PITCHES ITS colours in faraway places, a rectangle that flutters. Call it she and young men will think it's a damsel or their mother, and sometimes they end up like my brother.

Burn the flag and the country too will come back to you as the woman who, every day, brings in more peaches.

As I said previously, when I graduated from Stanford the army sent representation. A general they keep on the shelf for just such occasions. The world was ours for the taking, he said, but a small town is home for eternity and then a freeway. Such was the dream of a few bearded men who built the railroads, and dismantled them on learning the price of Congolese rubber.

The general spoke of those fabled campaigns in Europe. Something about tombstones and poppies followed by periods of austerity and shopping. Waged in defence of freedom and us, the nations progeny, now tucked safely inside his explanation. You could float an ocean liner between what was said that day and what I heard, but that's true ordinarily.

The good people of Michigan and Ohio kept the blast furnaces stoked. In the evenings they'd slide into the folds of what we used to call newspapers. Workers then believed to be constitutionally entitled to all manner of information, not to mention the coupons. Those Sunday cut-outs were a godsend after Passchendaele, the Somme and before we repurposed the railroads.

Buffalo Bill rode those locomotives too after launching his rodeo of riders, ropers and sharpshooters. But for those early audiences there was no difference between a show and a massacre, having recently obliterated the indigenous populations. That's why Bill had to kill his Indians repeatedly.

Prohibition followed on the heels of Bill's hootenanny. Ushering in those heady days when the Kennedys thought they too were Sicilian. All of that was before Joe built Camelot with the help, or so I like to think, of the above referenced Italians. By then you couldn't tell a cop from a gangster and people without beards were now bankers but, I know from the BBC, bristles were still hip in Afghanistan.

When I got home I bolted the door and moved back from the windows. Having survived Bob's inferences, I commenced to scrubbing their stench from my kitchen. Then I reheated some lasagna I had told Bob was a salad. I had to climb onto a chair to access that dish, and the handle on the microwave was as high as a skyscraper. In short, I was a turtle.

I did all I could to reconstitute, to prove my mammality, but I couldn't find my papers and I wouldn't have been able to reach them anyway. Soon I was lost between the couch and the coffee table, surprising since this was my house. I'd also been a turtle before, but that was with Kiki. This would never have happened if I were an elephant, I reasoned, and then reason crippled me.

The next morning I woke up in Idaho so I phoned Kiki. That's one fast turtle, she said, are you sure you're not a bird … what kind of bird … you called me … then no … you're not sure, or you're not a bird … I'm not a bird … I'll pick you up after school … what'll I do till then … pretend you're in Paris.

I made coffee and pulled out some biscuits I keep hidden behind a large bag of oatmeal. Then I went upstairs to watch YouTube. How, I wondered, did all those random people get into in my television. Among them a professor, a philosopher no less, from my alma mater. Or not, says my analyst. He's of the opinion one would have to attend Stanford to say that.

The lecture was about connectivity, or what engineers at Fort Meade call surveillance. In real time, and therein lies the kicker, said Edward Snowden. Soon we won't have to tweet or post to be noticed, we won't even have to fill in our census form. The archive will be dynamic, the professor explained. A living, breathing inventory of bodies per hectare, per metre, and the technology will correct for the hit-to-miss ratio.

For decades I have been lobbying to outlaw assembly of more than two people, it's still too many but I'm trying to be reasonable. I'm also wary of the third person plural, the creeping collective, of alliteration in general. But this not about poetry, it's about the fucking poetry down-cradled, on tripods, in the hands of our daughters.

Kiki dropped by as promised. In two years she'll be going to a different school, a large building I walk by and ignore daily, whereas Kiki sees it with her whole skin. It's next to the playground where she keeps her train and rocket ship. In Kiki's space time continuum all of her inventions occupy the same spot exactly.

Tell me about Idaho, she asked before she was through the door … you mean Paris … same question … I see … do you … no … let's talk about my new school instead … what about it … the kids are so big … you'll be big too … are you sure … think of them as food … what kind of food … meat and tomatoes … you mean potatoes … those too … why is it called middle school … there's nothing to the left or right … that makes sense … above or below … I suppose … one big middle … I get it … a priest and a rabbi walk into a bar … or not.

Then Kiki put on some music and we danced all the way to Alpha Centauri which, as it happens, was between the front door and the table. A good thing too since I'd already been to Paris that morning. I was tired, is the long and the short of it. You mean old, but don't worry, said Kiki, when I'm around the stars also make house calls.

125

I HAVEN'T BEEN OUT for a week, or an hour, not since I ditched Bob on Tuesday. Big city streets are no place for a turtle, so I waited until I could reach the fridge, the microwave and my passport before I set out again. I found that document this morning and the face in the mirror matched the one in the photo, thus confirming the club I was born to.

No longer reptilian I grabbed my list and set out immediately. Shopping is how I steer clear of the hardships in Palestine and

Burundi. Not knowing anything makes it easier to invent the particulars, it's the only way I can be sure of what's happening.

The anchor journalists who work for Rupert Murdoch and WarnerMedia do the same thing, so they must be in those stores with me. I can't say what endures of the things I'm not seeing, nothing perhaps, not even the perhaps I just mentioned. I am, after all, a dead man speaking.

Pure idiocy, says Blanche of my metamorphoses and journalistic analysis, that's how I know that she gets me. The population is increasing is all I have to say about that. About anything really, and tomorrow there'll be two hundred thousand more of us to share in the misery. Fifteen in New Jersey, not accounting for murders and suicides.

As for the exodus from Detroit and into the Garden State, that's more of a juxtaposing than a bump, an alignment, because they no longer do those in Michigan. The American family was brought to us by Westinghouse and General Motors, that's why they couldn't put any black people in those early commercials and placards. The fifties was Arkansas' favourite decade.

The seventies, by contrast, was not kind to white people. In a recent remake Archie is still working on his first million while Edith protects the home front from creditors. She's talking to realtors about selling their house in Queens for a bungalow in Nevada so they could bank the difference. On Sundays they drive past Archie's broken down factory, read the old postings for new instructions, since what they thought was happening has been ripped from the language. At night they watch reruns of themselves while eating spaghetti from Costco.

What happens in Vegas is counted, shrink-wrapped and shipped to the Caymans. Visitors are advised to double down on the dreaming. Fortunes were made to be lost, that's why the hotel windows don't open, but you can still take a bath with the hairdryer.

The front desk will spring for a plane ticket home if you're a regular, but first check to make sure your wife isn't bonking the plumber. If so, there are plenty of cheap motels on the border with climate control and even more hairdryers. Jesus too has been known to frequent those places, he likes to hang out with the Mexicans. Fortunately those people are seasonal, in with the lettuce and out before Christmas.

124

IN THE BEGINNING I was thick as a brick in a basket. I came, I saw, I wasn't – that's the gaze I'm after. A few months later I saw my toes, so I could no longer rely on my absence. I left postwar Italy before the Beatles went to India in search of the sacred. It wasn't there. They too wanted to be nobody once more, but not like they were before. I hope my saying so doesn't negate their negation.

Bob and I would meet decades later at Stanford. I remember it like it never happened, that's why I can be flexible on where that school is exactly. After graduating Bob too went to India - Britain's last, last hope after King George lost the Americas. Philosophers, like the Fab Four, were going there to find themselves, to be, which needs no explanation. But Bob gave me the lowdown anyway on the drive back from the airport.

I wasn't there, he said … where … India … how do you know … I looked … so what happened … nothing … is that bad … everything got worse … maybe that's the point … of what … going … be serious … I can't … why not … I'm driving … is there food at your place … some … let's go there … don't you want to unpack and then sleep for a week … I can do that later.

Bob's trip to India reminds me of my time in Tibet, except I never went because I didn't want to tarnish what I knew of that region already. Bob says there is no stand-in for going, but I find his contingencies tiresome. I took a job instead of travelling, mortgages, because that's where the poor keep their money, and then I locked the door behind me.

Before becoming a business guy I, like Obama, was a community organizer. I showed all manner of crazy people how to live without money. Doctors had stopped locking them up after watching Jack Nicholson play McMurphy in Hollywood. After which it was easier to be an angry idealist in movie theatres. Still, emptying those facilities was a good idea because we needed the space for Blacks and Latinos.

As to the resultant surge in streetside cranks and prophets, the government does not issue cheques without addresses. A zip code to every car and underpass and that, I explained to anyone who'd listen, is how we'll solve this and the next housing crisis. Space is space, as we used to say in the property business, people the standard anomaly.

Last week I petitioned the surgeon general because the health minister is refusing to talk to me. Through her to the minister, physicians should be dissuaded from playing name that condition. I know it's good for endowments and pharmaceuticals, for business in general, but it doesn't ring true atop subway grates or on the floor of an ATM vestibule.

In the seventies I tracked those shamans to their corner offices, down the hall from where they were keeping my brother. But not before my mother and I slipped him the stuffed eggplant we'd smuggled past the nursing station.

By a fresh water stream in Calabria we'd sprinkle sugar on lemons, and then my brother showed me how to catch the water. Such was the light before his diagnosis, the sound no sound makes when it shatters. A sound I knew well as a turtle, such is my Idaho.

To be clear, I believe in the clarity of blood and piss, the efficacy of those medieval beacons. Hell, find the pathogen is practically my reason for living. Madness too is a third party moniker and therefore immeasurable. My brother is his infirmity, I told those clinicians, but if you don't say so he can still ride the trolley.

I HAD LUNCH WITH Aristotle this afternoon because Nietzsche was busy. Soup and a sandwich, go now and tell Brian I did that. I saw and heard nothing, said the philosopher, but that's not how I wrote it. I had to answer for who I was not, otherwise it would have been next to impossible to get up in the morning. It seems Ari knew and died anyway, but I tried not to notice.

It's a thin line between art and complaining, so I always bring a knife to a poetry reading. My way of broadening the conversation, should I need to demonstrate the difference between knowing and fabrication. What one brings to art is their stupidity, how else could we have surmised the sound of gods laughing.

What was I to do, asked Aristotle … wait … for what … that has nothing to do with it … what has nothing to do with it … that's right … we wait to wait … approximately … without purpose … it's complicated … so I understood nothing … careful … not nothing … possibly … less than that … you're getting it … what of the searching … it's critical … really … more or less … which is it … neither.

I like books but television is faster. A story is so much more than the sum of its body parts, like when those towers fell in Manhattan and not in Damascus. There are places where the things we don't see happen more often. I'm sure by now we'd have grown tired of those New York corpses, had we known more about the situation in general.

Still, I can't get enough of those smiling TV announcers and every year they get prettier. With a wink, in the stir of a hip or a shoulder I'd believe anything. Therein lies the rub, but I swear it's occasional.

BEFORE NINE-ELEVEN THERE was war and there was terror but we needed a preposition to win. Or so I understood from the president`s speeches. Too bad he wasn't just talking to his dog Barney. Americans wore blue that morning but soon changed into their khakis.

When you're down in the polls bomb something, said daddy dearest, but leave the speechifying to smart people. Father … yes son … I want to kill you … I know … and then I'll finish what you started.

Words are a harness on which to hang a pause or the people. When I am done this work I'll go back to the beginning and remove all the periods. Collect and arrange those stops in some as yet unidentified order, and then I'll end it all on a comma so anyone reading this can write their own ending.

War is a good Idea, but the long game is in for-profit prisons. You say potato, I say per diem. Somewhere in America it's raining black people. What I'm saying won't reach the judiciary and it won't change the way police do their business, but it may confound the next generation. They've received enough praise and now we must prepare them for the world they'll inherit.

Murder is not wrong when the army concurs with the president, when it's collaborative. There is a time to kill and a time to choose between sedition and dreaming. As in the sixties, and more recently for the young people of Tunisia and Egypt.

Life, all up in their fingers, the pocket edition, Cairo tweeting or the Baltimore jitters. Admittedly those things could not be more different but a taste is a taste and then a habit, an engaged populace, in step, is what matters.

By the seventies full employment had come to the hills of Medellin thanks to an uptick in Manhattan discos. Kandahar too was awash with product, still is. The harvest synced, coincidently I'm sure, to my academic calendar, but at Stanford we just called that summer.

Yesterday or last week Tuesday, Blanche found a letter in my desk addressed to the president. I promptly attached a stamp, then several, and threw it out the window for express delivery. It's not there anymore so I assume that he got it.

That's not how mail works, she said … I don't understand … you're a nitwit … that could mean anything … not in this instance … are you sure … why do you bother … with what … the letters, the rants … because I don't own a bazooka … you don't own what … a piano … there are things besides … such as … travel … I travel … you don't … that's your opinion.

I disagree with Blanche, it's what I do when uncertainty fails me. Agreeing is the same thing but the former keeps the conversation more lively. Everywhere but here the evidence piles up, but there's no downside to that, no upside either, so you'll just have to wait for my signal.

Then we'll mount the alphabet on a spit and plant it on Sesame Street, put a picture of the same on every refrigerator. It won't mean a thing but it's important the kids see it pinned and wriggling before they start singing it.

Between the mark and its likeness there was a great bleeding, said Kafka. Blanche looked but couldn't find that sentence, so the writer and his editors must have taken it out on revision. The problem with substantiation is it could lead to surety, that's a metastasis in the brain or the larynx, in case you're not familiar. A forkful of nothing, followed by even more killing and literacy.

Why not a spoonful, asked Blanche … I don't understand … instead of a fork … surely you can see how they're similar … I cannot … different then … and why Nunavut … I didn't say anything about Nunavut … not recently … come with me … where … Nunavut … no way … why not … it's cold … it'll warm up … that's true … and we have to get in before the Chinese buy up all the good parcels.

119

I heard voices before I was born so I knew there'd be others. Mother, I surmised, but it may have been Mao Zedong. In the morning the birds would sing to me only. A song torn from a starling or a robin. Or the nether, said my brother, and some of those birds also work for the government. That's when I realized he was crazy already, but I don't know that now, not since my listening caught up with his speaking.

At Stanford I learned all there was to know about Stanford, but I swear I didn't inhale. I only went there so I'd have something to say in this sentence. It was there I realized never to underestimate a liberal's greed or a hipster's stupidity, and later I learned how to separate both from their money.

Now I study history, what happened and the way it was told to me. Paleontology too, because its practitioners could get blood from a stone. Thus I'm perfectly capable of conflating talking with knowing, but the birds will have none of it and given their numbers I have little chance of winning that argument.

Our species had a good run, geologically speaking, and then somebody threw a stick at a rabbit followed by a hellfire missile. That's why Syria now looks like Hawaii. Speaking of which, the Polynesians waited nine hundred years for Captain James Cook of the British navy. Only to realize those islands were never theirs to begin with. James is dead now but the English still visit those islands occasionally, more so the Germans. They come for the lava and stay for the pineapple.

118

I wake before opening my eyes, detach an arm or a leg so I can examine them closely. Reattach them after I discern their purpose and before I go shopping. Betwixt and between I have breakfast, oatmeal with a dollop of yogurt and a mountain of blueberries. Nourished, I recap what I know – my mother is dead. Then she and I commence to talking of all the dishes she used to cook for me. But after the blueberries kick in so as I can write down those recipes and append the day's grocery list.

I'm afraid when I sleep alone and when I don't, when I capitulate to the situation. The dead have a way of getting inside my head, but there's no room for regret in the things I don't tell them. That's why those gabs with my mother are in Italian and my responses are all in Hungarian. Easy peasy, said Kiki, since you don't speak the language. That's why when we're in Budapest she does the talking.

I did speak Chinese once – an address to the people's congress on how to grow rice in condos. A speech that had been festering for decades, even though Beijing then was no further than my kitchen table. I didn't mention Tibet on the advice of my handlers, or was it my analyst.

After which I attached a rope to a beam that spanned the ceiling above me, but it's clear that plan wouldn't have worked anyway. In those days I couldn't tell a hope from a rope from the rhyme those words just appeared in.

To the left is where I buried my mother, to her right is October. I came here to watch her sleep, to mimic her breathing. When finally I realized it would take more than my swollen tongue to keep her from leaving I took to whittling, waited for her death to begin. I'm happy once more but I'm not who I was in September. I wish I was back in that hospital room, her lips must be dry again and soon they'll need moistening.

A FLOWER WILL TAKE to the wind unless it's potted, out there in the universe everything is fine before vanishing. I had twenty such plants this morning, I counted them while I was on the phone with the editor. Bees are a better way to scatter those blossoms, after the frost and before they are poisoned, but those drones don't live in my living room.

The editor hung up a few minutes before me. I needed the extra time to conclude my side of the conversation. As I walked our talk back from the brink or the window I couldn't help but notice the sun was grinning. This would be a good time to restock the pantry, I said aloud, but I must not have been listening because I went back to bed. I did notice two more plants on my way there, so I made a note to update that total.

I'm for and against all manner of tabulating. The purpose of any list is to dispense with what's on it. Those logs also come in handy when tracking terrorists, or Norway as necessary. All script is tally, though I prefer to discard the words before I compile them. I am become French, as they say in Paris, but in Senegal the sequent still matters.

All that cataloguing was good for Sears Roebuck, during the dustbowl especially. The dream come to fruition finally, quarterly, making hay for recovering millionaires in New York or Chicago. It was Vanderbilt who brought the warehouses of Illinois to Nebraska, where no corn grew for a decade. On the farm they waited for toasters and cheap perfume all decked out in brown paper. But in coldwater flats off Broadway a kiss was more important than rain, and soon we'd have the movies to prove it.

A book is a pipe, as I said previously. A vessel, a hammer to stop the dark creeping, said Nietzsche or nearly, and sometimes we burn them. Too late, in my estimation, it's best to lay waste those scribes before they start griping. Folios, after digitization, are not weighty enough to clobber those of us who can't get with the program. As for the names, the geniuses who pepper these pages, they're just for show, or for Brian.

Accidents matter, I told the editor. She's a stickler for substance but I think she means context. When in fact those things only hamstring the howling. Every thought an adventure, I cried. But she does not impress easily and before our call ended she mentioned my betters. Everyone, is how she described them. She knows this will spur me to write something clever, even though she knows I prefer funny.

116

A YELP IS A YIP, or a piano, but it was for halibut that I took to the streets this morning, and broccoli because rapini wasn't in Microsoft's dictionary. Bob thinks it's a conspiracy, he says the language too is proprietary, but I think it's a glitch, or a calamity.

No matter, I speak as though from the bottom of the sea which, to my surprise, is not fatal. Not so for the folks on boats, those floaters that ferry Africans to Europe. I hope I never have to choose between death and Denmark, or wherever the stateless work tirelessly for decades before they are ejected anyway.

I could tell from the queues at the produce counter we were all pulling from the same psyche. Incidentally, the people in my neighbourhood also speak for Zimbabwe. I hitched my babbling to the couple next to me, even though they were there for something other than broccoli. They were cyclists from Montreal because that's what they told me. Q is for queue and Quebec, I said, holding up my side of the conversation.

They spoke to me of this city's mosaic while I eyed the vine-ripened organic tomatoes adjacent the garlic. Such is my Xanadu. Tomatoes are more important than intercity relations. Before parting, I told them about the fun places to visit within cycling distance, then I imagined their leaving. I had cycled to those places with Blanche, before she left me for her beloved redwoods. Why not the maple or the oak tree outside my window, I cringed.

I bagged the groceries and drove to IKEA, which was a little smaller than Sweden, closer too. Boomers rush in where cabinetmakers fear to tread, but I come here for the picture frames and the glassware, so my friends know I come here. My horizons broadened, I resolved to drive to this magical place more often. Cars, I thought, can be used for something other than transporting Bob and Blanche to and from the airport.

I pilfered, found and bought my furnishings in the seventies. Pressboard mostly, with a petroleum overlay, except for the pieces Blanche left with me. How was I to know we'd all be rich in the eighties. What's old is new in emporiums from Portland to Malibu, that's why I never upgraded the linoleum floors in my kitchen and why I'm still hip in Brooklyn.

Incidentally, that halibut, what I set out for initially, is delayed but not forsaken. Fish exists so long as it's still on a list, just like Al-Qaeda.

115

BOB'S WORK, *MEDITATIONS ON the Digital Lexicon*, is widely regarded, impressive, says the philosophical community, not to mention the blurbs on the back cover. I know from experience how monumental an undertaking it is to say nothing for six hundred pages, and what's left of that moan flies out my anus.

There is but one verdict, one story, but I'll say something anyway. Like a judge addressing the gallery before the rope tenses. They, in turn, will echo his proclamations on the way to the river. Justice was forged in the spectacle, so we'd all agree on the same brand of peanut butter.

Nowadays outsiders, and by that I mean black people and Latinos, are tracked, tried and fried in my living room. Whereas terrorists, their kin and adjacents, are exploded in place. What happens in Nevada stays in Nevada, now that Assange is no longer in business.

Allah's chosen are Jehovah's radicals, and the other way too, so long as we don't get specific. US foreign policy, as I understand it, is the president can invade whoever he wants, except for the countries that can blow up Massachusetts. He also can't target places that have never existed, like Palestine, for instance, as it morphs into Israel. That's how it is, said Beckett, except he was talking about something different.

I like to watch as much as the next gal, preferably while wearing red pantaloons over my armour. What better than a good whodunit to distract us from slaughter. Give the people something to think about and the state will save a bundle on jumpsuits and shackles. But you can't believe everything you see on television, that's why Al Gore invented the internet. Unless it was so stay-at-home dads can make pasta and pizza on YouTube.

Yesterday, while cooking a fine marinara, one of those padres told me the tomato used to be Mesoamerican. Its advent coincided with the arrival of Amerigo Vespucci. It was clear, from watching that internet daddy, the ten-thousand years before that didn't matter. Amerigo had little choice but to put his name on the continent. Diversity, culinary or otherwise, is rooted in our disembarkations, that's why the tomato is now Italian.

Pluralism thrives on proximity, said David Suzuki, he's a zoologist from British Columbia. I know it's true because pigment is no longer reason enough for a lynching but, if you're black, don't wear a hoodie. Dress for the job you'll never have, I tell young people of colour, and then don't worry because the bank will still take your deposits. I also told them to buy property with their student loans, seeing as that's the only time they'll pay posted rates for the money.

114

SPEAKING OF PIGS, OF pork bellies, more idea than actual, a swine in Ohio is an annuity in Chicago and bacon in Texas. They can't get enough of that species in Mississippi. Numbers plain and simple – the economy stupid – to the last hoof and toothpick. The hungry have always been hungry and they'll stay that way too, we have the billionaires to ensure their continuance.

Shop, said president Bush, as is the custom after planes smash into Manhattan. We'll still have the army for when we run out of everything, he said, without saying anything. Then he amended the tax code so he and his friends could move their money to wherever there wasn't one.

What's not here is forever, at least that's how I explained the president's tax reforms to Kiki. Over an American breakfast, if I remember correctly, yet another way to control the swine population. Then Kiki drew me a picture of the piggy that won't be.

In Vietnam they used napalm to manage the hog population, though I would argue Washington still owns those farms. Lingerings, vestiges in the rice and the water for which Dow Chemical still holds the patents. And there's more shrapnel than mangos on the Ho Chi Minh Trail, so that's theirs also.

113

For Japan the dream ended in Los Alamos. All things American for they who once, twice, swallowed the big one. From watching Clint Eastwood movies and BBC documentaries I know war was yesterday's certainty. Those crazy days when a chaplain, a rifle and a few cans of sardines comprised the machinery, and Jesus before he moved to El Paso.

His death preceded the telly, the telling, the English even. It's only thanks to Mel Gibson that we have the footage of his crucifixion and rising. British broadcasting is now the standard, the jewel, the shard in my noggin, and not those Hollywood blockbusters.

The BBC was even better when Churchill ruled and Britannia did its own killing. Luckily you can still buy an army in Bosnia, Botswana or Burundi, but let's end that list there because there's no B in Israel. This changes everything, thought Tony Blair. I know because Tony did his thinking on television.

Can you stick to one hemisphere, asked Bob … I thought you'd left … I've been here for hours … which hemisphere … you choose … how many hours … five … are you sure … reasonably … don't boast … roughly … that's better … is it … if only there were a witness … that would be me … a name … I have a name … a scar, a tattoo, a zip code … I have a zip code … to ratify, testify … to what … that you were here … I was here … are you sure … not anymore.

A child was born to save the world and when he returns he'll put the oomph back into our carcasses. I assume he's corralling the dead on some other star, some other galaxy. Should there be no space left for us in eternity, entire cities await their occupants in the people's republic. China builds is this century's mantra, Beijing rising on mountains of Manhattan money.

Bob doesn't believe in the reckoning, I don't either except it was true when I said it, and then I wrote it down to forget it. If Jesus gets to your town first, tell him we're here, we're queer and that we're home already. Convince him the money lenders must be left standing this time, because the only thing worse than the crumbs is not having any.

112

I WRITE TO DIE, said Rilke, subject to the usual vagaries. Then he proceeded to give us the blow-by-blow up to, but not including, the moment he perished. That's how I know he, like me, was just practicing, imagining a time when he would no longer be here. To be clear, I agree with his outlook, his verse, or I missed it completely. By way of explanation, I don't retain what I read. I'm against it.

The last time Kiki and I were in Switzerland, I pinned a note to the bard's grave. Congratulations, I wrote, on reaching your intended end. I'm happy to report your metrics, though they do not increase in number, continue to resonate, to permeate the academy. What was laudable is now vile, but your elegies are still the best way for fellows to seduce their students.

There's no accounting for what the dying does to our speaking, especially those passages in which you, Rilke, cracked open oblivion. Whereas I made up that stuff about pigs and Jesus, but I stand by my statements.

I gotta be me and by that I mean Frank Sinatra. Sammy Davis Jr. wrote a song by that title, but in those days a song wasn't a song until after Frank sang it. It was Ol' Blue Eyes and not his father who stitched Sammy's name to his skin. So Sammy learned to undo who he was by way of every gesture, from his first to his last lump of air. His pop was a dancer too, incidentally, because if he'd been a carpenter there'd be a hammer here somewhere.

111

Speaking of fathers, of mentors, agents, I allege, who have taken up residence inside my skull. Though actual encounters with the aforementioned are rare at my age. I'm explaining all of this to my analyst, but he's of the opinion the people we don't see are even more dangerous.

That's why he insisted on a standing appointment, two, since he added Tuesdays. Though most people call that Tuesday Thursday. We have to go faster, he said, because of the holes that we're finding. So to expedite matters I'm suggesting he restrict his observations to a nod or a groan.

He says I'm getting better, I return the compliment. He's a wizard with dreams but what happens there does not belong to me only. There are reasons for the people and things that we bury. He simply cannot see how we're failing, I suspect it's because of the progress we're making. On the plus side he makes no distinction between life and madness, but for a few belly laughs. Though I have yet to tell him of my conversations with Aristotle.

Personally I subscribe to the opposite of whatever is brewing. I'd stake my life on the last horse and all the wrong sentences. I'm simply not familiar with the races my analyst runs in and I'm partial to the things I'm not telling him. In for a penny in for a decade, he's a Freudian, apparently. I should never have agreed to that second appointment. On my back in the dark I capitulate to anything, and then I talk about tomatoes.

Obfuscation will only aggravate your condition, he says ... I'm not obfuscating ... oh ... I'm hostile ... and why is that ... because of my condition ... I see ... what should I do ... forgive ... who ... yourself ... never ... others ... I don`t remember where I buried the bodies ... we can find them ... why ... so you can move forward ... why ... nothing will happen otherwise ... for how long ... I don't understand ... for how long won't it happen ... that doesn't make any sense ... then why bring it up.

110

I've been to the end, it's not there, but that lack was magnificent. It's where I waited to wait, without depth and without miracle. To whirl like the dervish – I have the cone, a bucket really, but Kiki thinks it looks good on me. Each time I put it on she pretends I'm invisible. All I need now is the skirt and the sash to match, so I can wrap up what's left of the dancing.

Climb aboard, said Kiki, I'm sure we can find that stuff in Syria, and you won't need your toothbrush because we'll be home before dinner. I squeezed my head into that riddle and then into the cockpit.

We came in from the east, just like Bob Dylan, then we turned the drones over Iraq into pigeons. Whatever comes was our plan but, unlike Zimmy, we didn't sweat the lyrics. We saw broken villages at the mouths of great rivers, concrete where there used to be beaches. Hardhats dotted the shorelines. Above them necks of steel dangled massive quantities of glass and gypsum. Gone were the boats and the lofty birds that had been fishing those waves for millennia. Cranes for cranes, said Kiki. Three less words and she'd have said everything.

Christopher Columbus was no Marco Polo, but it's been my experience there's no bad time to talk about dead people. Especially if they're famous and I can get two in the same sentence. It's thanks to our ancestors, their trailblazing, be it on a boat or an ass, that there's a seaside McDonald's next to every fat farm from Fort Lauderdale to Jakarta. When I am done this book I'll provide a tally of the notables herein to save scholars, mostly Brian, from counting.

One man's tsunami is another man's fortune, minus the graft and a few points on the contracts. What follows every disaster are the residual condos. Still, I prefer a shack to those towers, more dirt to grow my tomatoes. We can't stop progress, but in a world without difference how would Kiki and I ever find our way home before supper.

109

I AM SO GLAD Blanche is back from the Rockies. I can only imagine the hole she left in those heaps, what the bears and the bees must be feeling. My heart goes out to them now that we're no longer rivals. To the ecosphere that must make do without her, and to the people of greater Vancouver because it's not Malibu.

It's natural to want to go someplace different but why not New Zealand, which is but a short block west of the park where Kiki and I play soccer. At least that's where it was the last time we visited. On the other side of that park lies Vladivostok, so instead of taking her plane, train or teleportation device, we just ride our bicycles.

Someday I too would like to discover something that matters. I'm not a scientist so it can't be a virus, or time travel since Kiki did that already. A moment, a story, dare I dream, in which nothing happens, for when I don't have my fingers to put these licks down.

I've always said yes to a blindfold, abandoned my ears to the muddle, the burning, the carnage in our rear view mirror. I'm simply not interested in the progress we've made as a species. I was also absent for the reckonings, the crosses, the crossings that emerged from our computations. I was and was not there for the taking.

How I understand things depends on the language. Yesterday I learned the meaning of everything in Swahili and then again in Hungarian. Both were coherent, but still hypothetical, like gravity, say, or the moon landing.

To go or not to go is the question, and the only thing Blanche and I talked about on the way to the airport. There are trees here too, I argued, bargained and pleaded. We'll watch them, they'll watch us and together we'll keep an eye on the government.

108

Marx politicised art, Sun Tzu aestheticised war and Walmart will put an end to both. The new annexations are not about borders, they're about product. Made wherever poor people work tirelessly to meet deadlines in Milan and Manhattan. Then come the knockoffs, Asia's initiative to bring style to Nebraska.

Kiki and I were in Bangladesh last week, last month, in the year of the snake, of our lord, as they say in the heartland. Late April, 2013, as per the console in Kiki's time machine. The workers in Dhaka were all smiles, teeth, actually amid random carbon. But in Paris and in LA no one remembers the deaths of one thousand one hundred and thirty four garment makers.

That's how it is in places where the fire code is friendly to denim and hostile to people. What happened in Dhaka happened to Prada and to your sister. Their stilettos are more leg than footwear, more leg than leg under a pair of Versace's. That ensemble is for yowling not walking, enough to forget my name and that sector's body count.

The new corporation is postmodern, subject to all manner of fragmentation and yet capital flows to an ever decreasing number of plutocrats. A sniper with an ounce of patience and a little strategy could take out the lot of them. Whereas it requires the whole of the Indian subcontinent to turn my frown into a jacket.

107

PEOPLE VOTE THEIR DREAMS not their conscience. Dreaming trumps liberty, trumps Trump even, that's why a vote in Mississippi always brings misery, or is it rain. At least that's what I told Bob over a plate of barbequed duck with a side of potatoes and string beans. Here, in the big city, life is not always about corn's versatility. I went to that restaurant with Blanche too, but then I ordered tofu and spinach.

Bob says I shouldn't indulge every thought and quiver … these are not that … not what … thoughts … how do you know … they don't go anywhere … I see … like that bridge in Alaska … what bridge … the one Sarah Palin talked about … oh yes … it's close to my house in Nunavut … Nunavut is nowhere near Alaska … a bungalow for me and the cat … what cat … it's in the living room … it isn't … try to think of it as unencumbered.

The cat I don't have is black with white patches and sitting on the windowsill. It's everywhere that I am as that which has no demeanor. In the West speech is not corked but it is immaterial, a distinction so subtle as to be nonexistent. That's why Kiki and I often speak in duck calls instead of diction. Kiki does not subscribe to that difference.

I stand by my assertions, the cat and my house in Nunavut. I've explained all of this to my analyst and the squirrels outside my window. I don't know if they understood because Kiki has yet to translate that language. It's a squirrel's way or the highway when it comes to inter-species communication, though a duck once told Kiki those rodents also speak Norwegian.

Inside the empire facts are dispensed before they are known and then fiercely debated on television. Just so everybody knows what to say and think freely absent all ambiguity. Tread lightly, however, verity is also how I lost my shot with Matilda. More on that later.

The muzzling has been with us continuous and they who transgressed sleep with the fishes, except the dank float and fish fly in this instance. That's your confabulation, says Bob. But I think his argument would've been stronger had he not said that. Confabulation, that is, the word is ridiculous.

In Tibet I took to the mountains, subject to the usual caveats, on that trip I told you about, the one that didn't happen. It's where holy men – they don't allow women – go to get right with a bird or a flower. Those things are everywhere, says Kiki, but I guess that's not enough for some people.

Abstinence is how holy men get the jump on the rest of us. All manner of restraint so the opposite of what I'd hoped with Matilda. The answer, they say, has no name, mute is our predicament. Up to and including their moment of dousing and combusting on some Beijing boulevard.

106

THE LAST TIME I saw Bob he was fumbling for his keys in the night while a cat watched and I waited. Then I took the long way home and dreamed he'd moved to Mongolia.

The next day I watched children running and laughing their hair off in the playground where Kiki keeps her train and her rocket ship. Children run at night too in some places, but their laughing sounds more like screaming.

The baseline for death everywhere is death in Manhattan. An eye for an eye, give or take a few hundred thousand. Those numbers are all about the apparatus, especially when you don't have any, as in Kabul or Ramallah. That's why they had to fly suicide Boeings into those towers. Whereas old glory's rocketeers lob death from wall-mounted Samsungs.

We know from what happened at Calvary, the rising not the hanging, there's nothing more powerful than a lack to compel the many. Nothing more terrifying than being seen and not seeing who's killing everybody. Theisms and flying machines raining fire-and-forget-me-not-warheads on the people we love to hate. The best technology, I've heard say, is one that was never there to begin with.

Bob says I should write the pope or the man from Tibet about such issues, instead of the president or Rupert Murdoch … why … for a consult … they do that … they might … outstanding … they'll help you crossover … to where … the hereafter … but where exactly … Missouri … that makes sense … how so … America has delivered more souls than Napoleon … that's true … or Himmler … what about the Dalai Lama … I don't think he's killed anybody … write him I mean … I can't … why not … he's busy with China.

105

I DECIDE THE DAY before what I'll remember tomorrow, while the present, the day of, disappears in the shuffle. It's how I connect the dots to where I am waiting. The hour is now and pending, but not like the weather or your run-of-the-mill calamity. I'm explaining all of this to my grocer from Palestine, while I pay for my yogurt and blueberries. A sponge cake too, but for that there is no explanation.

You said the same thing last week, said my grocer … impossible, I was in Vladivostok with Kiki … really … and the week before that we were in New Zealand … and I was having lunch on Neptune with Venus … the goddess … my ice cream supplier … Kiki will want to meet her … I take delivery on Tuesday … morning … afternoon … I'll let her know … cash or card … cash … do you have anything smaller … than what … a hundred … I don't understand … tens, twenties … I do but they're the same size exactly.

God created the universe because he couldn't wrap his head around its omission. Then he orchestrated the most famous killing in Christendom. For our sins, he said, but I think he needed to rise above the competition. When he finally had our attention he simply turned his back on our tiny awakening.

Yahweh's victories marked the beginning of our obsession with monogamy and fences. Followed by an uptick and then a tsunami of women seen running from split-level bungalows. I shudder to think what might have been had we not invented hair salons and electroshock therapy.

104

THERE ARE NO PHILOSOPHERS, no generals and no priests in this section. I try to live simply and mind my betters, alternate my philanthropic endeavours between orphaned children and high-minded assassins. I've always depended on the kindness of pipefitters because drones with explosives attached are just too expensive. Those prices should moderate, says my grocer, now that the Chinese have understood the robotics.

I am, I guess.

Shopping is how I steer the economy. It's importance cannot be exaggerated, said the president in his speech from the rubble. My accountant disagrees with that strategy and therefore the government. Though I've told him repeatedly money is only good for shoes, tomatoes and sometimes bacon.

There are places where pigs are food and not at all like oil or uranium. As with those hogs, people too are expendable, even though we can no longer sell them. Or eat them, at least not while there are still sheep in New Zealand.

Please don't take me literally, I was a poet before I was a parking meter at Stanford, or was it Africa. A veritable nomad until after I got into real estate. Madness was also an option, but my doctors would not be persuaded, and insanity is a tough slog without a state sanctioned label.

Nunavut then, come hell or high water. Both if we're to believe the science, after the clamor, the grammar and before we dispose of the bodies. If the warming is a cooling I'll go and build hotels in Haiti, or wherever locals are denied access to their own shorelines. Just me and my cat, the one Bob says is not happening. Outrageous, I know, but I have no way to counter his allegation since that feline does not talk to philosophers.

103

WHERE I LIVE IT'S mostly liberals and hipsters. A clump is a cluster and then a posse. They are who they aren't with a vengeance. Liberals vote their issues and hipsters don't fuck, I said to a large crowd in front of city hall, but my local representative didn't get the message. He was horse-trading traffic signs and dead-ending byways for his more substantial constituents.

Nothing says get out of here like that small-town feel in the city. Citidiots, as they say in Montana, will take to the streets at the inference, the hint, of falling house prices. In my neighbourhood near is the measure of distance itself, up to and including the piling of bodies. Only they who have nothing still need their boulevards.

It's easy to disappear when you have money and when you don't, but then you're the wind, the scenery in someone else's adventure. I belong to the first group, by the skin of my teeth, by the hair on my father's chinny-chin-chin. His choice was clear, work like an ox and then croak, making it possible for me to become a lawbreaker.

Set out or die are the rules that I live by, depending on whether or not I need garlic. I choose one then the other, both when I'm feeling reckless. Success is inevitable and therefore insignificant, but I still take an umbrella so those NSA satellites won't know it's me they're looking at.

Between me and my provisions there's a gaggle of indigenous people who are closer to death than is typical north of the forty-ninth parallel. The first are always the first to go, except for the few who managed to circumvent their annihilation. I wish I could be more specific but so much of what happened took place before we got television. Were we to do it again – guided by the beauty of our weapons, said Leonard Cohen via Brian Williams – we'd have got more of them.

Those stragglers are now a testament to the mosaic. We're one big tent, or so says the local residents association, their website specifically. But I still think that tent is a tepee, no room at the top, I told Kiki. She likes it when I wax idiotic. There's a place for the meagre – I'm thinking Winnipeg, the Chicago that wasn't – just not on those cul-de-sacs we gerrymandered.

102

While on a fruit run a member of that First Nation's pack recognized me from the ugly side of his drunken stupor. We'd spoken before – this does not bode well for my anonymity. The way to defeat death is to crawl up its ass, he said to me and to no one in particular. When this man speaks he speaks for everyone. Blanche thinks his suffering is the result of lost ancestry, mangled forests and poisoned rivers. The catastrophe that just keeps on giving.

On my way back from the market the man was sleeping, dreaming, perhaps, of a few square feet tucked safely behind some abandoned doorway. There's no grasping his situation, not since the hemisphere was wrongly identified by an Italian. The error has since been acknowledged, but that potted prophet will be forever fixed to what happened. I left water and some fruit in the crook of his arm, because the only thing worse than the day he was having is the same day without oranges.

I decided then and there, from the chill and the bustle, that it was the day before Thanksgiving. That's when we get tanked on tryptophan with all the trimmings and give thanks to god for the bounty, instead of the people we took it from. Thus my gift to the homeless man was both apropos and very last-minute, but I'd have done the same thing on any given Tuesday.

I resumed my journey home to weather the holiday with a little fish cooked in garlic and whatever Bob hadn't eaten from the fridge and the pantry. Later I told Blanche of my attempt to hydrate the man on the corner. She thinks I may have mixed up the seasons, but why sweat those details. After Galileo we know all Christians can be wrong. Let's just agree the Mayflower first appeared in the last paragraph, so we don't have to worry about what I said previously.

To recap, Thanksgiving is not yet, which is roughly between shortly and never, or what I sometimes call later. Never is never and later is later, said Blanche. That's when she lost me, but I still promised to keep those times open. Then we'll lie under the redwoods, side by side like cadavers.

101

In the West the living is easy or you've no life at all. I picked up my stride and tucked myself in behind the front door. Home is where the heart is but I can't vouch for the liver. Or the abdomen, the largest organ, but it may not be an organ so I can't say that either. Naming is surmising and springs from my genitalia, I reckon.

Speaking of which, the war between the sheets began the day after god chased the first couple from under the apple tree. Adam wanted to stay and fight. Honey, said Eve, think of all that wanton carnality. Adam packed both their suitcases and filled up the convertible. Eve begat Cain, and when she begat Abel god told Adam to trade in his drop-top for a Dodge Caravan. Then the lord explained matrimony which gave way to garages. The reason men still have cocks is so they know what to buy at Home Depot.

Pigs will be people too in the coming decades, vessels, repositories for livers and kidneys. Their organs will be worth more than bacon, than gold even, so I must remember to double down on those futures. There are no hogs in Nunavut, but I'm sure they'll get there eventually. As will apple trees and home improvement chains so long as America doesn't concede to the warming.

Meanwhile I wait behind my favourite window because I can't see through gypsum. It's been here since time immemorial, though the glass was installed later, as was the frame and the walls to hold it. It's where I go to wait for the temperature to rise, the sky to fall, for the next investment opportunity. From this window I can see Australia.

We should go there, I said to Blanche, as she packed for the Rockies … where … Australia … you have lousy timing … is that even possible … and there is no we … I can change that … how … I'll put the cart after the horse this time … sorry I asked … and the coachman in the trunk … stop … so he can't see anything … I get it … then we'll ride the elephant in the room … who might that be … me … I have a plane to catch.

Blanche left that afternoon and, I couldn't help but notice, I was the guy driving. We said goodbye at the airport and then we just kept on talking. In the cloud, which is different than teleportation or time travel with Kiki. When she landed in Vancouver I was right there with her. I'm just hoping the government wasn't there also.

I am the light, said Jesus. As do a lot of people, we have pills for that now so we don't have to crucify them. Crosses still bring people together from Manila to Puerto Rico. In fact, until recently who said what to a white person was reason enough to burn a few timbers in Mississippi. In Riyadh they prefer stoning, different strokes, I guess, for different deities.

Roman woodworkers were much revered before the advent of Swedish furniture. It was they who made those standing mounts popular, impressive little sellers in the empire's heyday. I can't help but wonder how different this world would be had our redeemer stuck to his carpentry.

I locked the door and put away what I had left of the oranges. Grapefruit too, because my friend on the corner refused to take them. There is time finally, hours and then minutes onto death. Two deaths actually, this is the one where I feel all the blows.

Shopping is more enjoyable while the city is all up in its business. Late morning to early afternoon, but on the weekends I avoid it completely. I make pizza with Kiki instead and then I send her home with the leftovers before Bob comes a-knocking. The squirrels see him first, but they don't report to me though they have the best vantage point. A mighty chestnut that's been dying for years, with dignity, admittedly, but that only adds to the spectacle.

It took a while after Blanche left before Kiki and I made pizza again. I had trouble climbing down from the ceiling, but Kiki came over anyway. She spent her time charting every chair and fixture in precise relation to the floorboards in between, so I could get right with gravity. I'd also been watching what

Bob referred to as a dangerous amount of television, alternating between Disney and Swedish cop shows.

In Walt's world Jesus was a gentile, Bambi was the fourth in the manger and none of the wise men were black. I guess his magic wasn't for everybody, but we are accountable for the things we don't mention, that's why I'm not saying Walt was a fascist.

099

I STEM FROM CAESAR'S peninsula, betwixt the toe and the ankle. I am susceptible to all manner of building, to erection in general. When I am done talking I'm going back to building houses with a guy named Gino. There's nothing more thrilling than designing the spaces I hide in. The weekends I'll devote to my hankering for the perfect tomato, no pun intended, sometimes a tomato is just a tomato, but I may have said that already.

Bob wants me to tell the whole story, from the bed to the shitter and back again. That would take decades, I explain, and a good potboiler must leave something to the imagination. In any case, I don't like what finishing does to my options.

I prefer the breach to the barricade, the ache to the rendezvous, no wonder Blanche left me. Where there are no roads there are no roads, said Rumi, without tripping on the same word twice. Sadly, I can't footnote that line because the poem it was in sold out in the nineties.

What this yarn needs is a bouncing ball, as in a Disney or a Looney Tunes song. Why not a plotline, a centre, says Bob. I'm fine with that so long as it doesn't interfere with the rattling. Who am I to decide events anyway. This morning, for instance, I had cereal with yogurt and cinnamon, but the whole time I was thinking chicken.

The truth about the truth is it gets into everything, and then I clear my throat. Still, I refuse to squander it on what the rooms look like and I'd have nothing to add to Kiki's renderings anyway. Suffice to say there are no dirty dishes here, no encrusted pans, no rotting meat, just me and a few sticks of furniture. As for what's not here, that's mine too, I'm lucky that way.

098

In Afghanistan carrots are not vegan, they're carrots, and watch out for falling ordnance amid the caves of Tora Bora. Other than that, a night in Kabul is the same as a night in Malibu, as beaches slip into the ocean. The world is our cauldron and poppy fields are just airports in waiting. Everything is and becoming Manhattan money.

God created Muslims so Christians would have people to kill, and the other way too. He concocted the rich so the poor would know to keep working, so they'd have dreams to die for. He's not a complex deity, suffering his opus, but that too is straightforward and no one could have anticipated the complications that followed. Servitude, annihilation, both in most cases, I guess he just wanted to see what would happen.

Razing is progress, this I know for the Bible tells me so. In Saudi Arabia they're handing out bonuses for killing coalition soldiers in Helmand province. It's a living, as they say in Kandahar, steady too since superpowers don't leave. If you're here you're family – Russians and, before that, the English underfoot.

I want to go back to the old ways, the old massacres, when armies ached for slower obliterations, so they could participate in the empire's rising. We didn't need a nuclear event to insinuate galaxies, the body count to prove relativity. There are theories, scenarios, we can't fathom or swallow. I liken it to thinking about elephants, but after they took to hiding in Smarties boxes.

What this story needs is a haircut, says Bob … what do you suggest … incident, sequence, a spattering of trauma … sounds good … after Freud … obviously … or Jung … why him … the sacred … there is that … so start … as a child I delivered newspapers … you're getting it … I was a paperboy … keep it moving … lock, stock and brain … I'll do the supposing … why … I'm the philosopher … I see … unless you'd like to switch characters … I'm not a character.

The void hunts, for me in particular, but I wouldn't read too much into that. I wait, perchance to dream my last will and testament, for a pizza while broccoli wilts in the crisper. There are ways and ways to mitigate the disaster. I do it by not moving a muscle.

097

I've circled the globe alone and with Kiki, I was looking for the back of my head. It was in the garage with an axe in its ear, a bull's eye, or almost, adorning a half sheet of plywood. I must have had something in mind when I drew it, but the note below was in Chinese and, as I've said elsewhere, I no longer speak that language. Not since I gave that talk to the People's Congress about farming in condos.

I was born within striking distance of St. Peter's Cathedral, but before I could mount an assault my mother put me on a plane to Ontario. I wish I was from LA instead, a poet, a boozer after Bukowski. A romantic haemorrhaging in some obscure hospital, if on my back I too had a monkey, I'd have ridden it all the way to the Booker.

The poet dithers and the man withers, once blessed is twice shackled for us middling artists. I will disappear in the buzzing, like a bumblebee or the wheat in Saskatchewan. I'm tired of my perfect life, and it conflicts with my plans to take down Lockheed Martin, or was it the government. Both are on notice until my thinking clears up, until I can discern which is what.

Peace is the threat and the problem, it's simply no good for the economy. Fortunately it takes almost nothing to keep it from happening. The nation state will be a footnote when they write the new guide to the species. Democracy happened, we'll say – it didn't actually – and later succumbed to conglomerates. The young will get old and die where they shop instead of the places we kill in. Children then, will be worth more than their proxy.

Everything is true, but after I say it. My friends have yet to come round to this way of thinking. Kiki gets it, she told me so on the way to Mexico. Lickety-split on the fastest train ever and did I mention her other car is a rocket ship. Easy-peasy for a kid like Kiki, whereas it took her forever to crack teleportation. Time was the hang-up, then matter, space too, the words not the science.

096

In the beginning was my end, but not before I said hello to Maria, or was it Matilda. I knew her as the babe in the crib next to mine. We happened, she and I, between consenting adults. After which only a priest could wash away the stain that created us. But the instant my father learned my soul would cost more than a mule, he converted to communism.

My name is an arrangement he made with the universe, before it spilled into all of my mouths. A side of ham to the registrar to certify the contagion, nothing moves without his endorsement. The hocks go to the midwife. Ratifying one's begets was complicated and costly in small-town Calabria.

I was not consulted or I'd have suggested the whole affair was unnecessary. The names are a cover-up for the tyranny of our having been in the first place, for the paucity behind our whys and wherefores. Between me and my inscription there is a child howling from a hole big enough to swallow the galaxy. But it might have been even bigger, says Kiki, had I not been given a map and a lamp to see by.

Before I die I'm having all of my aliases tattooed on my ass backwards, finally do right by my reflection. I will miss my hands in the hereafter, especially if I should run into Matilda again. I could say more about that but why mess with perfection. Everything will be fine in my absence, thrive on my carcass, what I do between now and then isn't important. But, before I go, I would like to test drive an anti-tank guided missile carrier hot off the assembly line to the Pentagon.

095

In New Mexico Oppenheimer exploded the wind. A day late and a dollar short, since Hitler's Berliners had already capitulated. Don't despair, MacArthur told the president, we'll suck the oxygen out of a few Japanese cities to usher in the new order. Truman was relieved, he knew the electorate might resist incinerating kids who looked like their grandchildren. The Pacific was the perfect real-world scenario to showcase the physics coming out of Los Alamos.

The oceans are expanding and taking on carbon to make way for plastic, the climate, or for some other reason. Experts agree our emissions problem is only tangentially related to the Manhattan Project. Technology is the problem and the solution, the mother lode, but not like it was in the Klondike. Wolves have offices now, lawyers too, so they will take your house but they won't eat your sandwiches.

Fish have the best vantage point but they don't understand what's happening, except for the few who majored in oceanography. The curriculum is too rigorous for your runabout sea urchin, and they wouldn't comment anyway for fear of compromising future proceedings.

A fish's best chance is calamity, so oceanographers of the two legged persuasion have been logging tumors and slow moving asphyxiations. Entire species are being sacrificed to the eradication of homo erectus. In reverse order – Africa, Bangladesh and finally New Hampshire. In a few thousand years a cockroach will trace and then notate our dismantling. Time, she'll tell her roach family, is more thorough, more devastating than a mushroom cloud or melting glaciers.

Bees must be talking to those fish because they too have gone silent, to preserve the integrity of upcoming indictments. But it is we who hold the patent to honey, so the few who continue to toil are sufficient to maintain the inventory. It's hard, I guess, to ignore a flower's come hither, such enticements reside in our cytoplasm, they are pre and post natal, pre twinkle even.

I will die of laughter unless my bald spot shows up on some screen in Nevada. I doubt those cockroaches will welcome me back so, like Elvis, I plan to return in name only. Without me mountains will be permanent once more and chickens will know dirt again. Bees will table their manifesto and squirrels, armed to the teeth, will spring from every treetop and dumpster. Violence is never violence enough when assembling an empire.

In a few million years all will begin again so we'll have to bring back the Chinese to rebuild the railroads, except this time I hope they're from Devon. There is precedence for this brand of racial fluidity. In 1492 an Italian sailing for Spain went to Venezuela only to discover the people there were all from South Asia.

We can begin the rebuilding in Manhattan seeing as the Lenape tribe didn't insist on an expiry date when they handed the Netherlands the deed to that Island. But that contract too is null and void since the Dutch only held it a few decades before they started slinging beer for the English.

THE EVENING MEAL IS a blessing and preparations approximate prayer. The hungry should skip this part, look elsewhere for truth and salvation – last week's bacon grease or the stench of yesterday's whiskey.

Jesus loves but he doesn't listen, and he can't feed us either now that his gathering place is on television. What the poor need is potatoes and what's left of that bacon grease to cook with those tubers. Those backlit preachers are neither animal nor vegetable, they are the wind's elbow, so check out the specials at Costco before you settle in for the evening.

Things change and begin again from that very threshold. Look to who's killing you now, I advised the good people of Georgetown Kentucky, home of the Camry. Kiki and I travel there occasionally, instantly thanks to her ground-breaking work in teleportation.

It was Henry Ford who first imagined America's highways and byways, and John D. who pulled up Cornelius' rail lines. The Rockefeller mansion in upstate New York is rococo, says The American Preservation Society. But then so is that rotting doorframe you've been meaning to paint, so it too can be studied eventually.

To understand is to render the other as other, but that's just so we can hurt them. What will be will be, but what was is subject to discourse and ranking. They who think otherwise are probably working a route at Amazon. The same people who used to stand shoulder-to-shoulder with the afternoon shift at Toyota.

Kiki and I have made inroads into the above demographic. Ex-autoworkers, a vocation whites, blacks and Latinos could take to the grave in generations previous. Now convicts, so we could still call them lifers, when they're not working a grill for the local hash-house because McDonalds won't hire them.

I prefer to think of them as sleeper cells, of the domestic persuasion. So when the good people of the bluegrass state finally realize what's happening we'll have people in place to show them how to explode a Toyota.

093

In 2014, jazz greats Quincy Jones and Herbie Hancock presented William Jefferson Clinton the Thelonious Monk Award for showcasing that art form at the White House. I don't know if Quincy and Herbie knew the president bested the Gipper and Bush, the smart one, when it came to locking up black people. Creating an unprecedented investment opportunity in for profit prisons for several modern-day moguls.

Willy also played the saxophone.

Culture is a corpse and its sphincter is New York City. As for those libraries in Baghdad, the ones we detonated, those manuscripts just made the troops dizzy. Wyoming is the soul of the union but they shit in Kandahar. That's a place on the internet, so Nevada, approximately, next to Palo Alto. I'll take you there, said Kiki, the minute that city comes to El Paso, then we'll dine on burritos and mangoes.

A mosque in New Jersey will do for a Hollywood shoot-'em-up. Nowadays anybody can be Tom Cruise, liberty's jawbone, its full-throated banzai. America has the guns and distribution is no problem now that his movies fit in my pocket. Our idols no longer have to go a long way to change the story. As for our boys in Jersey, some will die and then go for lunch. Return to a hero's welcome, before they are buried again in the heartland.

092

Yesterday, anno domini, I locked the doors and battened down the hatches. Hurricane Sandy was making its way up the eastern seaboard. Happily I don't live anywhere near there and I'd already described that storm before it made landfall. Thus I was perfectly situated to pursue any and all other commentary. Soon I'll tell you again what I plan for dinner and then we'll discuss the salad.

Staten Island will recover quick enough, now that it's no longer a killing place. Those burial grounds have long been surveyed, apportioned, insured and collateralized. Genocide lifts all boats, but that's your neighbour's canoe on the roof. When he comes for it, you can trade it for your flat screen TV lodged between his front door and where his porch used to be.

After the flooding bankers in pickup trucks will come to board up the houses, to shutter the light in those mortgage documents. Plywood is the new black, orange if you're black already. Then Wall Street will go to work on the margins while an army of actuaries argues the value of your wife's earrings. Finally, congress will enact legislation causing all restitution to disappear in a duck's ear.

I'm having fish and broccoli for dinner, try to stay with me. I shop for food daily because less is more when Bob comes a-calling. Just-in-time inventory, like they do at Amazon, after Toyota, but before you try this at home, in Florida, say, check for upcoming tsunamis.

Bob is familiar with my shopping habits, but he still gripes about the state of my pantry. I do too, but in my world grumbling and not are the same thing exactly. Bob would have no way of knowing that because I moan alone, like Kerouac showed me. A little more figuring, mostly twinkling and I'll be ready to publish.

091

WHERE THERE IS NOTHING, nothing speaks, but not to me. I have felt its breath, a light wind over the strings of some as yet unnamed instrument. At all other times I wait for tomatoes to ripen, the sun to fall, for the worms to talk to me only. For the record, I see no difference between a word and its absence, unless that word is a salad.

Worms don't talk to anybody, says Blanche … I don't subscribe to that demographic … which demographic … anybody … really … it's my gift to posterity … I see … and to the people who know me … right … I've also heard it's not worth the price of admission … what are we talking about exactly … membership … to what … the species … of course … and in general.

I'm in the kitchen, slicing and dicing with the surety of an old surgeon for whom disfiguration is simply the state of affairs. From inside the fridge a carrot swears it's a candlestick. Me too, exclaimed the cucumber. That would make me a baseball, the tomato insisted. They're hoping to circumvent the calamity that befell yesterday's lettuce.

Blanche likes my salads but thinks I have lousy taste in yard furniture and everything else, now that I think of it. I'm fixated on the smaller issues, as in the expiry date on that cucumber we heard from a moment ago. Blanche, on the other hand, focuses on global calamities, since long before she zeroed in on those redwoods. It's her fault I have a faux-wicker patio set to go with my synthetic decking.

Back to the salad. In produce we see how not to be, but decisions made with a knife are usually final. Longevity is untenable for an organic tomato. Know that I didn't lift a finger to prevent the disaster. Here I decide, everything was beautiful enough to cut and then I closed with a sweet vinaigrette. I move the fruit next to the sink and rinse the cutting board.

I guess we're next, said the pear to the apple … it appears so … I am so glad we don't subscribe to his premise … what premise … but maybe we should pray anyway … for what … a twist in the story … you call this a story … not me, the tomato … what did he say … that we should distract the narrator … why … the alternative is unthinkable … what's wrong with him … the tomato … the storyteller … dread … that's it … it's a kind of exuberance … poor bastard … he's looking for a solution … to what … the solution.

It's hard to pin down a nullity, but I'm forever the optimist and there's every possibility these ramblings could still be the result of a tumor. The house I live in is one in a sequence of sequences that dot this city. They were built for poor people and immigrants, and so well-to-do liberals, centrists really, would have a story to tell their dinner guests.

As a child backyards were all about rusting lattices and broken hockey sticks to prop up tomatoes, string beans and oversized pickles. In the front we planted roses. None of those cucumbers, or newcomers, were English but, like our tomatoes, we did live in rows and didn't own pianos.

090

Blanche did what she could for those redwoods. In her absence I went to bat for tomatoes and for those pigs in Iowa, who in turn took one for the numbers coming out of Chicago. Pigs would be pigs again in the world I envisioned. I also lobbied The American Astronomical Society. I proposed an adjustment to the planet's rotational axes, resulting in longer summers, but I have yet to hear back.

So I instructed my lawyer to write a strongly worded letter to the above referenced body and to file a retraction, in advance, with Homeland Security. What should I say exactly … that I was coerced … you weren't and nobody cares … are you sure … I've read your work … thank you … as instructed … let's not split hairs … you're not a threat … you'll speak to that … sure.

There is no god, but not before he told us who to fix in our crosshairs. We prayed and sang songs to keep the blood boiling in between purges. I will return, said MacArthur, said Jesus. To where is the question, so I can move there immediately. Who's to say when, where, which utterance, what gesture will open the rock in which my soul will have ripened. Though I suspect the then I know now will still be more relevant.

089

SOMETIMES I GET DRUNK and pretend I'm in Hebron. When in Rome, don't mention Mohammed and don't eat at McDonald's. I have been known to phone Blanche on such occasions, and in the morning we'd remember things differently. She arrived last month or on Tuesday, I'm still perfecting that indicant. Time, that well worn schema is too precarious for the dead man I'm becoming. The sequential simply won't work with my schedule.

Blanche is back in our midst, but I still worry about her. Those west coast mountain people will rip through your brain faster than a New York liberal, has been my experience. Don't start, don't talk, she said the instant she cleared airport security, whatever you're thinking won't clarify anything. Obviously, I said, but I had to go to Stanford and then watch every episode of Family Guy to develop that level of cerebral dexterity.

She didn't want to look back. That was also the subject line to all of her emails while she was in British Columbia. Why look at all, I asked … bring the bags before I regret having called you … as we were then … heaven help us.

I'm running out of friends, say my friends, but I can still hold my own with a carrot. Blanche was the dinner guest of my dreams, and she loved my salads. Perhaps she'd have visited more often had I not given her the recipe to my vinaigrette. She was my co-conspirator, a counter to my splintered mind, but the Blanche I picked up from the airport is ruining that fantasy.

Speaking of smart people, of Brian, he's the critic I told you about earlier. The sneeze behind the sneeze – the sneeze that won't be, if we're talking plainly. I'm still hoping to flush him out eventually, with my erudition, with whispers of Didi.

Incidentally, all there is to know of the Irish man who created that vagabond is hidden in this sentence. Not to mention my frequent references to the one we call K, who, by all accounts, is still failing perfectly. I will too, god willing.

Then there's Bob. Philosophers are like the canned fish in my pantry, but how is it only one of those things is endangered. I'm sure Blanche will think me enlightened, progressive even, when I kick my one-can-a-day habit to improve the state of tuna in Newfoundland.

When god closes a door, he opens a window, so there's no shortage of Spam in those coastal villages. Not since Johnnie got his gun, got his gun, made his dad glad to have such a lad, and he didn't come back until it was over, over there.

088

When I got here I understood everything, and then I was told otherwise. Eventually I took a wife, of the kind with an apartment and furniture. Not formally, since no magistrate or priest would or could legitimate our arrangement. I was happy, ecstatic even. Fancied myself an outsider inside the nothing, but not the one I'd studied at Stanford.

Which reminds me, on graduating a general from pages previous told me it was my turn to serve. But there were no wars to speak of, except for those dirty little massacres in Central America and they were mostly for spies and mercenaries. Not a mention, not even a glance towards the towns that were burning. As for the people who did not survive, they're the same people each time.

We descendants of the greatest generation are hedonists not heroes, we eat better too. I was juicing spinach when my honey told me she was pregnant. I'm also a lesbian, she added. My son was born seven months later so I'd have something to die for. He does what he can to help with that, but he's evolved his own hypotheses regarding his purpose. But what, I ask, is more essential, more elemental, than killing your father.

I went to work for the few who were bamboozling the many, for a fee because a cut would have been illegal. Always a bridesmaid to the people who already had everything. The brains behind the numbers, like a bloodhound circling ever wider to escape its own stench,

The first million is a bitch and the second comes anyway, but there still wasn't room for me in the manor. All of my contacts were intermediaries, more crickets than scorpions. I bet on their folly and they did too. Stupidity is key to upward mobility. On Wall Street they continue to sing for their dinner but in Bangladesh crickets are protein, and they won't take your house after losing your money.

Bob travelled to Bangladesh, or India, those places are the same for us white people. He went there to bolster, or embellish, what he didn't know already. To find his bliss. I suggested heroin, but by then all of the poppy fields were in Afghanistan. So I told him to meditate on a snowflake instead. Then I asked him to repeat what I had just said so I wouldn't forget either.

Where in hell am I going to find a snowflake in July, he protested. Luckily, I didn't have to address that conundrum because he'd already told me his ticket was non-refundable. Then I fell asleep because that's what conundrums do to me.

087

The last time I saw Jesus he was in Miami riding the ass-end of a Cadillac. A new low in my estimation, but he didn't have far to fall after the shenanigans he'd pulled in Palestine. Next to his likeness were the words "HONK IF YOU LOVE ME". Below that was a website advertising a slew of anointed whatnots at bargain prices, and the promise of my very own custom bumper sticker. I considered it, but no self-respecting messiah would be caught dead on the rump of my Subaru, so I ordered the t-shirt instead.

If I were an astrophysicist and stumbled on a black hole I'd mark the spot and move on. By the time I rounded the sun the earth would be the size of Einstein's anus – roughly. Before exiting the galaxy I'd count the bombs falling on Southeast Asia. I know those people are dead already but from that distance, says Albert, we're still living in the last century. I could also take another run at Matilda, that's just science.

I'm against all things sentient and by things I mean people, or maybe just geniuses. There's nothing more irritating than a brand spankin' new theorist, fingers attached and aching for isms. It's just too much work to dismantle and assemble them again in my speechlessness.

Speaking of body parts. When cleaved or extracted from the lower stratums, they can be recycled, find new worth in Monaco or Connecticut. A kidney, say, fresh from the slums of Calcutta. That, a plane ticket and a part-time job at McDonald's will buy you a college education in Newark. A pittance for a nearly dead tycoon, hereafter the customer. But a good moguls is hard to find, so feel free to slice up the one I just conjured, or round up the few in your neighbourhood.

After I log the bodies and fix the numbers all of my stories will be about tomatoes and those pesky squirrels constantly eyeing my vegetable garden. Humanity will begin again from its mangled end. Then we'll know birch trees once more, magnolias and those creeping no-nonsense ivies. In the meantime I'll look to Damascus or the Congo to understand what's coming. I could have also said Paris but then we couldn't walk to a massacre.

086

SPEAKING OF BEGINNINGS, what this story needs is a spacewoman's perspective. Kiki said she'd sort that out personally, but I may have said that already. It's important she not be too young, more haggard than pretty so we don't get bogged down in the flesh of it. Beauty is its own catastrophe and sometimes it's the slug in the chamber. When it comes to my house I like to pretend I'm not dying.

Blanche has landed. I'm hoping she doesn't come between me and the weather, the miracle I have become in her absence. Chance encounters are problematic at my age and in my condition, so I have to plan them ahead of time. I'll fix her whereabouts, and mine, after I review what's been said of my patterns and habits, of my strolls to the market.

In the eighties we lived together, it was easier that way to exist without money. People like that now commute from the margins. This city was even more affordable a decade later, on the bust side of a booming economy. Everything stopped in the nineties – the future, said Beckett – that's why it didn't happen. In Dublin they're still waiting for that decennary, but in Paris, his preferred city, they've all but abandoned the notion of consecutive history.

I've explained all of the above to my therapist, but time's vanishing is not enough to stop him from asking. He's like a dog on a bone when heads go missing. He wants to know all about my connection with Blanche, what did and didn't take place between us. But I swear I couldn't follow it and that, I suggest, is the version that matters.

We aren't, never were, said Blanche of our relationship to her Jungian analyst. There was one on every block in the eighties, before they all moved to New Mexico. It was swank then to be an adherent of an apostle, to speak in parable, wisdom's cudgel. Regret is a vessel, said Blanche's therapist during our one couple's session, what you put in will percolate to the surface eventually. I regret coming here, I said, so I wouldn't have to stuff it down again later.

That was then, though I can't say for sure because the apartment in the house we lived in is now a high-rise. Gone too is our cherished bistro. That's what we called cafés in the eighties, and in the nineties bistros were eateries. Blanche remembers our little sanctuary like it was never there, a few doors down from our acupuncturist.

Spinach salads were by then well established, and kale was slowly making its way from the Bay area. One afternoon, late lunch, early dinner – some things are best left to the reader, and I was hopped up on wheatgrass anyway – I noticed Carl Jung eating crispy tofu a few tables down from us. You know he's been dead for decades, Blanche was quick to remind me, which, at the time, seemed wholly tangential.

085

LET'S TRY AGAIN. IN the sixties I hit puberty, or it hit me. In the seventies I learned what women wanted and in the eighties they came for my glossies. In the nineties, a thousand years ago Tuesday, I resolved not to split hairs between love and dreaming. The changeup would have broken my brain anyway, and it's unnecessary. In fact I might never have noticed her leaving had Blanche taken a cab to the airport.

She was the yin to my wang, and then a bucket to carry my life in. I needed for nothing, still don't, but it's hell to find after Amazon. When Blanche and I moved in together I'd fix the toaster and sharpen the blades on our food processor. Things aren't made like that anymore, so soon I didn't have to do anything. That's why she left, ostensibly. But I think it's because not all women marry well and die of pain like their mothers.

The secret to a good relationship is communication, but not talking makes it go faster. As luck would have it, our living room was too small for deep conversation, so I kept all of my opinions in Sweden. Such was our life together. We also took long walks and wondered why more daughters don't kill their fathers.

Blanche is back and wants me to drive her to IKEA. How's Tuesday, I ask. She's made a list of things I wouldn't do before she left for the Rockies. As for the things I did do, I'm keeping those in the vessel, as per her eighties analyst, the disciple's disciple. Unless it was Jung himself who told me what to keep in that urn. He talked to his receptacles, his pots and pans, squirrels too. Why not carrots, is the obvious question, then everyone would know I'm not crazy.

As a journalist I'd go down every rabbit hole, bypassed the story to where no one was talking. There never seemed to be enough time to record what was actually happening. Those silences were further redacted to conform with community standards, altering fundamentally what the people weren't saying. A mineshaft would not have sufficed to fit what was left on the cutting room floor.

In coal country the numbers are the numbers, and the other way too. Employers don't sweat the details and they don't pay for X-rays. Death is more affordable without a diagnosis. Eventually we'll do our mining on the moon, says New York's smallest mogul, the president. Permits will be issued and concessions apportioned immediately since there's a flag there already. The coal miners of Appalachia await his instructions.

I can't wait for the first lunar skyscraper, I'm sure it will happen soon because approvals are no more than a wink for the president's children. That's how a blind trust works, sons and daughters sorting out what's what for the father. Meetings on top of meetings amid a tidal wave of hotel reservations. When that tower is built I'll sell my house in Nunavut for a view of what was the Arctic, and it will be spectacular.

083

THIS MORNING I SAW my general practitioner. I didn't make an appointment because, as I explained to the person behind the desk, there was nothing wrong with me. I was looking for answers, specifically to two questions I had asked in my sleep. Why talk when you can spit, and when is a cucumber a cucumber and not a zucchini. You may have come to the wrong doctor, said the receptionist. But I insisted on waiting anyway.

Before I had time to sit, a toddler with his tongue and whole face to the window turned to me directly. Look, he said. Which I did immediately. Then we made the rounds of all the fenestration, while he pointed to everything that I wouldn't have seen otherwise. The rug, the ceiling and a ladybug that had somehow made its way onto the windowsill.

That tot went in before me, but not before making me promise to keep an eye on that ladybug. Which I did unremittingly until I was called into the examination room. There I asked both of my questions simultaneously so the doctor would have more time to answer.

She thanked me for being brief by reminding me there were sick people waiting. It seems she wasn't connecting with my side of the conversation, so I thought it best to surrender to her agenda. Breathe, she asked. Certainly, I replied. Any pain, she inquired. What's the difference, I countered. We never did get round to the point of my visit.

082

AFTER NINE-ELEVEN I spoke to the students at Stanford as their teacher, or groundskeeper. Let's see where this goes before I choose a vocation. Who on earth, they asked, would want to kill such good-looking people.

Those kids were anxious as many would soon be dispatched to the towers still standing, where they would dream the dream and reap the disaster. Graduates ready to garrison, hold the line in Lower Manhattan or Palo Alto, because nobody gives a fuck about Arkansas.

When disaster strikes again Kiki and I will already be in her rocket ship. A few more calibrations, by Friday, she said. So Tuesday I figure. Einstein is here too, and he simply cannot believe the progress she's making. I probably shouldn't have gotten hung up on the concept of explication, he said. That's right, said Kiki, it just doesn't work in all instances, pointing to me as her primary exhibit.

I agree with Kiki. I'm nothing if not consistent, both actually and in all instances. Blunder and bluster is how I came to know everything. But what really opened my eyes are thc things I'm seeing and not seeing on television. Why, for example, is the president still breathing twelve to eighteen times per minute.

The editor called again this morning, I've read more of your work, she said … oh … it's a lot of nothing … thank you for noticing … why twelve to eighteen times per minute … I googled breathing … and I don't like that alliteration … which one … blunder and bluster … I see … talk about what you know … I'm not familiar … with what … what I know … make something up … I just did … something else … it is if I say it is … that's right … what about if I say it isn't … what … it … then it isn't … got it.

081

I WORE BLACK TO the Reichstag to complement those bone-chilling syllables, crimson red to the Pentagon in deference to its incessant bloodletting. I decide the weather from the clothes that I'm wearing. The Center for Atmospheric Research is, or should be, tracking my laundry cycle. Every morning I choose an ensemble and then I put on something different, and again after I look out the window. I'm up to my ears in failed exits.

There's no difference between me and Obama, we both have a list and neither of us owns a cottage in Yemen. I'm a hunchback by trade and temperament. It used to be an honourable profession, when we still knew the source of our misery, the whip and the master. A hunchback is a frog and a prince, says Kiki … obviously … and a chicken … why a chicken … no reason.

Presidents don't do their own killing, yet another similarity between me and Barry. We'll just have to agree to disagree on the difference between guns and keyboards. President's also have spy agencies for more discreet murders. With drones and pickup trucks now that Ford's famous, or infamous, green Falcons have gone the way of Allende's Chile.

Neither a patriot nor a terrorist be, I told those Stanford fledglings, but they were already too dazzled or too stupid to listen. So I showed them footage of bearded men next to Toyota Tacomas, searing a buzzard in the Yemeni desert.

Speaking of grilling, I'm going shopping right after this sentence, the minute the guy behind my eye concedes to the evening's adjacents. We've agreed on heirloom potatoes and chicken, a carcass surrounded by half-rounds in my trusted Dutch oven. The dispute now is between string beans or broccoli. Why not both, he says, and we'll cook one tomorrow. I hate it when my apparition is the sensible one in our arrangements.

080

I MAINTAIN A LOG of Bob's comings and goings, for months now I have been dodging his company. He visits less when it's cold out so I keep my long johns on and my short pants in the attic. Easier since a few pages ago I said it was Thanksgiving. So October in Saskatoon and November in Billings Montana, so say the Amish because the Navajo don't acknowledge that holiday.

Columbus stubbed his toe on what would be Guantanamo. Radical for his time, whereas Kiki charts the impenetrable and she evaluates weapons systems in Andromeda. She says they're more advanced than neighbouring galaxies. When she's not doing that she scours the planet on the wings of a butterfly. She decides the destinations while I, her trusted assistant, mark the stopovers, essential when negotiating large bodies of water. Butterflies won't stop to fish, or cook, so I also bring sandwiches.

What I don't know is bigger than the list in my pocket, and smaller than what I could fit in a dirigible. What I don't know is a lot, which plays well in Paris but in Texas they put a name to it anyway. There's no upside to crazy on the streets of Laredo.

My son says my thinking is splintered, broken, were I to quote him precisely. He's a creature of unspeakable frailty, that's how he gets things to open. He also smokes a lot of pot so he too is really good at not knowing anything. It's another way of seeing, he says, a glimpse into what a glimpse destroys and we'll never die because we are already the sequel.

I spent his formative years bent over a boardroom table, pants to my knees, as I took one for the team, the queen or the mortgage. By the time I crawled back into his life my boy was already armed, camouflaged and dropping bodies. Still, I like to think he got that zip from me. He didn't just lick it off the ground as they say in Budapest, except they say it in Hungarian.

Bob credits the academy for my son's erudition. But when my boy stopped to smell the roses at his alma mater all he could detect were the Rockefellers. Those flowers, those colours, were only good for forgetting, he said, seeing things as they aren't.

I agree with him, it's becoming damn near impossible to articulate what we've always known anyway. But all of these tangents, these beside-the-point references are making me hungry. I ransack the fridge and the pantry, I was thinking cake but I settle for almonds and dried figs from Egypt.

The Egyptians invented rope long before somebody thought to put a neck at the end of it. Autoerotic asphyxiation came later. A tug is the same as a pull, said Matilda, and then the earth disappeared for a jiffy. There's not much difference in the faces one makes upon tasting eternity, and who am I to say between ecstasy and terror.

Gravity makes lynching possible, the fact not the theory. The falling as opposed to the flying specifically. So if you're walking in downtown Manhattan watch out for flapping fund managers, but if one should fall in your soup we'll call that ground zero. The most exalted, though by no means the biggest, ditch in history.

Kiki and I visited mid October, roundabout the time the president announced operation Enduring Freedom. Known around the world as the day Kabul changed forever. All that was airborne had fallen already. Heroes, said Bush the acorn, ready to die for their brokers, pulled what they could from the rubble. Evidence, digital and otherwise, before body parts and finally enough artifacts to fill a museum.

When it was all said, sanitized and ingested Rudy threw a parade for his first responders. CAT scans would have been better, but they were summarily rejected by the committee to re-elect the president. That precedent, Cheney cautioned, would spread like a cancer through the coal mines of Appalachia.

Kiki and I didn't stick around for the wrangling, the speeches for and against the campaigns in Iraq and Afghanistan. We had to invent what was said while en route to Peru, via Mexico before it was Mexico. What we're now calling Texas. We waited there for the Jesuits to bring in the census and the Spanish to sail past Gibraltar. For the English before they were Protestants. We left before losing our heads.

When I left Stanford opportunity knocked for white college graduates, so I hightailed it to Europe. The story on campus was that intellectuals had finally deserted the Parisian café and were quietly pooling in Spanish cemeteries. I was working my way there from Kalamazoo or someplace analogous, later I would change that word to similar.

By the time I got to Madrid the anarchists had all moved to Honduras so I caught a plane to LA. Like Henry Miller, I too wanted to grow old with my hard on but, try as I might, I never could match his narcissism. I did walk in his shoes for an hour, or so, so we must have worn the same size exactly, but I'm sure that's coincidence.

Eventually I made my way back to Blanche to regale her with tales of drunken nights from Hollywood to Madrid. In the morning she went to work and I'd crawl back to bed as Rimbaud or Bukowski. There have been so many poets, it's impossible now to recall their shoe size. I woke to the sound of Blanche's key in the door, to face the night while I could still put a little muscle behind it.

That was years ago. These days I walk in the shoes of a guy named Antonio el Camborio. Tony, for short, a fictional character from Franco's Granada or Guatemala. We met a few minutes ago in a poem, at that little café where Blanche and I raged against the machine. Where I still live and breathe and occasionally read Lorca.

I'm from Spain, said Tony … oh … and Guatemala … how does that work …. I'm not real … I see … I generally have coffee and pastry in the morning … interesting … for breakfast … I understand …. it's a Latin thing … I know … what about you … oatmeal … just oatmeal … with blueberries.

This story was supposed to be different. Only what fits in my mouth I promised myself and the editor. There and no further than where I buy my tomatoes. I bypassed the factories on the outskirts of town and stepped over my family to get here. The gulf war was raging, the president, soon to be the president's father, unleashed the storm so we'd all know he was the president. I remember it like it was the nineties, the real ones this time, or so said thirty-five million Iraqis.

Evolution is fine for most species, but things just get worse when it happens to people. I'm here now, late Monday morning in the Anthropocene period and the work week began several hours ago. Time for me to chase a squirrel up a tree and then count down the minutes till dinner.

077

After Blanche left I moved a few blocks closer to Bob's apartment. Now that she's returned he no longer reports his plans or his whereabouts. It's not easy to track a philosopher when he's not blabbing. He says I don't need to know his coming and going, and yet there was no getting rid of him while Blanche was still in the Rockies.

As I said earlier, the squirrels are refusing to help me keep track of Bob and they're easily distracted. I've taken to sitting and eating my meals at the bay window. I have a clear view of all except one direction, there is no end to my apprehension.

Blanche grudgingly acknowledges my real estate acumen, so I was able to maneuver her into an apartment next to my favourite everything. We're all three together again in the same neighbourhood, but she has to walk past my window to get to Bob's building. She's beginning to suspect the motives behind my consultancy.

I will have to part with some furniture seeing as Blanche left the mountains with what she could fit in a backpack. Hers, mine, let's not sweat the pronouns. She's a poet now, it happens. She's done with the revolution, or was it photography. What's important is she's here, around the corner, lighter than air on the main floor of a three-unit dwelling.

Regards chattels and poetry, one must be nimble to work the disaster, I explained, and there's really no difference between the floor and a chair. I'm happy you feel that way, she replied, I'll send a truck round on Tuesday.

I ache for a time when she loved to hate me and I pretended to be Stanley Kowalski. We'll discuss that again when pigs fly, she said. So I marked that date in my calendar. I wait, which is not nothing, and now that I've said it philosophers can go to bed early. Besides, Blanche says I do it better than anyone.

076

TRUTH IS I DON'T like poets, at least not while they're alive. I seem to forget that every couple of decades, and then nothing happens until I can extricate myself from whatever the situation. I'm here to take back what's mine, Blanche texted, as she pulled up in front of my walkway. She's bound to fancy Bob more than me, especially if I don't relinquish those furnishings and why, I ask, must both their names begin with a B.

This must be Tuesday, is all I can say about the preceding paragraph, since there's now a truck out front and two men at my door. Blanche walks in behind them and we talk in the kitchen while the furniture disappears from my living room. What's happening is inconceivable, as was her leaving, beyond me, so Blanche sees no reason to speak of it. On the bright side, I'll have even more reasons to drive to IKEA with the Blanche of my dreaming.

In her defence, I have been known to mistake what's hers for what's mine, what I want for proximity, but I generally go back and delete all those references. I'll never understand why she chose those redwoods over our life together. It was only to fill that hole that I built houses for aging hipsters and liberals. Sooner or later we all circle round to the real estate channel.

Absence and the occasional bump in a Subaru kept our love

alive, back when Blanche spoke to the moon – her mother. I can't say for sure but I think that was her death talking, or what I like to call talking in general. I still see very little light between Blanche's fear and her supposings.

We had a thing, is all, more or less the sum of our parts. We talked about the doors we would someday open. I was young and she was from Philadelphia. Tomatoes cost fifty-nine cents a pound and rapini had finally made it out of New Jersey. Strange I know, said Blanche, but in Pennsylvania they still don't understand it.

075

WINTER CAME EARLY AND stayed late this year, so we'll have to wait until summer to catch up on our walking. Nowadays atmospheric conditions often diverge from meteorologic history. No matter, I prefer the opposite to whatever the forecast, the sky inside out. In Sri Lanka they call that a catastrophe, but in Alabama it's still just the weather.

I suffer from an indolent, contradictory state of mind, but I am certain of my imbecility. As for the warming, there will be consequences outside our fields of inquiry, anomalies beyond the purview of the scientific community. I'll tell you what they are in a minute.

We don't know how to think the disaster, that's why we need miracles. CNN is reporting one on the Hudson, though several Canada geese might disagree with that characterization, as they were sucked into the engine of a 320 Airbus. No fish were mentioned. In the weeks following the Port Authority gassed thousands more of those birds to prevent similar marvels.

The passengers crawled, barely able, onto the flat expanse of a wing while the cold wind blew. All that floats, came the rallying cry for small to smallish sized vessels. In minutes they mobilized against the river steadily rising into the hull of that aeroplane.

On this day the river spit back its victims, on television, because New Yorkers matter. No shit, is how you say that in Farsi. Miracles happen in Afghanistan too, but then there are no PowerPoint presentations, no experts to explain the explanation. Stories never seem to make it out of some places, I know for I was a journalist in previous pages.

Moving on. The networks frantically blasted those images, because the only thing better than a loop is the looping. After days of milking that string of rattled passengers, those hesitant first steps, like ants on the wings of an eagle, networks began trimming that footage. They put a few less spikes in their nail guns, to make time for analysis.

Book the pilot, said Oprah to her producers, before he ends up on CNN. Captain Sully accepted her invitation, all invitations, but soon disappeared. Familiarity is not a good look for the valiant, though sometimes they come back as a movie. There's the splash, and then there's the drowning that happens after landing a plane on the Hudson.

Americans love a good rescue, but there never seems to be enough death to hold their attention. After a New York disaster, and this applies to hits and near misses, all parties must be seen to be outraged. Floating fuselages and falling buildings are good for the polls and the ratings, thus there is no discord then between the state and what they're saying on television.

074

I THINK TO SLEEP and wake to dreaming, that's how I square every circle. Certainty waits in the room next to the room I'm in, so you know that I know where it is exactly. At Stanford we called that an enigma, the word is Greek but nowadays only the French appreciate its meaning. They say everything needs saying again.

Speaking of speaking, the tomato is also a miracle, the fruit not the vocable, the notion behind the notion, as in a sauce or a salad. You'd think with such phrasing, such insight, Blanche and I would have more in common, her being a poet, but we can't even agree on a semicolon.

What we did well and what I'm hoping to do again is a night on the town, one leg showing from her calf to her elbow. There's salt in your eye, she'd say, catching my gaze, except she called it drooling. No glaring without consent, no grovelling without her say so. Imagine the dreams you'll have tonight, she said hailing a taxi. But I know she'll be back because the only other thing we talked about was her poetry.

073

I USED TO BE a numbers guy for bankers and lawyers. Without shame, but that went with the office. I left because I wanted Blanche to see that I left. I hear that job is even funnier now that the rich have all the money. I'm a sucker for all things jocular, while the customer bleeds out in the margins. Violence, it seems, has lost its aspect.

All you can be and a college degree, said the army video, so Floridians would think dying is simple. I know from scientists who study motion, the mechanics of fluids, the bottom is the most likely of places. Blood and piss will find their equilibrium faster than a severed head or a finger. Viscosity is key. Personally I prefer a gush to a trickle, though I know there's nothing more persuasive than a drip to spur the unthinkable.

We're all in this together, said the president. He, like me, is too old to fight and die in some as yet undisclosed location. Everywhere borders accede to the market, that's how tacos got into Sweden, and then more borders until entire generations fall into the ocean. All of my thoughts are to die for. When I run out the list I'll draw a picture of the things I've not said yet, should someone younger, with a penchant for munitions, choose to pick up the pieces.

Neither a Texan nor a Mexican be, I told Kiki. Gringos go south for the weekend and return with a headache, whereas Mexicans head north for the harvest and go home with their tumors. Even Kiki couldn't tell me what that meant exactly, but she did say it was wacky enough to post on the internet. In a moment we'll both know what I was implying.

It's the pesticides stupid, said somebody on Twitter, pharmaceuticals the sequel, made by the same companies so Wall Street can underwrite both sides of that story. We built those towers strong – Bob swears that's a song – to subvert all other economies. Incidentally, autumn is whenever I stock up on organics.

Bob says it is not we, but I think he means me, who decide the seasons … what about the harvest … stop … the weather … nope … why not … because it's the weather … I see … which reminds me … yes … you're out of tuna … thanks … and mayonnaise … understood … those things you can plan for … I agree … life as we know it … before or after Freud … neither … I knew him … you didn't … when I lived in Vienna … you never lived in Vienna … my mistake.

072

Before Blanche got here I had nothing but time, like a cancer patient a few days into their diagnosis or an old man in a Portuguese barbershop. I'm delighted she's back and undeterred by her commentary, her reticence to resume our relationship. Anyone but, she vowed, when she picked up her furniture. Whenever you're ready, I said, I didn't want to seem desperate and waiting, I'd argue, is the best part of conjugating.

The game is the game, afoot, said Sherlock, but I think he got that from Shakespeare. Yesterday I made a list of important places to be, my very own elsewheres for when Blanche and I meet inadvertently on a regular basis.

I hear Odessa is dancing again. They who had reason to complain are now dead or in Miami, unless I'm just a glass half full kind of guy. Now comes too late and the future is just a theory, but this time I'm keeping the Cadillac. I could get used to this, death as my opus or the meal I cook this evening. A run-through for when Blanche comes a calling and then I hope nothing happens. A lot.

All day long I've been pretending this is that evening, my time to shine and that there is nothing strange about how my legs attach to my body. I spent the day shopping for books and ice cream. An odd combination since I had but one bag between them, it's the least I could do to save the planet, though Blanche says I should also buy local. A movement that is steadily growing in popularity, except among the six, or so, billion people who can't afford the idea.

My conversations with Bob are full of meticulous and gigantic thinking. Blanche, on the other hand, does not impress easily. My talks with her sound more like weeping, especially after she visits. I'm not a fan of the figuring that happens between two or more people, so I do most of my braining alone. It's easier that way to change the story. There will be tears, but I will decide the reason.

071

It's true, the population has increased, but you didn't hear it from me because that would be plagiary. A word tracking a smell is how I came to know everything. I do love statistics, especially the ones that aren't here yet. N-u-m-b-e-r-s is how I spell catastrophe, how I cracked the secret of southeast Asia and the Americas. I use them to bludgeon the pope, the president and the population in general. As to the facts, the thing as given, I have no explanation.

Sums broke my noggin, I told my analyst … they didn't …. how do you know … I'm a doctor … they teach that in medical school … we need to access what drives you … which is … the hurt behind the numbers … is that where it is … the feelings behind the words … I feel those … really … deeply … good …. or you'd have found them by now.

070

I DON'T LIVE IN most places, but that's just an estimate, or coincidence. If your here weeping it's the company I'm keeping, so said my mother. Luckily, it's a short distance from the brain to the screen and back again, but who am I to decide between a man and his pixels. All as nothing, I am insofar as I am already semblance. Clearly, I am spectacular.

I say I, except when I'm sleeping, so I know who's speaking. When I'm holed up in the Himalayas with a bear, for example, but that and dozing are usually concurrent. The bear is the bear and I'm the guy trying to wake up the guy screaming.

God knows I'm not a traveller but for my expeditions with Kiki. Not going is what makes those places interesting. Bob has come round to my way of thinking, but only after his trip to India. He did his travelling while he was young, before he was conscripted to fight in Vietnam. As a gunner, or somebody's driver, whatever sticks is my motto.

There'll be no storied soldier here to explain away murder, its aftermath, what might have been a small pig or an infant. Why do they who have everything still want to kill us, with prejudice and all manner of applied mathematics. For Kissinger it was the inconvenience of living witnesses, but he told his wife it was the lack of raspberry jam with his blintzes.

Always the statesman, entire villages became craters in the instant he learned of them, so no one would notice the burnings adjacent. We will win this thing the secretary told the president, that and the opposite. A bizarre bunch those walking talking specimens of the greatest generation. They had but one thought between them, to the exclusion of all other outcomes.

In Europe we learned that it's damn near impossible to exterminate everyone. I'm sure, after that, people would insist on showering before boarding those transports. Especially given them postwar innovations in indoor plumbing. There would have been no place for trains or showers in Kissinger's mode of diplomacy.

Our war will be different, said Henry, so Nixon would know what to say to his constituents. The kind of war that makes presidents and generals envy their predecessors. There are dividends to every catastrophe, the secretary continued, and there's no better way to empty our warehouses of incendiary acids.

069

Presidents slaughter. Perhaps we should log their totals before they take office. Wars to come will then have already been won and victory ascribed to their genius. We can even inflate the numbers, or not, as the situation requires. To each an airport, hell let's put all their mugs on that rockface if it distracts them from marching. Something new, something blue, something shiny to keep them from chasing their legacy.

Personally I've done well by my leaders or we wouldn't be talking. Especially since the planet is now the size of a melon and the NSA can track a terrorist from fetus to cherub. Longer, should they survive puberty, there's just no escaping those screens in Nevada. It's true the people they kill might have died anyway of madness, the water or the governments they elect to protect our conglomerates.

God bless America so they don't accidently bomb Sweden or the dumpling house I go to on Tuesdays. The one Bob doesn't know about. Always crowded, which is a good thing given the military's aversion to collateral bodies. Alternates, decoys, in this instance, and I'll be the guy eating.

068

LOVE IS FRENCH, DEATH too, so I'm expecting a kiss and a wink as the train leaves the station. I know from Blanche's postings, her emails, her new favourite colour is yellow. The streets are abuzz with talk of her recent arrival. Bob says it's just me, but I don't catch his meaning. I've told him repeatedly I am more than my singularities, than the sum of my sums, than my scars even. Cut me and I will bleed yellow, or whatever hue the situation requires, but please don't mistake me for a canary.

The difference between opening the abdomen of a goat or a virgin is that the goat would disagree vehemently. The Aztecs built pyramids to sacrifice both, resulting in a bonanza for clothiers, as they struggled to adorn society's daughters. By contrast, the animals had to be tethered to take one for the sun or harvest.

A drip is a trickle and then a river, all monoliths will be rubble eventually. Try burning those women, Cortes and his priests announced on arrival, and those goats would be delicious with a little rice and potatoes.

Nowadays we can take down any structure and the city it's in with the stroke of a key, what we used to call a pen in decades previous. Still lethal in the hands of the president, and you could use it to stab your boyfriend.

God favours Americans, because so few of us would survive the alternative. But those signing ceremonies, proclamations really, are more necessary than ever. Especially now that Jesus does not always tag along when our troops go a-butchering. As for the harvest, we have machines for that now, so we won't need to open your sister to bring in the corn.

Skyscrapers are more susceptible than pyramids to wayward Boeings. I wouldn't have believed it had I not seen it on television. We'll fight them over there, said the president. That too is a place in my living room, between the clicking and the flickering, approximately, and so is Manhattan. Incidentally, gravity would also have defeated those towers, but not in my lifetime.

We are the beneficiaries of an ever expanding economy, consumers of news, shoes and shrapnel. Luck notwithstanding, our survival will depend on they who think otherwise. Now try to guess which one of those things is not like the others. It's the shoes since, when thrown, did not lodge in George Bush's noggin.

Kiki and I have been to the end and the infinite. It's nothing, in the making, so light can pass through it. The universe is vast whether or not we have eyes to see it. A marvel of linguistic engineering, but astrophysicists have yet to buy into that theory. They will not admit to what doesn't exist, at least not consistently. A certain flexibility is required to find and record those positionings but, until then, Kiki has marked those spots with an X so we can circle back later.

067

EVERYONE IS LOOKING FOR their place in eternity. A mention or two in the third person, an echo, since it will continue to ping in our absence. But one is never so alone as in a room full of torsos. Three of us – call that the problem – will meet one day soon in the market. Wednesday, said Blanche, so Tuesday I figure. A diner with a new age motif, the community's much talked about secret and this year's best eatery ever.

Blanche reads the room while I scan the periphery. We agree on a table next to a window that rises from the floor to the ceiling. Tempered, so it won't kill the patrons should someone need to put a chair through it. Locals come here to see and be seen, to talk about what's happening in Haiti and in Burundi. Funny how geopolitics just rolls off the tongue from behind café fenestration.

Bob and I hover, more out of instinct than reason. We wait for Blanche to choose her seat, but our hesitation is awkward given the table's modest diameter. She's the prize, but you didn't hear it from me because she'd stab me with a fork and then smack me with the furniture.

I talk to Bob while my ghostly other, the fourth in the trio, tracks Blanche's leanings. Later he'll report and then berate me for what will have unfolded. But, in my defence, you could land a plane between what he'll say and what my friends will later think happened.

Good things come to those who wait or they would have come anyway. Sometimes they follow me home and slip in before I can notice them. Either way I collide with what never arrives and then I put the future behind me. Unless I forget to forget, in which case I have to do it all again with a crowbar.

The dying is easy in my neighbourhood, for all but those misfits I talked about earlier. Though it's gotten better for them too, now that begging cups are disposable. I'm sure those receptacles have by now reached the streets of Burundi where, but for a spoonful of soup, people would have died an hour before they died anyway.

Death did wonders for Marilyn Monroe, also a misfit, but not like my friend on the corner, the guy who prefers oranges to grapefruit. Being rich, and ample, she had to find other reasons, other ways of becoming perfectly thin. A career requirement for young women in film, aspirants too, except women in Hollywood don't always know that they're starving.

Blanche points to our bloated lives as the root of all pain. Bob jumps to agree. Our living is out of kilter, she says … what about the dying, I ask … what about it … are we doing it right … it's the same thing … how so … living is dying … that's a song … it's not … it should be.

To my eyes Blanche is still twenty, Washington is burning, an obvious prophecy, and Kiki is eating ice cream so she won't lose her sweetness. I've learned to make do with a muzzle, solutions that disappear in the larynx. Ideas-cum-murder over coffee and pastry. Neither a way nor a way out, there is no time left in the time that I'm talking about.

Back to the conversation. A meeting of minds, of discipline, a convergence if not a consensus. I concur, then disagree with the thing I acceded to. That's when the machetes come out. But in my little life it's the swing and not the cuts that matter, those botched finalities from which we always come back.

There are many ways to say nothing, but after you know the shot, said Al Pacino while he was a real estate agent. I bide my time. Stack sugar cubes to better defend my place in the circle, but before I could put in the last brick Blanche moved the bowl to the table behind her. What would Al do, I asked myself, on scanning the tables adjacent, and then even Blanche couldn't stop the next thing from happening.

066

If I die before Bob he's promised to explain everything to my son. If Bob goes before me I won't say anything. Happily, sins of the father preceded my moppet, so telling him would do nothing to help his predicament. My boy needs to know I died for no reason. I'm also working on the opposite theory, the why of my dids, in case there's a heaven in heaven, or in Missouri.

There are no words for the words I'm unpacking. These pages are whiter now than before they were written. The facts I've also set aside for safekeeping, but I don't think I'll need them. I know so much more now, than when I knew everything.

Let's get back to the café, again, so this must be later. Sorry for the uncertainty, the spinning, lord knows I'm no Finnegan. The grumbling is more important than meaning, and there can only be one voice in the labyrinth. This is not without risk. I circled the block in a cold sweat before entering. A stitch, maybe two, is what I came here to unravel. Will I be the first or the last to arrive, and is that my cannoli.

As I wave down the waiter Blanche tells Bob about finding enlightenment in the Rocky mountains. My friends don't subscribe to who we are really. Luckily, I'm the narrator and the pronoun in the preceding statements. I take a minute to find my demeanor, to decide who is speaking. Harder now that places have been described and people identified. This is the place where I could lose everything.

Bob knew this would happen and is quick to take control of the conversation. Everything he's saying will need to be unsaid, until it breaks in my direction. I survey the terrain. The table is round, but we knew this already, no right, no left flank either, we're exposed on all sides. A glance, a phrase could take out all three of us. When will it come to me and how will I know when I hear it.

The waiter comes to take our order, desserts are not on the menu. He rattles off a list of pastries and puddings. The gelato, he says, is artisanal. The things you hear when you don't have a bazooka. I ask for a macchiato and a cannoli to tie in what I said previously. Bob and Blanche do the same, this I could not have predicted, I assumed constancy, its lack thereof, was at my discretion entirely.

065

ONCE FIRED, A BULLET may lodge in the sinews, but we know from the spent cartridges most will succumb to gravity, no matter the skill or the gun's calibration. By the way, a bazooka is just one way to thin out a café, but the thought alone won't break the skin, or there'd be an ear in the sugar bowl and brains in my coffee.

I prefer a gap to the story, but a mind in freefall gathers no moss so it's best I keep talking. Bob is dipping into his bag of authors to demonstrate his grasp of the poem Blanche is working on. Something about how everything is washed away by our inattention.

He queries, elaborates and finally agrees with Blanche's premise. Heaping is but one way philosophers say nothing, but Blanche will have none of it. She knows the game and is becoming irritated with Bob's hodgepodge of nuggets and pauses. Hold on to your hat for the inevitable wrangle. As for the conversation itself, I ignored it completely.

There are two doors to this place and no exits, but I don't need a portal to rack up these absences. Bob and Blanche argue while I catch the show in the window. In medias res because the whole won't fit the ambit. I pull my rucksack closer and wait for my friends to notice me. One must be seen to be leaving, there can be no ebb without onlookers, but I'm in no hurry. I have nowhere to be and all of the numbers in my phone are wrong. I'm sure that's coincidence.

Blanche likes to talk about poets, dead ones, or those who at least speak the language. Stubborn pricks who swim upstream and then pull up the river behind them. A bard's best chance is no chance at all, and some commit suicide. All the while scholars, like fiends on a sausage, turn those hard nights into treaties.

Poets are like the last dinner guest whose parting is endless, since they must first plant and then grow their departures. They know how to finesse their insignificance. Much like those dragons we talked about earlier, or that unicorn who caught a plane back to Jupiter. Kiki`s friends, now mine, also trumpet their nonexistence, but they don't attend dinner parties.

For Celan it was the Seine that offered up the broader perspective, that's why the bard said yes to the river. By my own hand, he whispered. But I still think his death came from Germany. As in a few decades prior when Jews were made to squat en masse to accommodate the arm's extension and a bullet's trajectory. Two deaths then, since Celan checked out again when his hair hit the water.

Kneeling is fine, better than shooting fish in a barrel for your workaround genocide but, said Himmler, nothing scales like an oven. Sixty years later a priest wrote a book about the Reich's fastidious tendencies. A folio good enough to be a CBS documentary, in contrast to the absence of data coming out of Tel Aviv or Nevada. Times change, and given the preponderance of fire-and-forget shelling, they wouldn't be able to log those bodies anyway.

We're all poets, at least to the end of this sentence. Who hasn't, in this day and age, gone to war with the language. Such were my thoughts from behind my line of sugar cubes. I also thought about zucchini while Bob and Blanche discussed all things serious and beautiful. But mostly I thought about how the conversation was too high a price to pay for the dessert that came with it.

064

July, 3020, I remember it like it was Tuesday, Kiki and I were at the park next to the fire station which, on that day, was just west of Albuquerque. From there we flew to India. In futures prior travel was, is and will be more talk than actual. Kiki has the technology.

On arrival I spoke to anyone who would listen and then with the resident ascetics. Will I ever go clear, I asked. No, they said, but you will go insane, or at least digital. I decided then and there to ask somebody different. Why not try the monks in Tibet, said Kiki … when … next week … on Tuesday … why Tuesday … no reason.

Until then I'm in the wind, not literally or I'd have hitched a ride out of this coffee bar. As a hummingbird, say, with a pressing engagement. Then Blanche would know I'm important.

Though I always leave twice regardless, any which way I can and then better later.

A twirl to flash my ensemble, the wing-tipped shoes in particular. They hurt like hell but I wear them anyway. Indigo, to match my belt, a tip from my father, that I might access a better class of people. Or not, which is why I left home in the first place. He was a tailor who also loved books, that's why I always keep one on the coffee table. I think of him each time I reach for the clicker.

Books, says Bob, are how we know almost everything, but that almost is bigger than the all that he's talking about. So we just kept on arguing like three kids in a dorm room, tinkers who still believe they could change the way governments do business. But, being artists, not all of our alls are about politics.

When the empire succumbs to mob rule our gardens will no longer need trimming, hastening the return of the wolf and the grizzly. Weeds make the best stranglers and soon all of this will never have happened unless Elon Musk makes it to Saturn.

I'm fine with either eventuality. I keep a list on the fridge of what we'll need then, and one in the cloud should the world end while I'm shopping. In the basement, or is it the crisper, are a few atomic devices for when Elon resumes building castles.

You've been peddling that crap for decades, said Blanche, and you've no eye for fashion … yes I do … I take it you're leaving … why do you say that … because you're standing … I see … you don't know … that I'm standing … that you're leaving … I have places to be … you don't … I might … where … it'll come to me … could you be any more conspicuous … I don't understand … sit down.

063

I HAD SO MUCH to say at the café, but mostly I worked on my pauses. Bob, on consulting his pecker, knew my next stab at an exit would be irreversible. He waited until I was on my feet to announce he was hungry again. He ordered Blanche's favourite dessert, French, with two forks which, were I to subscribe to that schema, was one shy of mine.

It's for the table, he said … really … too bad you're leaving … is it … I'll pop by after Blanche and I finish talking … thanks for the warning … sure … sooner rather than later … why sooner … so I won't have to feed you … of course, but do pick up a little something so we can have tea.

When Bob gets to my house he'll want to rehash his conversation with Blanche even though, by then, I won't know where it's been. Bob may have manoeuvred himself into a pastry without me, but he has not yet grasped the true cost of that delicacy.

He'll come for tea and leave with a headache. I will need to know what was said after I left the café, so I can inform what he assumes happened. I try to stay current with what I'm not hearing, the rumours, the suppositions, with which to beat back oblivion. Absent Blanche I'll be the voice in Bob's noodle, so I can highlight and then compound his misery.

Broadly speaking, I prefer sedition to moaning since all of my gripes are political. In my kitchen there's no discerning a coup from a whimper and next week I'm going to Guatemala with Kiki. There was food all year round in that little country whereas here, in the north, eating was seasonal. That is until Chiquita started growing my bananas in Central America.

On the way home I picked up a few essentials for dinner. Broccoli, because Bob doesn't like it, and tomatoes, though Blanche thinks my interest in the fruit is unnatural. There was still space in my satchel for a few canned goods to boost my reserves for upcoming cataclysms. My next meal and the apocalypse buttressed, I put away the groceries and waited. A machinegun in every window is how I imagine it. Sadly I have but one son and many openings.

There's clarity in waiting, so say the sages in India, specks on a mountain, rust on a rockface. There have also been sightings of those teachers at Starbucks, since they too are now on the internet. A good thing since It used to be damn near impossible to find a guru unless you played guitar for the Beatles.

Before I left the café Blanche gave Bob and me the address to her favourite studio. A real estate office repurposed for healing, above yet another well reviewed eatery. We'll meditate, she said, and then go for salad. How will you manage that, asked Bob, as I grabbed my carryall, but not before they invited themselves to dinner. Thursday, said Blanche, so you can write about it on Friday. Sounds good, I said. But I'd already written those pages.

062

THE UNIVERSE RAGES, GENERALLY lets up around seven. Thank god for television. Between the burbling and the blazing lies my salvation. By nine eastern, seven mountain time, I'm fully anesthetized in the confident, soothing tones of the BBC.

It takes focus to shutter my brain, especially after I talk to people. I'm concerned about what my friends are saying at the café. I know from experience Blanche can really stretch a French pastry, so it's not likely Bob is on his way here. I'm also fidgety about what the squirrels outside my window are up to, their so-called playing.

I prepare a sandwich for this evening's documentary. Something about miracle cures for whatever ails me, currently or soon to be in clinical trials. Every night I wait for a breakthrough, for some good doctor to rebuild my eyelids so I can stop seeing actually. At ten eastern, seven pacific, the First Lady will address the nation from her vegetable patch because the rose garden belongs to the president. Sugar, she says, is not a vegetable. The message plays well in Seattle but in Mississippi they just don't believe her.

In my left hand is the remote, in my right is the sandwich, without which it would just be my dick I was holding. Always an option. All to say I won't move a muscle, my gift to democracy and the people we're bombing. I can also block the sun with my thumb, its rising so called, here and in Australia.

Here it's my version that matters, though I often feign ignorance. Who am I to say these are my thoughts and those are my footprints. Like a sitting duck in a cyclone I dodge tsunamis and chase fires in Buffalo, because they don't report murders. All from the comfort of my four-legged furniture.

There's a ring at the door, or a knock, a lesser scribe would have felt compelled to decide. There is no bell, no toll either, somebody should have told Hemingway. That'll be Bob on the stoop with his jitters, a mishmash of body and absence. All there is, a Buddhist once told me but how, I asked him, did it get into my living room.

Talking to me will do nothing to help Bob's condition, so long as I stick to the script. I've been anticipating his arrival, though I prefer his departures. In fact, I can't get enough of them. I press pause on the first lady's initiative. As I walk to the door I'm thinking that silly rabbit was right, Trix aren't for kids. That's why them corporate types had to take out that bunny.

061

I PREFER AN AXE to a blade since tanks are illegal and you can't pick one up at Home Depot. There's waiting, and then there's waiting, I realized as I unlatched the door. But I must have said it out loud unless Bob was thinking it also. I agree, he said, though I prefer to wait for someone or something than to wait for no reason. Logicians will not commit to an inkling without a proviso.

These days only the French will go to bat for a deficit but here, in the colonies, we plug those omissions. I believe Bob because I believe everything, something is not nothing, but a lack is not a loss as I see it. Clear as day for the Buddha and

Archimedes, or that's what they said when Kiki and I visited. I took pictures, but Kiki says it is forbidden for time travellers to modify history.

At the restaurant Bob and Blanche spoke with great eloquence about art, art and art, and then they talked about quinoa. I'm thinking barbeque for our upcoming dinner. Beef just tastes better when a vegan is present, pork more so, the animal not the futures accruing in my portfolio. Not all pigs are for eating.

Bob is still glowing or gloating from his time alone with Blanche. He's a hair's breadth from despair but he doesn't care or know it, yet. I am the truth and the trouble ahead, through me, said Jesus, to the next debacle. Except he said it in Aramaic and the English never did translate that sentence. So I'll just keep on sinning – happy sinning, said W.C. Fields – now there's a stipulation our saviour could not have envisaged.

The fog will only worsen, I told Bob … what fog … your surmisings of what Blanche may be feeling … no it won't … like a toothache … I don't see the analogy … what analogy … between Blanche and a toothache … it'll come to me.

I believe in the mind because the body, I know from the dead pigeons accruing at the foot of my street, is inconsequential. I am, or so goes the theory, and have always been an ambulance chaser, there's actually no difference between me and a German pharmaceutical company.

A yelp is a word and two are a muddle, that's why there used to be only one yelp in this sentence. Two now, for clarity, but I wrote the second one first so they're not consecutive. There's a dead lake between my ears, it's where I go to make my connections, betwixt and between runaway fragments.

Your bits are your bits, said my grocer, and hopefully you'll never have to retrieve them from beneath fractured concrete. People from Gaza say the darndest things, and they make the best space travellers. Why only last week that storekeep had lunch on Neptune with Venus, his ice cream supplier, and on Tuesday he introduced Venus to Kiki.

BOB LEFT DAYS AGO, shaken, but not enough in my estimation. This morning I put out more cuts of meat than three people could eat in one sitting. Nuts too, because Blanche needs her protein. I'll round out the feast with a tomato salad, local. Then the pickers go home for the winter so my Palestinian grocer can sell me blueberries in January.

Bob arrived early to examine the bounty, he will forego it or admit his hypocrisy. I wouldn't trade that moment for all the pigs in Haiti. Which, incidentally, is what that country did in the seventies. The entire population slaughtered to make room for the Yorkshires of Manitoba and Iowa. That's just how it is when third world herds get the sniffles.

My plan is to say everything now, for practice, and then again after Blanche gets here. That way she'll see Bob is muddled whereas my thoughts are perfectly collated. I continue preparations, tactics really, consider the seating while slicing a crisp English cucumber. Haiti will choke on the plastic it came in.

Speaking of swine, of the two legged persuasion this time. The eighties was truly our decade, our time to shine, even if Blanche remembers it differently. I see her still in the attire we picked out together, the regalia, the machinery to keep my eye twitching. When in Rome, I like to watch women walking.

Vegetables, long-time staples in Lahore and Calcutta, were finally making their way into American second tier cities. That and cocaine is how everybody got thin in the eighties. Taller too, women especially, because of the hair, though some men kept their platform shoes from the previous decade. When the recession hit in eighty-nine women couldn't afford to maintain all those updos. Big hair went the way of elective surgery.

The nineties delivered a terrible blow to Dow Chemical and to silicone sales in general. People should not have to choose between the mortgage and augmentation. The salons closed down and then the factories. A tailspin the experts agreed and the recovery foiled, buried in the swill we call lower Manhattan. Then things got worse, but it didn't matter because we were told otherwise.

The best way to get people spending again is to attack a small Arab country. The go to enemy was Iraq in the nineties, as four letter names were all they have a mind for in Kentucky, and before that it was Asia. I have earned my senility, scoured these streets with a knife in my teeth because here, in my three syllable city, no death can reach me.

When it's all said and said I plan to come back in name only, but I may have said that already. Blanche says I left this realm years ago but, far as I know, I have yet to get hit by a bus or a missile. I wouldn't have known anyway because once bombing commences consciousness is not recommended, so said my brother. Sensible, since as a toddler he would never have been able to outrun German ordnance. He also said the rats all wore sunglasses for fear they'd go blind from the flashes.

059

When the going gets tough I like to pretend I'm George Clooney. So does everyone else, but I'm not deterred. Only the insane and the indigent can really imagine what it's like to live in a movie. Easy since all they have to think about is their lack and they don't shop. No place to put things, I guess, so any benefaction beyond soup would only add to their burden.

That rusting Cadillac represents the last five year's rent and every trip to the food bank from now until Christmas. General Motors is still king in Detroit but if you trade that heap for a good scrap cart you can still keep your flatscreen.

Waste is the point of acquisition. Better a deluge than a trickle, like an ill-timed piss at a truck stop. Garbage as the first rule of progress, the measure of the modern family and Wall Street's primary indices. Our gift to Bangladesh because they who have nothing don't have that either. They put the zero in supply chain economics.

America spends to temper the pangs of being them, of being in general. There are millions of little brown hands bred to accommodate that very purpose and no end of ways to accessories fabulous. Why else would god have given us walk-in closets, storage lockers for those of us who don't have garages.

058

I MARINATED THOSE CUTS to perfection, shank, chuck and sirloin. Bovines were harmed in this sentence. Ethically, presumably, but the concept is extraneous to their point of view, to the way they live actually. Cows are lucky like that. I know for I was one once and then Kiki sold me for five beans exactly. Jack was her name on the day she did it, two hundred years ago Tuesday.

Kiki, Jack, Jacqueline, say, planted those beans and by morning that vine was through the clouds. She climbed and she whistled, climbed till she bested that still growing foliage. There was a man there, she said, tall, bearded and lacking in gray matter. So I've heard, I replied. That very day Kiki and I cut down that beanstalk, but we never did find his body.

Bob is asking what I put in the marinade. Cows, I said … be serious… oil, garlic and a few spices… that's a lot of meat … is it … good cuts too … the best … why three steak knives … Blanche is coming … she doesn't eat meat … I know.

Before Bob left the restaurant he and Blanche arranged to meet again on Tuesday, but I wasn't invited so I'm refusing to write about it. I was both hero and narrator at the aforementioned social. I should have known what would happen.

When a man meets a woman everything he knows is the first thing to go. So I must have written that statement before Blanche and I met. No matter, I'll fill in those blanks later when I, the ousted, the mulch, become the shovel.

As to my upcoming exclusion, I'm relieved, but that hardly matters. I needed first to refuse their invitation and then be admired for my tenacity. That's how I reason when I'm not watching television, and I never take soap from a eugenicist.

I have one hour before Blanche's arrival. Plenty of time to grill and then display the meat prominently. In Blanche's world the cow would have hosted this dinner, with its cow friends and I'd be the slab in the oven. But that's not how this ends. I know for I've written the last scene already, a backhoe operator digging a hole for a skyscraper or to squeeze in more bodies. He won't know me from Genghis Khan or my great uncle Charlie, but he will know, from the shape of my skull, that I wasn't a bovine.

057

I DON'T KNOW WHAT I don't know about soap, hygiene, about asphyxiation in general. There was a list. Death is always the death of others, slow or sudden, memorable as a sneeze for most people, or a last puzzled look from those ill-fated bovines. Curious, but hardly worth worrying about. Whereas people, unlike cows, will lay down their lives willingly, for the president or the patria, one and the same in Nebraska. They say they too have a list, a stash and a dream that's worth killing for.

I'm envisioning, planning, a more dynamic script for my own atomization. An old style obliteration, with cameras, where I will finally be at one with strangers, just not with my maker. The law and a courtyard, a dimly lit stroll to a platform from which my crimes and then the verdict will be read on television. A death for the cybernated, more enduring than marble, than flowers even and before sentencing I'll allocute to the chickens I've tortured.

It's never too late to learn a new language, said the New York harbour girl to the huddled masses. These skyscrapers won't build themselves and I'll need people to pick up my dry cleaning. The editor doesn't like it when I quote monuments, she also says I shouldn't speak for cows or that unicorn who hightailed it Jupiter. She especially doesn't want me to engage them directly.

I listen intently while my redactor is speaking. Unicorns and cows, she says, are not credible as bona fide characters … what about statues … nope … what about if they speak the language … what language … English … that won't happen … French then … if they're from France you mean … sure … that would confuse the reader … the what … the reader … the what … never mind.

Onward, though I don't grasp the concept, to the debacle at hand, commonly referred to as an evening with friends. When they leave it will be up to me and what remains of that witless bovine to make sense of what happened. The editor says readers are also resistant to exchanges between leftover meat and protagonists. Such conversations, she explains, are not of a kind that can be understood later.

I blame the Greeks. It was Socrates who battened down the hatches, and before that reason was optional. It doesn't work, said the Buddha, the last time he deigned to climb down from my ceiling. I can't fault the French, there were none. The English too had not been invented, so no genial middle, no erudite paladins to tell brown people what's what before strapping them to the mouths of cannons.

It would be a thousand years before European kings carved their names into those torsos. In defence of monarchs, and to this very day, it's easy to mistake greed for a calling, the either-ors that have never existed. Hostage, terrorist, either way we need walls to contain them, from Gaza to the Mexican border because you can't be too careful.

There are two sides to every story and then there's the noise only. Peace talks won't last the morning. The bullet points we'll get from Wolf Blitzer because the fine points are not meant for us onlookers or he'd have blurted them out decades ago.

Gaza, in case you're from Oklahoma, is that wedge between a wall and a shoreline Palestinians can't get to, a target plain and simple. Whereas each time America closes its borders Mexicans can walk down to Peru to keep from getting murdered. But, said the torch lady, I'll still need that dry cleaning.

Bob scours the fridge, finds and unwraps the cheese. That's for later, I said … later when … after dinner … Blanche doesn't eat dairy either … what won't you eat is the question … grapefruit … good to know … let's have pastry later … there is no pastry … so you say … I do … why did you invite Blanche to a barbeque … there's plenty else to eat … did I mention I'm moving away from meat … really … for ethical reasons … good luck with that.

055

When Bob is down he talks to the floor and when he's up I don't answer the door. He snags a baguette from the counter and a plate from the cupboard. For the cheese, he explains. He pulls up a stool as I pick up the cleaver to resume hacking. A carving knife would be better, but I like how the axe flatters my knuckles.

Bob is reworking his discussion with Blanche at the café. I attend carefully, focus on the parts he can't access. He's dreaming of another kick at that talk, to correct the should haves and could haves he left on the table. A do over, and he's using me to hone his performance, but it will not go well is my plan and my reason for hosting this dinner.

The future isn't such a hard nut to crack, I was there yesterday and tomorrow I'm going back to buy grapefruit.

Blueberries too, to help revive my dead brain matter. Moving forward I'll need even more antioxidants to neutralize the free radicals. As evidenced in that BBC documentary and echoed soon after when, from her vegetable garden, the first lady took on big sugar.

As to Bob's fixations regarding our three way café fiasco, four if we include the narrator, and then two because he and I left together. I remember it like I don't remember it, so there's no difference between the part I attended and for which I was absent. Blueberries are fine, recommended, yet minds still break despite our best efforts. But I cannot allow my friends to come between me and my synapses.

All of this reminds me of those translators, those Afghan assets who worked tirelessly, optimistically, for their American handlers. The ones who were later abandoned, captured and tortured anyway. America is the blueberries in the preceding analogy and those translators are the people who eat them and die regardless.

I digress. Not to beat a dead horse, but I think it's those dead brain cells acting up again. Those gaps are more than their numbers, more than my all. Bob says I won't need or miss that brain matter since my thinking is all holes and no substance. I agree, but I don't see a downside in that analysis. Did I mention Bob also hates broccoli, other things too, I keep a list in my pocket.

Speaking of produce, in 1994 the tomato was reengineered as a tomato. That patent is now in Virginia. The fruit looks better than ever proving once again, we can eat our experiments. I'm sure those same scientists will soon get round to people so I'm requesting to be genetically rearranged as Franz Kafka. A few tweaks should do it and then everyone, Brian too, will pretend to like what I've written.

At the café Blanche spoke briefly of how she missed this city, while I talked about the opposite and then the same thing exactly. I don't mind beating a dead horse once in a while but, for the record, that was before I got my cannoli. After which I turned my attention to less poignant commentary.

Coffee, say, and the sacks piled high against a decidedly unfinished wall. Brick, wood and burlap, made you itch just to look at those totems. On the plaster surfaces were pictures of the café's Austin location and then photos of smiling Hondurans. The scene meticulously curated so we'd know poverty was more than just an aesthetic.

Not everything is controlled by multinationals, said Blanche scanning the pictures, big business is only good at splitting mountains and melting glaciers. It's not true, I said, or there'd be fish in the Manhattan subway. The coffee had kicked in but my plate was empty, therefore the fiddlefaddle. You're an idiot, said Blanche, on registering what I was on about. I agreed, but I don't think she believed me, it's hard to argue across one's own stupidity.

Truth is I never know what to say while I'm saying it. I follow my mouth, go wherever it takes me. Panic is how I run out the nights and the mornings, but what's killing me now will still be here tomorrow. Kiki is working hard to remove that day from our lexicon, and then she'll go to work on the previous. We were in Texas this afternoon. People there are still waiting for the death that was promised them, different than the one indicated on their hospital bracelets. In Texas waiting is lethal.

The meek shall inherit the earth, said Jesus. Not in my zip code, replied cousin Calvin. You tell him, whispered the local residents association. Don't despair, there's plenty of room at the margins, sole to toe in the direction you're facing, so you won't need a map to get there. The meagre are the beneficiaries of what the well to do set in motion. It's nothing really, but that nothing could feed all of Africa, so long as they agree to mine and then buy back its petroleum.

053

I KNOW FROM WAITING, the colour and feel of my unripened kiwi, the magic does not happen here, but elsewhere. There, is always where we need it to be. A good thing too, since it's no longer politic to trade trinkets for continents, now that anyone can buy those doodads on Amazon.

When a black president dreams of murder the list is ratified by the joint chiefs and emailed via a secure server to an underground bunker. A win-win for those generals-cum-lobbyists, and there's no lack of places where the worst should be done after mounting it to a predator drone. Justice is blind, finally, and flies out of Nevada.

Afghanistan certainly, Guatemala as necessary, it's only a matter of time before that little country is ready to receive our technology again, to be awed by our progress. Presidents do what they must for our conglomerates in the tropics. Dole Foods and Chiquita Brands International, formerly the United Fruit Company will, in turn, ensure the hemisphere's agronomics cohere with my fruit salad.

052

I TOO PREPARED FOR slaughter because it should not be excluded. The occasion never came so I joined forces with the squirrels and racoons in my neighbourhood. But first I had to rearrange my hearing to fit their speaking. Being a mammal, I thought I'd be better disposed to my kindred species, but the rodents were clearly more charming, and they were fluent in the other's palaver.

Their plans for insurrection were well in advance of my own and had been fomenting since the last century. Thus they were eager and promised to introduce me to their New York contingency, the power and the brains behind the organization.

They'd been conspiring since before the Clinton administration to take out a few money managers, and then as many as necessary. Together, I thought, we could set an example.

Truth is I can't tell a billionaire from the rhinoceros Kiki and I befriended in Africa. His name was Frank. After which Kiki spoke at length of the mastodon's peculiarities, its modest footprint. Apparently rhinos, despite their size, are practically invisible. The way to tell a billionaire from a rhinoceros is by their excretions, Kiki explained, because if Frank were a billionaire there'd be slime all over these pages.

Tonight we barbeque and tomorrow I'm going shopping. For grapefruit, in case you've forgotten, seeing as Bob doesn't like them. I buy what he eats at Walmart because that's what it takes these days to stretch a ruble. Grapefruit then, bananas and five kiwis to coincide with the empty cells in my egg carton. The fruit is good this time of year and Bob won't find them because he only eats ova that are cooked already.

Then a quick swim with Kiki in Saint Tropez, drifting, glistening by the light of the moon. In the French Riviera they remove all the dead fish and plastics. Not in Indonesia, said Kiki, and in 2004 those dead fish were people.

I attempted to console her, downplay and then distract her with the science behind the tectonics. Try as I might, I couldn't compete with Zuckerberg's mission to bring us together, so those bodies remain lodged in her noggin. Tsunamis, I said finally, are just a rumour from Sweden. Don't be ridiculous, she said, everyone knows those storms comes from Jupiter.

051

IN RUSSIA FORTY IS the new sixty, the new seventy in Appalachia because of the vodka and the moonshine respectively. There's little difference between Marx and McDonald's in a market economy. How did the good people of Siberia ever manage without just-in-time inventory. The dream is the dream because you can't eat it, meant to be, so you can still scratch it. A dog that won't hunt, as they say in Vladivostok.

Everything these days happens in hours and festers for centuries. Like those mountains we've been decapitating so we can get to the numbers inside them. Geological time, but faster say my racoon comrades. I beg to differ, said the triceratops in the tailpipe of my Subaru, since it's taken me sixty-five million years to get here. Then she spoke of the meteor that knocked out her zucchini.

History is the two hundred year old lamp I'm rewiring and time is a crack in the bedrock from the lithosphere to my kitchen faucet. That's why the surgeon general is recommending mom smoke on the porch. It's no good for the kiddies and after a good frack it only takes a spark to explode the domicile. No matter, those structures are a drag on the value of whatever is beneath them. I know for I was in real estate before I got hooked on tomatoes.

From the Amazon to the Arctic, places in flux, in transit to their nonexistence. We had to make room for the cows. Cars too, said the triceratops, and I know from a previous incarnation there's even more oil in them there glaciers. We can use it to make more ice after the melting. Such is the plenty of our disappearing.

The earth just keeps on giving, though it's looking a little peaked, bald in some places, but for the garbage. The plastics, the packaging, the branding, as they say on Madison Avenue, is bursting with colour. Then off to Bangladesh where it's scrubbed and sorted for pennies on the ton before it's shipped via China back to Seattle. The system works, but for a little mercury and cadmium in your salad.

I'm not a chemist or an economist, though I have been known to say otherwise. A mere raconteur, but Bob thinks that too is debatable. I can tell by his breathing, quick like that of a bunny, that he's taken a turn for the worse.

I had to thwart his every hope to find that panic, but it's not hard to take down a philosopher. More like hunting in

Cornwall, with hounds and footmen, as opposed to Tajikistan. The English are no match for a doe's focus, her singular purpose, that's why they kill for sport not dinner.

050

To BE HAPPY IS to think one thing only, as in commerce or genocide. That's a line from a poem I wrote, read, both in this instance, in which a Congolese woman wields a machete while eating spaghetti. Silly I know, but there's no other pasta that rhymes with that implement. I checked.

The house I live in is in good repair, tightly sealed against the weather, bees and the occasional yelp, unless I neglect to latch the windows before I start screaming. I fix what I must to ensure it outlasts the speaking, even an amoeba is hardwired to resist its dismantling. Home is where I forget to forget everything.

To be or not to be is too convoluted a statement for the shells we inhabit. But we don't know about the second part of that statement because Shakespeare whispered it from the wings while listening to the prince's soliloquy.

Bob thinks I should move to a condo, less maintenance, he argues … I like fixing stuff … you don't … really … you're thinking of somebody else … what about my tomato plants … you have no tomato plants … not now … how do you decide what to fix … inadvertently … does that work … probably … cook the steaks … no … why not … we're waiting for Blanche.

I consider Bob's suggestion, sit mostly, so much depends on the things I'm not telling him. I cannot listen and apprehend simultaneously. What he says conflicts with how the words arrange themselves in my noggin, so it takes even more work to hear them regardless. People whose names begin with a B are becoming a nuisance.

What I don't know is good for the nation, what I do know is still being edited and what I just deleted could land me in prison. The cure is always worse than the malady. To live is to be a long time sick, I told Socrates. Who in turn told Plato and his treaties, so mine in this instance, would outlast the future. Then I said the same thing to Blanche, but she'd heard it already.

When this fails, and it will, said Blanche, you can always go back to real estate … that won't be necessary … oh … my lawyer and I are talking to Ingmar about a screen play … who … Bergman … he's dead … what's your point … I'm not sure … then everyone will know my work … your what … my worth … come again … my address.

049

WHILE BLANCHE WAS STILL in the Rockies I wrote her a letter. Philosophers, I said, are only good for recounting yesterday's errors. Out the window it went, along with that other epistle I wrote the president. It wasn't delivered, so I gave her a copy the minute she stepped out of the airport.

Recalling my conversation with Blanche, the one about Ingmar Bergman, caused me to purchase more meat than was necessary for this evening's soiree, and then I reduced the salad. I continue to refuse Bob's frequent requests for steak before Blanche's arrival. I offer him an espresso instead. He volunteers to make it, I ask for a double. I'm just hoping Blanche gets here while he's still miserable.

Coffee helps me discern one grouping of words from another, methamphetamine would be faster but then I wouldn't know who is speaking. Shakespeare plays Shakespeare in the story you're reading. He's taken to reciting all of his sonnets verbatim and to illustrate their dexterity he's inverted the syllables, to prove he too was postmodern. When he's done reworking his legacy I'll hogtie and dump the body.

Next time I go shopping I'm taking Will with me. I'll introduce him to my buddy from Winnipeg. The one who hates grapefruit, but you might remember him as the guy who likes oranges. Like the dramatist, he also speaks for his dead, but don't look for them in the who's who of cadavers. In Manitoba you don't have to be a prince to get murdered.

The meat is marinating and the salad awaits its dressing. Tomorrow my indigenous friend will put a knife to Shakespeare's ear. Seeing as Blanche is late I may as well tell you straightaway how it happens. I'll be coming home from Walmart with those grapefruit we talked about earlier. I'll stop to give some to my friend from the Midwest and that's when he'll take the bard hostage.

That's Shakespeare, I'll say … who's Shakespeare … a playwright … who are you … also an author … I prefer oranges … to authors … to grapefruit … I see … do you … no … writers make everything worse … perhaps that's only true in this instance … leave the grapefruit … sure … now go fuck yourself … I can't … why not … this hasn't happened yet … tomorrow then … certainly … bring oranges … you got it.

048

A CELLO IS A cello unless it's a radio, essential for those nineteenth-century winters on television. I stop barbequing in the late autumn, except for a few sunny days in September. For now my winter is still in Nunavut, about fifteen degrees north of here. I can't wait until it dips a few latitudes, as Bob rarely goes out past October.

I've been known to mistake music for hunger, the disaster with what I don't have. Bliss with the list next to the cash in my pocket. I regularly conflate Nike with the rape of Kashmir, though it's well documented women there were forgetting to button their blouses. So said their protectors.

In South Asia farmers are mules, miners, or Maoists, it depends on who's hiring. One must be nimble in the east.com, all of my electronics and small appliances come from there via Amazon. Should you still be working your little rice patch in Sri Lanka count yourself lucky and click express delivery. Lest before then you should lose your address or get shot in the brain or the elbow.

There's only enough money for the rich in what we pay for everything, for a decreasing number of globetrotters. Competitors, as they say at the Chicago School of Economics. The spoils to the third person sailing, the supplement that supplies nothing. Nowadays moguls need only fabricate zeros, in sufficient quantity to choke a horse or a small island nation.

For bees every gunshot is fatal, but they're harder to hit than a Tamil. We have only this flower, that one and that one, a worker once told me from the inside of an oil painting. Bees can't talk, I said to her, and then I switched out that canvas for a cityscape I had stored in the basement. Soon art will be the only safe place for bees and homo erectus, at least that's what that drone said the last time I did laundry.

047

Perhaps I'll take up that cello, having recently mastered the radio, anything to keep me from hosting these dinners. I hope it comes with a manual, better yet software. I'll ask Santa to get me one since it's coming up to October. Easier now that he's online with the rest of us. Honey, said the missus, it's high time we went digital. Then she packed a lunch and together they hightailed it to Portugal. Now Santa can get his bride something other than thicker socks come December.

I'm fine with the warming, so long as it doesn't lengthen Bob's foraging in my fridge and pantry. Does Blanche know you're going vegan, I asked … don't be so drastic … that you'll be eating less meat … not entirely … I hope dinner won't be awkward for you … no you don't … what have you told her …

nothing … really … it was more of an understanding … I see … a meeting of minds … over what exactly … everything … cows too then … exactly.

In the kitchen I'm searching for more words to complement and then compound Bob's bewilderment. Something more specific than the blurring in general. I'm sure Blanche will find my attempts at subterfuge ridiculous. Obtuse, she said, on witnessing the same at the café. She also suggested I jump from the Peace Bridge into the Niagara River, but I know she didn't mean it because then she told me to shut up and eat my cannoli.

Did I mention women scribes were men too until recently, there's no end to the muddle, no hilarity till we raze the academy. While at the café Blanche felt compelled to interrupt that thought, so I finished it later. Bob says he felt his character was also being misrepresented, the third man, a foil to my genius. The guy behind the guy who was not saying anything.

046

YESTERDAY I SLEPT INSIDE a rock where I met a man who said I could appropriate his solutions, just not his name, to express what I'm thinking. All I have to do now is find out what those answers are and get them down pat before Blanche gets here.

Let's begin. This man says god and I made our debut together … hasn't god been here all along … perhaps, but nobody's seen the here that he talks about … I see … that's why we don't know what we don't know … but it functions … what does … what we don't know … where … here … where's that … everywhere … roundly … that's right … subliminally … exactly … impossible … why is that … it doesn't exist … what doesn't … the unrevealed … when it does, you mean … I don't understand … it doesn't exist even when it does … how do you know that … my analyst told me.

I talked to that man till he screamed, which gave way to prayer. Then I hit the books. Philosophy mostly, it didn't make a dent, but I was able to increase, exponentially, what I didn't know already. The fog grew again after I took to emulating the buzzing … the what … the buzzing, of my Irish betters. One couldn't help but admire those modernists, there are so few clackers who've managed to say nothing really, what the French call language.

Women wore black and we, their boyfriends, pastels by the time I left Stanford. Manhattan was the place to be, daiquiris and heroin in case you've forgotten. Roundabout the time Giuliani locked up Tony Salerno, an obvious irony. Smoothies, though not in the Bronx, permeated the village. Soon to be the epicentre, after LA, of the kale revolution, but I never did like the age I was born to so I chose another.

045

MEN WAXED THEIR WHISKERS in the time of my choosing and never apologized. Women, pre-formed in hoop dresses, ambled beneath parasols and a wobbly sun. Boardwalk gallantries, after botanicals and African ivory, were all the rage in my Xanadu. Swans next to cats on the banks of slow-moving rivers, emptying into lakes like mirrors, to fragment beneath the brushes of some up-and-comer, changing forever the state of my looking.

Scholars at Berkeley had recently discovered sociology, but at Cambridge it was not taken seriously. It doesn't exist, they said, across hundreds of books and thousands of articles, at Cambridge they get paid by the syllable.

In New York and in Massachusetts they turned those theories into a campaign to start flappers smoking, what Madison Avenue would later call advertising. After the women we'll strap in the children, said Edward Bernays to The American Tobacco Company. He, like his uncle Sigmund, also got paid by the syllable. Perhaps Brian, or someone of equal erudition, can find and footnote that reference.

Thought was mostly European in those days, wars too. That continent has always been everyone else's predicament. It would take decades before the rabble on the other side of the pond realized there was cabbage in carnage. Cabbage is what Jimmy Cagney called money, and the new colossus wouldn't come into prominence until after we saw him on television. Though that box was not yet the source of all knowing.

I was hatched long after the advent of behavioural science. After Rorschach splattered my brain on those ink blots. A Tuesday, I think, but to confirm I googled what was, at the time of writing this, the current president, Barack Hussein Obama. Thanks to Donald Trump he'd recently posted his birth certificate, establishing Barack as my age approximately. Before that he was a Muslim, Kenyan and a communist probably.

When the union elects a black president they follow it with the whitest one ever. Winning is calamitous for African Americans, but I know theirs is not my story as I'd already written that stuff about botanicals and ivory. I lifted the details from a Monet painting because the nineteenth century was there for the taking.

I used to have a cat, like the ones in those landscapes, still do when the mood strikes me. Except Claude's cats were swans, for some reason. I also have flowers, of the kind that need watering, so I'm guessing the life I have really is still too fast for his canvases.

It was never my plan to blacken the sun, to level mountains for the sake a toaster. We came for the barley and then we went back for the chromium. Yet flowers still bloom as the objects of much lousy poetry. A rose is a rose and a rose no longer. As for my cat, well it could be a rabbit, light be its arbiter. The eye is a crooked broker, so if you see a flower here feel free to kill it, or just delete it. I said all I had to say in the title.

I KNOW NOTHING OF Monet's work, but there must be a cat in it somewhere, or there will be eventually. Being dead, so I understood from my talks with Ingmar Bergman, is not reason enough to forego one's artistic practice. Especially now that we've established cats can be swans on occasion, rabbits too. Art is sublimation, gnarled imitation, the space of our finishing. I could go on and I will, but after Blanche gets here.

I came here to topple civilization, to sell plastic forks to the Chinese. I'm no smarter than the cows in this story, but I'll know for sure after they review what I've written. I grow less confident with each word and lesion. They're one and the same in this instance, judging from the mangled mess in my head and on the cutting board.

In the Democratic Republic of the Congo I traded water for diamonds. I furnished the bottles and the Congolese supplied the river. The contract was signed in New York so I didn't have to go there. On the advice of my lawyers I put what we planned, what we pulled, in the fine print, and the bodies we left in those mine shafts.

I always save the best for later which, by any calculation, is never. And the way to get there, said Kiki, is on the wings of an eagle. From those heights we can see what happened and what's happening in Jericho. That thing Moses did at the Red Sea, because it's not his version that matters. If only the prophet knew then what we've learned since, that you don't have to drown all of your neighbours to take their olives.

In 1948 David Ben-Gurion spoke to the United Nations. One must have a story to oust a people and found a democracy, but all Ben really needed was a wink from the English to step up evictions. Yahweh's blessing had been secured a few thousand years prior, so let's not pretend now to be distressed by the numbers.

Besides, shelling Gaza is not the same as ordnance hitting, mostly missing, Tel Aviv. Israel's enemies must perish, or perish, that is the middle ground, and don't even get me started on planes flying into Manhattan skyscrapers. Even the Knesset knows there can only be one ground zero, that's just arithmetic.

My father's war was good for everybody except for the dead and the maimed. The defeated are less accommodating now that the greatest generation is done and buried. Washington no longer steps in to help clean up the rubble. Never again will we kill with such clarity. That's why, after Indochina, journalists are vetted before they're embedded, to stop people from dying on television.

043

I HEAR A KNOCK, a bell or the door was unlocked – why choose when you can catalogue. Bob is elated, beet red, if I were inclined to such characterizations, but I just don't see them. Blanche lets herself in, throws off a few layers, feathery, diaphanous as they say in Paris. Hugs and cheeks just like in Barcelona, but it's difficult in that city to discern between a kiss and a smack.

You're late, I say, as she sashays towards the counter. She got to talking to her yoga instructor, her spiritual advisor, her afterlife pundit. They meet on Tuesdays in the studio above what is quickly becoming her favourite diner. He says they'll meet again in the hereafter and then Blanche won't need a credit card to seek his counsel.

The steak would need time to cook, giving scope to the salad. I begin preparations immediately so as not to prolong the debacle. My spirit lifts as I pick up the knife, but I'm choosing to keep my fantasies out of this paragraph. Blanche looks at the meat, then me. Her glare is like a kick to the groin.

There's salad, I say, and nuts for protein, I don't want to lose control of the calamity unfolding. I'm fine with Bob's pining. Their touching is the problem, that's why I can't let it happen. If I'm not careful their knot will tighten, an impossible thought, the meat and the day wasted.

DINNER IS OVER so there's no point talking about it. Into the breach, or the living room and then back to the table. Everywhere there are pictures in which Blanche and I appear happy together. Yet, like Napoleon at Waterloo, I can't break the enemy's momentum.

Panic is the only way out of this pickle, because cutting Romeo is illegal. Romeo is Bob, but just in this instance. He sits a-gawk at the table, ignoring me completely. I place what was left of the meat squarely in their line of vision. Greasy plates and napkins round out the arrangement, lest this should be misconstrued as a romantic moment.

I need time to think, but it pains me to leave them alone with the kiwi. A good house is like an old shoe, except bigger, and Bob is the pebble to turn my foot purple. Still, I take heart in the fact that a room will generally outlast its occupants.

I wish I was more like that homeless man who knows death by its anus. The one who put a blade to Shakespeare's ear for the sake of some oranges. His copious lack of friends is what I find so appealing, his abundance in general. I'm here and with him simultaneously, but my friends know to look for me in both of those places. Where and where I am approximately are contiguous to my way of thinking. They know I'll show up eventually.

The two of them were still talking as I stepped back into the kitchen. Bob had slowly, skillfully, obscured the mischief I had so carefully concocted. He was suggesting Blanche take the longer view re his flesh-eating proclivities, at least until farmers exhausted all inventories bred for that purpose. An argument I found infinitely reasonable, so imagine my surprise when Blanche also agreed with Bob's pleadings.

There's a city out there, I said, so many places you've not seen together … we're fine where we are, said Blanche, and you should thank your lucky stars for the company … what happened to the kiwi … we ate it, but we saved you a pastry

… what pastry … the ones we weren't supposed to find in the crisper … there were six … they were never there and still one remains … your point … once again, hat and glove, the impossible comes out to greet you … fine … and next time try something besides nuts for protein … like what … rice and lentils … anything else … better tea … I'll make a list.

041

I'M NOT HERE, AS at a luncheon, but I can still tell you what I think from a distance. I have been known to drink bottled water, like they do in New York or LA, it's no better than tap but the statement still matters. Except when those bottles are dispensed from the back of a truck, then keep your head down and steer clear of the army.

All this talk of style, of people who don't live in war zones, reminds of the woman whose name is, whose-name-is-not-Rita. She convened with poets in a state-sponsored huddle and together they pulled doggerel from their collective navel. I could not adapt to all that urbanity, her casual brutality, so I crawled back into the holes that made me. For every little thing there is a forgetting.

Such were my thoughts as I tidied, because my friends were refusing to talk to me. So I'll just dribble on till the washing is done. In Palestine sparrows no longer perch because they've been eaten. Their flight belongs to the ages, to rumours of treason. To the children, because there's just not enough meat on those tiny bones to feed a family.

There's hope. While there is still breath to slap the wind and the skies yield to a wing's laceration. Paradise now, as the kids say in Gaza, is gained for the price of a little shrapnel strapped to your abdomen. It takes focus and plenty of heart to blow open a portal to the hereafter, whether or not there's a bus in front of it.

I have never known flying as such, but I do speak to birds. I can't seem to get enough of what they're not telling me. One in particular, also a sparrow, he travelled widely for liberty, the republic, for the CIA, as it happens. He was always already where he was going, blind. Dead, he corrected me. I didn't believe him till he showed me his cardiogram.

Everything I say is true, said the bird … really … and important … is that because you're dead … no, that was a day like any other … I see … I flew kicking and screaming into the light … there's a light … then I heard the sound of doors closing … how many … two … which ones … sound, light, breath … that's three … pick two … can I think about it … you do that.

Of death I have no curiosity. I plan to spend my forevers – there's more than one – in Calabria, but I may have said that already. A pulse is only necessary for swimming not floating so, with time on my side, I'm bound to get there eventually. Perhaps I'll run into that bird, unless he's been reassigned. I've searched heaven and earth, Baghdad to Brisbane, but it's hard from this window to track a single sparrow across time and continents.

I've asked Bob to keep an eye out, and before Blanche left for the Rockies I drew her a picture. You could look for it there, I suggested. You're delusional, she replied. So I said nothing of the bird's contribution to national security.

That bird knew me when, I told Blanche one day over coffee … I don't understand … it's an expression … meaning what … the significant past … but when exactly … it's hard to pin down … the year, the decade even … a certain fluidity is implied … is it … in the phrasing … I see … the meaning … what meaning … the lack of it … clearly … because of the war … the what … the situation.

040

EVERYTHING I NEED IS within walking distance, and it will stay that way too so long as Arizona doesn't start killing migrants. It would just be too difficult to get my produce from Tijuana, and

I don't speak the language so there'd be no way to tell between tomatoes and broccoli.

In the seventies Starbucks was a donut shop in Seattle and laptops were the size of refrigerators. We couldn't see Iraq from Nevada, but it didn't matter because the people who needed killing were in El Salvador anyway. So said Jimmy Carter. Now there's a president we could believe when he lied to us.

In New York People stayed home to write screenplays about bone-crushing afternoons in coldwater flats. How we healed ourselves in the bathrooms of the city, just like Al Pacino. After which we worked all night to take down the man or the government, and to cover our tracks we simply rolled down our sleeves.

In the eighties American anarchists and junkies were becoming vegetarian in alarming numbers. Mushroom caps and zucchini sticks bore the mark of sophistication, but that was mostly in Winnipeg. In Thatcher's England the workers of South Wales were being told to pull themselves up by their bootstraps. As were the coal miners of Appalachia, and then nothing happened because the Gipper was too busy rethinking Central America.

I was at Stanford when congress approved one hundred million dollars in military aid to Nicaraguan death squads. On top of what they received covertly before, during and after the Iran-Contra fiasco.

As a result, students weren't coming home from school or the store in that little country, so father didn't always get his beer and tobacco. Siblings and classmates turned over dumpsters and freshly dug pits at the fringes, while mothers made official enquiries. Matriarchs are revered in Latin cultures, feared even, but there's only so much a mother could do while her other kids are still living. Thus everyone pretended not to see the few drops of blood on a fresh pack of Marlboro, in the shirt pocket of the local contra.

I HAVE THIS DITTY and a child that needs killing. Who am I to say it doesn't take forty years to buy cigarettes. Everything has too much and too little meaning when bodies go missing. Those campaigns were just business anyway, how else would Chiquita Brands International have secured my bananas, my bananas today.

A terrorist is forever in Virginia, but he'll bleed out in Afghanistan. Peace, finally, locked and loaded to take on all comers. It's about the economy stupid, the filling and emptying of warehouses. Same day to your stoop, or from eighteen thousand feet into multiple living rooms in Kabul.

The best way to stop the violence is to educate the people, says Blanche. But that's only because she thinks murder is unreasonable. Voting is important too, says Bob. He's thinking up new ways to agree with Blanche's solutions, but I'm not worried. The minute she shows a little leg he'll forget his address.

In the eighties Blanche packed me up and took me to some god forsaken place in Saskatchewan. I needed rescuing, she said, from the poems I was writing. I was becoming unstable, deaf to the world, the word and its meaning. A lunatic, were I to summarize her depiction succinctly, but I couldn't see it. Lunacy is subject to all manner of interpretation and besides, I argued, I write the lines as I find them.

I didn't mind the prairies and the coffee she brought in from the motel diner was fine and so much cheaper than those burlapped beans in the city. There was a time Blanche thought it was cute when I, her very own oaf, worked through the night and ate all the bagels. I didn't see it coming when she began planning her transition from me to her garden overalls. Try to remember this life is a river, she said, walking out the door. But I think it's a coffee cup next to an unmade bed in Saskatchewan.

As for those poems, they were mostly about travels to Arcadia. That's a place in Greece, so don't nobody call it heaven. From Jupiter Kiki and I would set a course for those islands, but we had to recalibrate because each time Berlin flushes Athens floats a little closer to Libya. A trickle in Frankfurt is a gusher in Alexandria, and what follows German largesse is austerity and a spattering of suicides. Following which even the sheep will concede to IMF money.

038

I'M DREAMING OF A death that has everything, ice shavings, Jell-O and an old nurse who will lie to me about things in general. A free-for-all, to celebrate my crossing from this place, this face, to its omission. The first time I died those things disappeared in the same sentence, and then my life continued. Roundabout the time I bamboozled my way into Stanford. Boondoggling is how I stayed out of prison.

It was that or digging a ditch in this, my father`s land of opportunity. I graduated summa cum laude without a single botched suicide. I took to higher learning like a cadaver to oxygen, whereas these days I prefer the smaller queries. I like how they accentuate and then quicken my insufficiency. A hat or an umbrella, for instance, string beans or rapini and that cod would make a fine dish but the chicken is funnier, I told Kiki the last time we had dinner.

How so, she asked … it arrived in a tuxedo by way of Toledo … you don't say … the butcher told me … I see … his name is Frank … the butcher … the chicken … that is funny … the fish is from India … how did it get here … it rowed a bucket from there to Nantucket … really … emptied it into the Boston Harbour and went back for another … why did it do that … to save the Maldives.

I no longer understand houses and shoes, I don`t understand what it is have neither. I need at least five bathrooms to live creatively, two with a view. Other artists follow the indigent, before they too are ousted to make room for more substantial citizens. Except you'd never know it now that money managers and dotcom sensations have all gone shabby chic. One, then the other, it depends on the venue.

Each other is the look they're going for, the same as the same because different don't mean shit if you're the only one doing it. The objective for us real estate professionals was to anticipate and then expedite those migrations, show low income esthetes how to live at the margins. Location, location, location because the rich don't live in those places.

There are no bad exits, and there's more room to paint and store art in those suburban houses. The old neighbourhoods are being reimagined and soon there'll be enough main floor powder rooms commensurate with civilized living. Then the meagre will arrange themselves cordially along major arteries and yield to the best fed dogs in history.

037

Dinner was a hit despite my best efforts. There can be no rest after people, now come the hours we will not speak of and the worst, as always, is still to come. Before leaving Bob eyes the uncooked steak, asks if I have eggs and proposes to stop by for brunch on his way to the library. Luckily I had a doctor's appointment at the ready, which I'll now have to go to and talk about later.

I locked the door and watched from the window as my friends rounded the corner. Out of earshot I turned with a few choice words for the host, who is choosing to remain nameless. Traitor, saboteur, I hissed, I marked your every word, your twisted dance, from the rafters. He respects no boundaries, he's my cellmate and jailor. It takes forever to recover from a night of his chatter.

I need a change of address, I told my analyst … why is that … my house has been compromised … by whom … the occupant … I see … he's crossed over … to where … the other side … what side is that … theirs … of course … I can lose him in New Zealand … who … him … who … me … New Zealand is far … that's the point … but moving isn't … isn't what … the point … what point … changing address won't help … why not … it's not the house … how do you know … it's never the house … what about the city … nope … the country … still no … so it must be the hemisphere.

036

The bible speaks well of those who communed with sheep in Palestine. But they're no different than the herds one might find in New Zealand. The vistas from the shores of that tiny nation are simply to die for. Cliffs for jumping and souring after Jacinda reversed privatization. I know for I pretend to go there occasionally and I can say, without hesitation, everyone is friendly so long as you're not Muslim or Asian. That's how it is in a country where calamity is a story below the fold in Melbourne, Australia. That is until some freedom loving Kiwi decides to shoot up them foreigners.

I invented geography, except for those places where Jesus still dangles from behind every bedpost and lectern. Such haunts were written into our skin before we got here, but those cliffs will still be there long after the black he's concocted. Blanche says deserts and oceans will also do fine, positioned as they are for the long haul. But I think that's her guru talking, now mine, since I joined his flock the minute I learned her schedule.

In 1948 god returned to the holy land to review the disaster he'd set in motion two thousand years prior. He was happy to see the situation was stable, finally a hate he could count on. The promise run aground, about ground, and to think before him Jerusalem was just a city of neighbourhoods.

It was Tuesday when I set out for that doctor's appointment, the one I used as an excuse so Bob would think I was busy. It was also raining or why else would I bring an umbrella, every day an adventure so long as I don't tell myself everything. Betty, the receptionist, watched me come in from behind her desk.

What are you doing here, she asked … it's Tuesday … it`s not … roughly … you don`t have an appointment … I do … you don`t … I logged it in a previous paragraph … that doesn't count … I told Bob … who's Bob … a philosopher … what did you tell him … that I was coming here … why … so he wouldn't come over … you lied to him … that's right … and then you came anyway … it would seem so … take a seat … certainly … better yet proceed to examination room three.

I walked past the lollipops next to the mannequin with her organs showing, to a door at the end of the hallway. Why are you here, asked the doctor … I already told Betty … are you sick … how would I know … is there pain … of course … physical pain … I see … well … I'm thinking … are you … probably … you're due for a prostate exam anyway … then will you know what's wrong with me … I'll know something … good … or nothing … even better … I think we've talked enough … I'll say.

035

Each time I admit to the tree the apples go missing, so near and yet further than the wind whistling. I'm tired of these serial astonishments, these flashes that won't leave the starting block. The facts, says Bob, are too big for my britches, thus my circumspect approach to the actual.

I will put an end to the rambling, or the other way around. I'm trying to find out what doctors are for before I next assume the position. Until then I best stick to smaller miracles, like the custard tarts I found this afternoon behind some leftover chicken. I put them there a few hours ago, but that in no way diminishes my incredulity.

As to the imbroglio unfolding, indelicate as it may appear, seeing Bob two days in a row would have been a catastrophe. Betty said she'd strangle me with a stethoscope if I show up again without notice, so I'll be in Bulgaria the next time Bob comes a-knocking.

Which brings us back to the woman with her finger up my ass, though she too is refusing to accede to my booking. Deeper, I said, but first let's agree touching is everything. This is clinical, she said, forgive me if I don't find your pending cancer more interesting.

Obviously we're talking about a general practitioner, my analyst would have understood perfectly. He studied the Sufis, ascension in general and then we'd go there together. How was I to know a woman in bleached whites could get me there faster. The room began to spin, or I fall in love easily. I am death, I said, or whoever you need me to be in this instance. Not yet, she said, but you will be if you turn up again unannounced.

034

Death happens, with or without a pronouncement. I was shaken when I left the doctor's office, as is wont to happen when one is called upon to be both stud and specimen. I said goodbye to the mannequin and stocked up on lollipops. I gave one to Betty, seeing as she allowed me to lie without consequence.

Words, in the mouths of doctors make boatloads of money. On the subject of medical science it is their and not my version that matters. All I could do was watch when they killed my mother. Nothing is bigger than that nothing, not even language. Such were my thoughts as I waited for the elevator. It also occurred to me that I could be from Sweden, but that's true of anyone.

On the street people followed my every step, while pretending to ignore me completely. Twice injured, I took to the alleyways. I feel at home in these arteries awash in graffiti, all smirk and no quarter. Night falls to a gesture, a spray can, apparently. There is also garbage in my tinted gardens and empty beer bottles, but Kiki still thinks those doodles are pretty.

These aerosol miscreants are all that's left of a dream. The same dream I abandoned for the perfect tomato after I cut a deal with a Subaru. Our kids know we failed, so here's to the few who defile what we've done and the fewer who research their targets. Be merry my friends, for tomorrow will bring even more kids without hope or reason, so the rest of us can concentrate on our driving.

033

I ENTERED MY HOUSE through the garage in case Bob was out front angling for leftovers. The exchange with my doctor still troubled me so I re-enacted it as two penguins talking. In Swedish, so I understood perfectly, the sound not the meaning, their warbling specifically. I enjoyed our conversation immensely, unlike the one in her office. I have yet to meet a penguin who takes this stuff seriously.

The bird who was now my physician vowed to retract her diagnosis and I promised to do my dying in Stockholm. We moved to the window that faces the alley and the moon, as usual, was there to greet us. We basked in that glow while we talked about the stars adjacent, love and my next anal probing. A colonoscopy, she said, this coming Tuesday … seems like overkill … it was booked already … really … that's what happens when you show up arbitrarily … I see … I'll have Betty call you on Monday.

I ended that conversation and called Kiki immediately. Let's go to Brazil, I said … when … next Tuesday … you got it. Rio is as good a place as any to postpone the inevitable. One must be gone to think clearly and I wanted to get a jump on the cancer that, purportedly, wasn't happening. My doctor's findings will be pointless without a body, if I'm not there to hear them. I'll be like that tree no one sees fall in the forest.

Ridiculous I know, but my days won't be the same after she names my condition. I will not suffer this life as her patient, and she gets paid for whoever walks into that office. By Wednesday Betty will have noted my truancy and by Thursday she'll have forgotten it. And then I simply won't write about it.

How else could I fit the unthinkable on the head of a lollipop, see my mother in a sunflower next to songbirds forever. I don't need a doctor to tell me what time it is. I'll decide when to cash in my pork bellies, and when I have eaten my last tomato I will return the favour. Cycle of life, said every poet since Homer, that's why I'm not going to.

032

I WEAR A HAT so the government can't see inside my noggin, walk opposite my intended destination until I get where I'm going. I whistle to keep the police from hearing what I'll say shortly. My mornings are full of urgency and purpose, and then I make myself an omelet.

It takes a notion to muzzle an inference, five media cartels to befuddle a people, and then as many docudramas as necessary. We are still building the old conspiracies, everything is and becoming what it was anyway. The teachers at WestPoint no longer differentiate between Kabul and Honduras. Any war will do, say the shareholders at Boeing and Lockheed Martin, so don't nobody mention Toronto.

Bob didn't visit today, or he was here and I wasn't. It doesn't matter, there are no end of things to complain about. Obama is on television. When he smiles I forget to remember the empire is collapsing, that we're cooked already. What I thought I thought before he started talking.

That smile launched five hundred sixty-three drones to Pakistan, Somalia, Yemen and Afghanistan. Better than a thousand ships, but we can't know for sure because there were no drones when Paris snatched Helen. The president has since been immortalized in bronze and in stone, just like those Greek lovers. In centuries to come pigeons will continue to shit on his torso.

Sudden death is fine, as they say in Kabul, preferred if it precedes the bleeding. We've heard enough screaming and children can still play so long as there's cloud cover. Calamity has many facets and refusal is as near as the implements in your garage or the first lady's garden. In France they make no distinction between pitchforks and politics, and sometimes pitchforks are improvised explosive devices.

When I go I'm taking the music with me. Scatter my ashes to the houses I died in, better yet next to Trump's Mar-a-Lago so I can catch a wave to Havana. Then I'll pay my respects to Fidel and together we'll hitch a ride on a dolphin back to Miami. I've already tagged my big toe lest it wander, just burn it with the rest of me. When I die, by and by, I will still have everything.

031

I PHONED BLANCHE THE minute I stepped in the door. I was hoping she'd confirm that it is not I but my doctor who's crazy. It's you, she said … really … you're delusional … I'm not … and you overreact … to what … everything … is that possible … talk to your analyst … I did … what did he say … I'm delusional … there you go … what if he's wrong … what if he's right … what difference would that make … go to bed … I'm worried … there's nothing wrong with you … I'm delusional … you're impossible … and impossible.

Blanche and I used to walk these streets together, but after I'd agreed to her cat's provisos. That puss and I were still working things out when she booked her flight to the Rockies. Blanche, that is, cats don't have passports and they don't submit to society's protocols, that's why they fly as cargo in cages. The point is Blanche took that feline with her whereas I, apparently, wasn't worth saving. Regrettable, since an agreement between that lynx and I was all but inevitable.

A pact with a feline is so much more complicated than an accord between people. I argued before and after I agreed to everything. No meaning where none intended, said Beckett approximately. As far as that cat was concerned, it had not been invented. How else could she have boiled weeks of wrangling down to a single syllable.

030

Blanche went west and I commenced building houses because I couldn't play the piano. I ordered my lumber from British Columbia to preserve the connection between us. She kept the roots and I got the cuttings. On the seventh day, a Tuesday I'm sure, I rested like any maker on seeing the mess he'd created.

A house is a box with smaller boxes inside it. With a little maintenance it will typically outlast its inhabitants barring hurricanes, airstrikes and forfeiture. Sometimes a box is a casket, the light and the music plowed under. Those crates are then matched to a stone at city's ebb, a monument, if you will, not far from the boxes we pissed in.

Now that I've told you what's coming let's get back to what ails me. Bob, obviously, philosophy, and Blanche, because I couldn't have her. Everything, its lack, its deluge and all the pretty dresses I won't unfasten. Idle hands are the devil's playthings and then he burned all the bridges behind him. I am so tired of his successes, his ars poetica.

I wish Blanche and I were back in our beloved Guatemala, the café three doors down from the fish store. A continent between it and the favelas. Such coffee houses are remnants, testaments to those American anarchists who marched arm in arm with their Latin compatriots, before accepting their commission at Berkeley.

I too have a long game. My plan is to come back as a movie, just like Bin Laden. I'm here and he isn't, hence more nimble than the army that wasted him. The burial was discreet, for the sake of his Saudi name and their Texas partners. Now Kathryn Bigelow, à la Clint Eastwood, could finally tell Bin's story correctly, remake that book by its cover.

The war on terror is assassination made simple, or legal. Winners take all and the losers go missing. They're fine with that in Oklahoma, but in Brooklyn they're far too sophisticated. Outrage is their preferred response, then brunch, but I don't think the government will kill them for that.

As mentioned, I'm talking to Ingmar Bergman to direct my story. I hope his being dead doesn't complicate matters, but I'll leave it to the lawyers to resolve that conundrum. Who'd a thunk it, Blanche will say when I invite her to the premier. For the lead I'm thinking Clooney, then I too will use my celebrity status to end the genocide in Darfur. I am, and George is too, in case you're wondering how that will happen. I liken it to winning the lottery.

029

I'm expecting a chicken for dinner, fully dressed from the churrasqueira. But first I had to Google a Portuguese-to-English dictionary to find that word's correlate. I ordered that bird for sustenance not erudition and I will not be dissuaded by its lingual equivalencies. When it gets here I will dismember it again, deny it its last tryst as a cockerel.

A chicken that was is still a chicken, that's how it is with tenses. The biddy I'll be eating was already prone to its syntax and its rigidity. A constituent of the choir immovable, ever since we began crating galliformes. Ambulant hens have since become too costly for your workaday grilling enthusiasts. Luckily, only goldfish forget faster than chickens.

In Gainesville Georgia, poultry capital of the world, the first death is a bitch and then it gets worse. Though factory farming and steroids have shortened that span considerably. As at Perdue Foods, not to be confused with Perdue Pharma, seeing as their chickens are people. Still, you can't beat stacked, sixteen-inch cages for distending the bestial and them new fangled tumors. I like to fry mine up with some fava beans and a nice Chianti.

Those chickens are born crazy because the alternative would be unthinkable. People too, though my analyst vehemently disagrees with that statement. Dying well is a fallacy and having been is not really a thing, a Buddhist once told me. Why else would we torture stone to keep from vanishing and why, I ask, are there still Romans in Brittany.

I'm still on the phone with Blanche, or I called her again. She says my thinking is becoming splintered … you mean is … is what … splintered … how's that working out for you … do I have to decide now … you don't know … not at the moment … later then … possibly … when … when I'm not thinking about it … what happens then … I wait … for what … what do you mean … what do you wait for … I don't understand the question … perhaps you should stay out of the sun … skin cancer, right … that's right.

028

EVERYTHING BLANCHE SAYS IS reasonable, but that's not how I hear it. I believe in the muddle, the meat of our bickering. To live is to differ, or suffer, why quibble over a couple of characters.

Always be closing, said Al Pacino. Did I mention he too was in real estate, before he was a junkie in New York City. Blanche said I may be conflating the man with the actor. But what, I ask, is the difference.

I'd also like to cite Aristotle along with that Hollywood icon, for emphasis. Good enough is good enough for what that logician won't have said anyway, but wait till it comes to me. For your edification, Goodenough is also a chemist on YouTube.

Quoting geniuses is just easier when I choose the phrasing. A philosopher will always say which way the wind is blowing, but after the buildings have fallen to be erected again. There, not there, and there again, I liken it to Aristotle's unmovable movers. A stretch, you say. Or a way back to our national obsession with real estate and Al Pacino.

It was not I, but Blanche who mentioned his name again. She's talking about the housing crises, bankers, bailiffs, sheriffs and agents, obviously. I know from experience those jackals don't go easy when payments go dry. So hunker down, wait until they come to turn off the water before moving in with your cousin, and then don't despair. A market economy is all about second chances, contingencies, a restructuring of what was yours anyway.

027

In the South Pole most of what was flesh is now frozen. Petrified, but not like those chickens in Georgia. Antarctica is a naked place where one might still stumble upon penguins laughing. As was the case when I went there with Kiki.

We flew to Argentina on the wings of a pigeon. His name was Henry, if I'm not mistaken, and then we hitched a ride on an iceberg that was going there anyhow. Step lightly, said Kiki, even here species have been known to go missing and we wouldn't want to wake up this continent.

America eviscerated its enemies before going to work on its citizens. From bunkers in Nevada they're picking off stragglers from Libya to Pakistan, because in the Congo there just aren't enough targets. The situation is more complicated in the homeland, it's better in a layered economy if the people and buildings don't perish.

It was I who dreamt the Manhattan project, the numbers not the science, indices of what the fuck happened. A measured response, for what was dropped on Pearl Harbor. Sushi has since come to the heartland but nobody then, or now, gives a shit about cherry blossoms.

In Amarillo they're still learning the names of those cities the joint chiefs must have pulled from their asses. Some good people in Texas and Arkansas still won't drive a Toyota. There are things, Horatio, that only make sense in the heartland. I guess a few hundred thousand Japanese, skin attached, then not, would make it awkward to keep up relations.

Last week I emailed Blanche to tell her the world was getting smaller. Then I panicked, deleted it, and called her instead, but the NSA had already seen it. Perhaps you should come over, I said … why is that … I think they're listening … nobody cares what you write or say. I agreed immediately, it's not the content but the rattling that matters, I said what I had to, to keep that call going.

026

At Stanford I read the romantics, and then I learned to think otherwise. With a knowing that was not knowing at all, Wordsworth bamboozled a flower. I did too, but without all those adjectives. Poetry is just noise until it screams, until it chokes on its busyness.

There were no wars to protest while I was at college. Reagan's little campaigns in Central America were, on the whole, too small for primetime. This story was about real estate before my Palestinian grocer introduced me to the people who weren't dying on television. The amateurs who blew their audition.

I commenced to logging those bodies until that sparrow, the one who visited me in my mother's hospital room, let slip that, but for a single breath, all death is fiction. It was then I decided to write about tomatoes instead. As for the final tally, the reckoning, we'll just have to wait for the movie.

In the beginning was the word, more likely a grunt, but I'm no theologian. God will have been here a nanosecond when the planet finally stops spinning, but he did make it easier to kill Muslims in Yemen. In the end he too will be called upon to confess to nothing and no one in particular, before being refused entry to the next thing in general.

Kiki and I draw our own maps to nowhere, so I really can't say what it's like to have Jehovah in my corner. I assume he's white, why else would he have allowed us to lock up all those black people. The feathered were the first to detect those massive prisons, even the almighty can't cordon the sky. Still, I don't believe everything that bird says, so I've asked my mother to corroborate his reporting.

025

I COULD TELL BY my breathing, the panic specifically, that soon I'd be alone for the evening if we don't count the people on television. I'm here too, said the cat I don't have and sitting on the windowsill. I have things to do, places to go, said Blanche … so do I … you don't … it's possible … you need to hang up now … I see.

I know where I stand with a pod in each ear and when I'm with people, at all other times I could be in Myanmar. I suspect Bob had a hand in Blanche's plans so I phoned him immediately. He didn't answer so I called him as Brandon or Barrett, but by then he was on to me or I don't get the technology. It's possible Blanche didn't want to talk to me, but there's clearly no point to that line of reasoning.

I called my son, but he wouldn't talk to me either. I didn't ask the reason because then I'd have to move to Spain or Australia. It's a thin line between love and loathing, though he says not seeing me does help a little. He wants to have done with his name, its grip and its grin. Me, in a word or a hat, and is that a tube in my cock. Too late now to forego all that happiness.

My son knows all about fascism, he says it's making a comeback, as are god's conscripts. One and the same in Tallahassee, Jerusalem too. I shudder to think what the holy will do to my boy when he gets to heaven. It was they who made the desert bloom with water from Hebron and Jericho. The people who were shot and later bulldozed now feed an explosion in organic farming, but that's as true in Bavaria as it is in Palestine.

Murder is history's hovel, its pigsty. The media's job is to roil the nation so governments can throw open the coffers. Every week I write the president, or tweet, it depends on the occupant, and sometimes I copy Time Warner. I end each sentence with a sentence so there's no need for pauses. I sign off as Pedro on matters of immigration, Osama when the Prophet, peace be upon him, is top of the news cycle.

024

THERE'S NO GREATER PROMISE than serial disasters, no better future than the world in ruins. Think of the bargains, the rezoning, the ocean views from Bangladesh to the parishes of Louisiana. Those structures weren't worth restoring anyway. A house, after all, is not an old Chevy.

Isn't it odd how god and the army always arrive at the same time exactly. They're part and parcel of the same plan, so I assume they work for Wells Fargo. After a tsunami It takes money and purpose to eradicate ways and mores dating back to the last ice age. To transplant who or whatever was here so they don't get in the way of our surveyors.

As for the levies, we'll rebuild them after we send out the notices and before we flatten the existing inventory for code violations. We will make those spaces safe for the former occupants, so they can come back to sell us trinkets and cocktails.

Everything is carbon and before that it was a Pleistocene tiger named Tony, proof finally that there is truth in advertising. Oil is about the babies Benjamin or the Benjamins baby and thanks to Ilhan Omar I know to apologize in advance for that statement. Her point, as I understood it, is there's no difference between a tsunami and bombing Gaza, but for the places to run to.

023

TORTOISES SNICKERED WHEN MOSES came back down the mountain. Two thousand years later they got together again over pizza and beer to watch Charlton Heston do the same thing on television. They're of the opinion more could have been gleaned from those tablets before Moshe's scratchings. Rules aren't really a thing for most turtles, much to the chagrin of the Catholic pedophile society.

That which could be thought was here before Jesus, we just needed a scientist to go the Galapagos and explain it in English. When Darwin returned to London he was free to pursue his theories. Queen Victoria, unlike the pope, was reluctant to kill the messenger, especially after that fiasco between Sir Thomas and Henry. That and inbreeding is why monarchs grew fairly stupid. On the subject of clotted cream I have no opinion.

The iPhone was invented after the current sovereign acceded to the throne and after we levelled Hiroshima. Roundabout the time we dropped even smarter bombs on Baghdad. How quickly we repurpose the bits to grow the machinery, a rate of progress Darwin could not have predicted. America's secrets would soon be ubiquitous, but what government wouldn't forego nature's crawl for the glow of nuclear physics.

Still, there are unwanted consequences to every experiment. We needed more testing and five million sorties over Hanoi to perfect the technology, our delivery especially. That's why it only took twenty-five thousand forays to level Mesopotamia, and don't even get me started on what we can see from Nevada.

Technology is making the world smaller, and bigger, but that's smaller too. More and more of what I don't want to know now fits in my pocket. Mornings were easier when Oprah still ruled the airwaves, when she spoke to me directly. When the remote was a dial en route to the fridge or the pisser. Oprah talked to everyone, still does, says Bob. But it would take more than the obvious to change my remembering.

022

I BUY DATES FROM Senegal and noodles from China. I've tasted ice cream on five different continents, and on the same day after Kiki dismantled the space-time continuum. I'm part man, part sofa, a dead ringer for nothing doing. That's why I left you, said Blanche. That, and so much more, I corrected her.

Rub-a-dub-dub three men in a tub, Tolstoy and Shakespeare are vying for my attention. My mind is my own, but that's hard to prove, like gravity or the value of money. Suffice to say, I'm the guy bathing.

My accomplices are suggesting I turn up the temperature. Books need warmth too, they insist. Lest I forget it was their nose before mine in those pages. Bob's in the basement, I must have forgotten to lock the door. He's looking for a screwdriver to fix Blanche's cabinets. Kill him, said the playwright. I agree, said the novelist for six hundred pages. The bard has always been somewhat circumspect on the subject of murder, whereas the Russian, when wet, makes a fine projectile.

Before bed I make lists so I'll have something to read in the morning. That's why there are no holes in this story. Then I fix myself an espresso, two shots exactly and wait in a chair at the window for the world to start spinning. We have to start somewhere, though the words are but adjunct and the manifest broken, the repudiation of purpose and notion. I am become furniture.

Let's begin again. Food shopping is all about choices thanks to corn's versatility. Every night I dream the perfect meal while indexing the things I would have bought anyway. Fish and spinach are what I woke up to this morning, reason enough to get out of bed but too few items to warrant a shower.

It was late afternoon when I set out. I took some leftover pizza to the yard because raccoons know a good thing when they see it. They don't look at me and I don't see them while they're eating. Then I put out my returnables for the less fortunate, empty bottles of single malt because heroin is illegal. Finally I walked to the market, upright, just to fit in.

021

I suspect Moses was going for dramatic effect when he made the people of Israel wait before he brought down those carvings. Roundabout the beginning says the Vatican, give or take a few billion years. What is mine is now yours, said the prophet, but that was his too. It seems our dispatches have always been subject to time's moratorium. Later we would call that the post office.

We were hunters before we were farmers, and then we went digital. As for the dinosaurs, their extinction, there are no end of theories, though archeologists have confirmed their fingers were too big for the keyboards. Their mobility too crude for the quill and the ballpoint and there were no Jesuits to teach them penmanship at dinosaur school.

020

WHEN I GOT TO this country there was a chicken in every pot and a rooster named Foghorn on television. Villains, more Russian than Russians, would invariably meet their fate before the last Kellogg's commercial. The moon landing was one of a handful of programs we watched as a family. The future is here, said my brother, so long as Kennedy doesn't mistake a goose for a missile.

I considered murder, for its own sake, but that was before I owned property. I also thought of killing for the team, the queen or the fatherland, but I didn't want to take a job from some kid who couldn't afford college. I've had to go a long way to shorten the journey, but I knew the crimes I was committing would pay off eventually.

At Stanford I learned what not to think, but had I waited I could have simply asked Kiki. She's nine, hence quick with the blow-by-blow of what I'm not seeing. I have since returned to my childhood happiness – same bliss different sofa – while bullets whistle past my ear and disappear into the speakers behind me.

Yesterday Kiki emailed NASA. Their last notable campaign was the moon landing which may or may not have happened. The moon is a place, a race and an idea, to paraphrase Kiki, there's no difference between the orb and its absence. Whereas Mars is in the schoolyard next to the fire station and down the street from her favourite ice-cream shop. She attached a map and a photo so NASA could update those coordinates.

There's more to that little girl's brain than can be apprehended in our chronologies. I'm saving all her notes and doing my best to chronicle her methodologies. Timelines are important since it must all be recorded and annotated before she forgets she knows everything.

I live in the north, a curse, and a blessing as we'll soon grow our own oranges. Fish from the equator will come ready-cooked and people there can just eat each other in what we'll come to know as the great deserts of Amazonia.

Living is dying, a Texan once told me. A songster, but even he found it hard to do both simultaneously. Time is a growth in the belly, the brain or the liver. A drug induced heart attack, in the case of that minstrel.

Fish and spinach prompted me to take to the streets this afternoon. It's the chase that makes shopping interesting, the tomato before the tomato. The tomato in your mind, said Kiki. Before stepping out I put oatmeal on the list, having run out ages ago or on Tuesday. En route I'll add yogurt to keep readers riveted.

I know from a thousand Looney Tunes mornings astonishment is better than certainty, except in the mindset of Wile E. Coyote. I found the fish, but the spinach was on its last gasp. I set a course for another store, another shore, to complete my adventure.

019

I WAS YOUNG WHEN my mind broke, but I'm not looking for accolades. A swing is as good as a bull's eye in the things that I'm saying. I stepped out this morning and the rest I don't understand. I learned to speak with other people's mouths, poets then bankers, matching both timbre and content. I needed to know how they were running their businesses.

The English came and went, and the ones who stayed were from Texas. When I am done shopping I'll restock the pantry and then I'll tell you all there is to know about the economy. In the meantime put a pail under that drip in the attic, it's as good as a tarp while you wait for the bank to tack those credit cards to your mortgage. Like they did the last time the roof needed fixing, and will again so long as you keep making those payments.

Everyone is in hock to the tits or the dick. A bonanza, as we used to say in the real estate business, then we'd sit back and watch the billions roll in. The juice is in the arrears, a fee here, a point there. Small cuts help the medicine go down, the medicine go down.

Detroit is growing carrots where there used to be architecture. All factories will be gardens eventually, houses too, but do pull the eaves and the copper before they send in the bulldozers. The vig is forever though your crib is no longer, banks have longer memories than Sicilian gangsters. Thus concludes the education I promised you.

018

ALWAYS BE CLOSING, MCNAMARA told Johnson, when explaining Vietnam to the American electorate. Go win this thing, hollered the president. That's hard to do with aimless volleys and wanton sorties, replied the secretary.

Fascinating, said Bob, but I will need a reference for that conversation. Regrettably, I had yet to construe a source for those statements, but had the president lived a few more decades he'd have heard the same thing from Al Pacino.

People are numbers too after burning, and correspondents are not qualified to discern a limp from a defect, a char from a birth mark. It's best to set those tallies before shelling begins, so CNN can plan our consent.

America, like all great nations, will put off until primetime the crimes they've committed already. Real time reporting was fine for the Mekong Delta, but death and internment were more or less instantaneous in Iraq and Afghanistan. We've come a long way since those rolling barrels.

I found fresh spinach next to Blanche's meditation studio. Above that eatery I talked about earlier, where gatekeepers spin words into barbwire. They come to mimic laughing, to fix anthropology. I endure their chatter with a plug in each ear, but I still think the meals in that bistro should come with a salad. By way of explanation, studios are safe spaces for they who already have everything.

I was born bloody, like you, like anybody. Learned to speak after I'd put a significant dent in the grasshopper population of Italy. I was working my way up to lizards, but for that I would need better armaments.

Bows were cutting edge in mid-century Calabria, arrows fashioned from the spokes of English umbrellas. Sadly I wasn't strong enough to tension that instrument, so I got myself a stick and turned my gaze to the cat next door. I could manage those bows now, but nobody makes umbrellas like that anymore.

Before I could let loose on that feline I was conscripted by god the terrible. You wouldn't believe the stories, but all I could glean from his ramblings is that my bloodlust need not be senseless. We still talk occasionally but, after the inquisition, he wouldn't know a mass from a massacre. In heaven, he explained, we never stop dying so there's no need to mechanize killing. But I think he's just jealous of our innovations.

017

Big cities are small-towns too, so I must get home before I am noticed. I see the store that carries the sheep's milk yogurt I'm looking for. Reputedly from a small farm in the foothills of some enduring village. Cow's milk is cheaper, tastes better too, but Blanche said we have to stop factory farming to save the planet. She also finds people who eat bovines less interesting.

I like the packaging on that yogurt container. A pilot smiling from behind his goggles, sporting a leather cap and jacket, his scarf flying high above rolling greenery and roving sheep. Evoking a time when aviators were more susceptible to crashing, to gravity in general. Hence the leather. He's flying over the Swiss Alps or Poland, but more likely Germany because the sheep in that picture are so good-looking.

What happened in Warsaw accrues in Geneva, and then it's unlikely victims will return to claim their possessions. Nations plan, plunder, and then sell it all back to the people they took it from. The powerful must be free to recoup their expenditures. Such is the invisible hand of the market, a movable plenty. One death is tragic and ten will send a message, but when you kill in the millions you're talking real money.

Youth wants what it wants, Nike, or the same thing exactly. I wish I could show them a pickaxe or a gun, deaf to the call, the mall and the marching. Kiki is beginning to sense our brutality and yesterday she drew two circles corresponding to places she'd seen on television. Labelled one Ramallah and the other Jerusalem. On noticing there were too few roads between them, she drew a line so people could go back and forth without incident. This will come in handy, I thought, for weddings and funerals.

I've been walking all morning. I wear sensible shoes and carry a stainless steel bottle. I'm tired of buying back my water and Nestle can choke on the plastic that, thanks to my canister, will have never made it out of the factory.

In California water is a statement, especially if the brand you drink is from Europe. Hydration is a sign of intelligence, like what books used to be in centuries previous, before we backlit our stories. Some say the sun shone brighter then, but it still wasn't enough to see by.

These days people read with their fingers, identify with whoever is trending, be it a dancing bear or a fascist hotelier cum president. In Tucson they're insisting the government not let in more Mexicans, but in Fresno they're worth their weight in tomatoes. Don't blow this for us, I wrote the president, Arizona wouldn't last a week without meth or spaghetti sauce.

All scripting is afterthought, thus I've exhausted my shopping list and its addendums. I entered that bodega after I'd already left, so things were bound to come undone in the telling. That's just how it is when the yogurt one seeks is Bavarian.

016

I HAVE LIVED BY way of a motley of faces. Prefer a yip to a yap and a yap to a word, it was never my intention to join in the speaking. If something is worth saying it's not worth repeating, and you probably heard it on television. Those words would only fail again in my mouth, I told Bob a week ago Tuesday but, so he has it, I'll tell him again when I see him.

It's getting so I can't distinguish between what I do and don't know. That was also Socrates' problem, except he couldn't do it first. I got here after Cornelius Vanderbilt and a few million Asians threaded the Rockies. Their deaths were so simple and his was unspeakable. That's how it is with moguls, and yet not nearly as consequential as middle managers jumping from burning skyscrapers.

Dreams made of glass and steel will generally outlive their makers but, unlike the pyramids, our citadels won't last forever. Those structures are about progress, the bonanza that is obsolescence. The breach not the thing, synonymous in this instance, and there's money in both, so try to stay with me.

A school is an armory, but only after we bomb it. Presidents have been known to use munitions to right the polls and the economy. As in that war on terror, the one we're still winning. The same one that makes nations long for the days when they were just miserable.

When the dust clears it's not uncommon to find an ear in a sneaker, and then there's no telling who it belonged to. You can't see inside a Toyota all the way from Nevada. As for local footage of children transitioning to their atomized futures, we cannot confirm its authenticity. Our correspondents are mostly in Paris or Istanbul and the people we bomb could be related to those would-be journalists.

For a few crazy days in September ears were toes too in Manhattan, though the shoes, in this case, were Ferragamo. The day bankers plunged, some flew, to their last appointment. Then Bush the acorn signed up a coalition of forty-nine – to pop's thirty-five – countries. Allies, he called them, though not all of them knew it, and together, sort of, they set out to find the enemy.

I can hear you, said the president, and the people who knocked these buildings down will hear all of us soon. A Tuesday, as luck would have it. So a day like any other but for the fact that Iranians, Afghans or Iraqis, anyone but the Saudis, took down the World Trade Center. Outrageous, exclaimed Tony Blair the minute he had Bush's ear. Then he and George talked about how there's no comparing those deaths to death in general.

015

New York calamities have consequences, I told my analyst … do they … legs too … what are we talking about … nine-eleven … why … you brought it up … I didn't … when … when what … when didn't you bring it up … I'm not doing that … let's talk about the disaster … what disaster … in general … this is not that … how do you know … it's smaller … than death … less cogent … than death … extraneous … to death … I take your point … what point.

I'm happy to report I didn't get hit by a trolley again while en route to that therapy session. It seems I have mastered the coming and going, not to mention the telephone. The thermostat too, so long as it's analogue.

What happened in Manhattan is being written into the skin of America's adversaries. It reminds me of that story by Kafka, the one with the apparatus attached to the carving needle.

Though I doubt the author would know his invention now that it's been modified and expanded to its full invisibility.

While shopping I bumped into Bob, unless he was following me. He was waiting for Blanche. She's taking me to lunch, he said, for fixing her cabinets. And that's when my thinking stopped happening. Bob didn't notice because I just kept on talking but, try as I might, I couldn't derail his plans and I couldn't stick the landings. The reader will have to imagine our conversation about the upcoming luncheon, what I might have said and done to stay true to the genre ascribed me.

I should have gone home the minute I'd exhausted the list in my pocket. The last item was the yogurt I talked about earlier. Chance encounters are not a good look for me. On seeing people who know me I freeze, like a tot under the spell of a ladybug or a hellfire missile. Not to equate stumbling into Bob with what we hurl at Kabul. Where I live there's no falling ordinance, but it's not inconceivable the people dodging those shells might have also been out buying spinach.

Several blocks from my front door I'm fumbling for the keys in my pocket. Nothing will happen between here and there, but that too can be unsaid if need be. The precipitous is what I take seriously, the next thing in general. I'm thinking salad, but the salad instead is the salad that interests me.

014

THE KEY IS IN the door, but before I go in I thank the squirrels for their industry and all the pretty people who didn't speak to me. I feel the tension leave my body to prepare for the wave that is coming. I listen for the lie and the miracle but tomorrow, I think, will bring better phrasing.

I put the yogurt in the fridge, two containers because, unlike the produce, its shelf life was considerable. In the bag, unbeknownst to me, was a tin of my favourite biscuits. The tomatoes would do fine on the window sill. I pull out a large jar for the oatmeal, fill it and put it back in the pantry. Finally, I place the spinach next to the knife on the cutting board. If those leaves could speak, we'd know more about spinach.

In the seventies I was a whiskey-drinking gringo and Cesar Vallejo was a cadaver in a sombrero. I had to swallow a glossary and then forget it to receive his message but, as luck would have it, poets then went wherever heads needed breaking. The words always come too late and too early, said the bard. He was teaching me to subvert my liberal education, but at Stanford they have yet to reference all the things that he told me.

In the eighties Central America was going the way of all boneyards, but it didn't matter because Dole had already secured the pineapple. Vegetables too began making sense. I wore Birkenstock to connect with the earth in general and Blanche in particular. When in Rome, as they say, don't piss in the Tiber. In countless yet distinctive cafés we listened to ballads, recited poems in support of our Latin comrades. Economists would later suggest a correlation between our then solidarity and what we now pay for coffee.

Salads were bigger then, though they've gotten smaller again. Tofu had burned through LA, inspiring the chefs of the West Village. As New York dithers so goes the world, but thanks to the Mafia you could still find a good linguini in Jersey. Coppola did what he did with those crime families, but the heads he planted on the banks of the Nung River were simply spectacular. The horror, said Marlon Brando, and that's when Americans realized they'd lost a war but gained a movie.

013

I KNOW FROM TRAVELLING with Kiki we are in so far as we are where we're going. Not here, clearly. Last week we were in the Congo, thanks to her ground-breaking work in transportation technology. Such brainstorming is common with little girls everywhere except, in some places, dreaming is susceptible to breakfast.

In Kinshasa, formerly Leopoldville, there's no fuss between blood and profit, just like in Manhattan. In Honduras Chiquita Brands International is finding new ways to skin a banana, so said a panel of experts on the HBO special I watched yesterday. A subcommittee within a larger initiative bringing technology to agriculture in developing regions. This group was tasked with studying the impact of mechanization on existing practices, its relation to hunger, hunger and hunger respectively.

It took hours to recover from the day's errands, eventually I seasoned and ate that spinach without altercation. While reading an article online about the witches of Salem, how torture brings us together. Suffice to say burning women is now frowned upon in the Boston area.

Muslims say the darndest things upon ingesting a little water through a common rag to modulate oxygen. Romanian operatives call that waterboarding, or enhanced interrogation techniques when speaking with their bosses in Langley Virginia. Who'd a thunk insurgents would make even better canaries than those burning witches.

Kiki is here to help me make pesto. She plucks the basil while I run the blender. A play date, she says. Ergo essential. Before we begin I prepare our workspace and wash the utensils. I don't like this part so I do it while pretending I'm Marlon Brando. I notice Kiki is counting and arranging the stems carefully after the plucking. I'm going to replant them, she explains, as apple trees and blueberry bushes so next year we can make pies.

I took Kiki home after sunset, but not before we drizzled that pesto over some butterfly noodles. My favourite, she said, better than the pasta I had last week in Italy. The geography may vary, but she says that of whatever I feed her. When I got back I warmed what was left of our repast and went upstairs to watch television. In the morning I watered and fertilized those stems, as per Kiki's instructions.

That which never comes will still come as such. Thinking is its own dislocation and salvation is wherever the body ends. Though sometimes there are delays in the form of a little flour from Denmark or Canada.

We, in the first world, recommend waiting in lieu of murder, for trucks to come, the rain to go, for a yes or a no. In Yemen they call that the future, so no different than what was promised them the last time they died.

I'm tired of a world even weeping can't fix. Bob says I don't have the stomach for it, but you'd never know it from the fun that I'm having. People have been dying without me for ages, and then again on the history channel, after South Park and Family Guy. How many times must we kill Kenny to know death is just temporary.

Atlanta was nowhere before CNN pitched its tent. They're the most trusted, but not the only stand-in for what there is to think in America. CNBC is naming names this evening, having assembled a handful of cold war soldiers from before the first Bush presidency. Generals mostly, so different than that HBO panel on agriculture. The same chieftains who would later instruct the president's begat on how finish what daddy started.

Any oilman-cum-president can start a war, but one must have heirs to kill the same people repeatedly. Bush, Bush and Bush then, because Blair is Bush too in this instance. There are a lot of Bs in that sentence, but I'm sure that's coincidence.

Those warlords are talking about Iraq after Afghanistan had already been decimated. We only agreed to a few weeks of strafing, they contend, and nobody was supposed to die incidentally. But the Iraqi people refused to be occupied, especially after Paul Bremer fired the Baathists and decommissioned their currency.

Dead is not a good look for our species and the back of a Toyota Tacoma is no place for cadavers, unless you can't see the corpse for the flowers. Those freewheeling beds, so adorned, are reminiscent of Mexican gardeners in Malibu and greater

Atlanta. Funeral processions are also good for the ratings, said Wolf Blitzer to his videographers, without sound so everyone can hear what I'm saying.

CNN hides bodies on both sides of the question. A steady oozing of dissenting analysts, as per The FCC's fairness doctrine. That's why our brains cannot bend to what Wolf says is not happening, or this sentence, for that matter. Good enough until the enemy is exposed anew in some upcoming Hollywood blockbuster. Don't think, roll, said the CIA to Kathryn Bigelow, then go home and watch all of Clint Eastwood's movies.

011

Bob's on the phone, he's looking for something to do. I'm watching a documentary and then another. Why not try skydiving, I suggest, or a game of Russian roulette with a goldfish. I eventually agree to tea and talking only during commercials. The doorbell rings as I put down the receiver and before I can hide the biscuits. Damn them new-fangled mobiles.

He goes straight to the kitchen, prepares a tray for our viewing pleasure, salmon salad on crackers with a side of olives. He puts the kettle on low, takes out a small plate for biscuits and a box of Earl Grey from the cupboard at the end of the counter. Tea after canapes, he says, as per the Queen's English.

Bob is requesting I restart the documentary already in progress. It's about the pine beetle creating havoc in the Canadian prairies. I refuse, turn instead to a piece about that redhead from Murdoch's stables, the one who hacked into a murdered girl's telephone. She resigned and was rehired to run Rupert's London operations. It's good to know the boss rewards silence.

That story is soon over as are the sandwiches. I rise for the second and final course of our soiree. It is I who will decide the cookie allotment. I return from the kitchen with tea and four biscuits exactly.

On screen Bush the acorn is peddling his memoirs. He says everything happened as it should during his presidency, though he's not sure what that was exactly. It's all in the book, he explains, and Iraq is still Iraq, but with one less tyrant.

He's lying, I told Bob … how do you know … I have the book … and … what I didn't know I don't know even more after reading it … right up your alley then … how so … like Beckett or those French guys you're always on about … sure, but without all that genius … you mean the buzzing … ah yes, the buzzing.

010

The truth's in the spittle, and Rupert buys his by the barrel. These scratches are a kind of blinking, some twitching, because you never know who's listening. People talk, while media moguls learn surveillance, but that doesn't stop me from shopping. For all of my speaking there will be a reckoning, or not, which is the same thing exactly. Did I swallow the world or the word, this prattle is the hole I was born to.

There was a Bob before Bob, but that was Bob too. On the phone he told me his visit would be mercifully quick as he was meeting someone for dinner. That's hours from now, I protested. Are you sure, he replied. Knowing full well that question would rattle me. I had no choice but to retract my statement.

A new meatless restaurant in the market and the tofu, he said, is the best in the city. He stopped short of telling me it was Blanche he'd be eating with. He's subtle that way, like a toddler closing in on the tail of a kitten.

Why eat now then, I asked … protein … I see … do you … I'm not sure … the restaurant doesn't serve meat … I got that … how are things otherwise … sometimes when the phone rings I pretend I'm sleeping … why pretend anything … so I don't have to answer it … just don't answer it … when I don't hear it you mean … how does that work … I have to pretend that too … I see … when are you meeting Blanche … I'm not … what time is dinner … six-thirty … it's six o'clock … time flies … really … arguably … but does it … it's an expression … as opposed to what.

Tomorrow Bob visits his mother so I won't have to see him. She's dead, sadly, but that in no way impacts their scheduling. She, like Bob, keeps her appointments. Life is a crossing, said [insert philosopher here]. To where is the issue, I hope it's not Winnipeg. Before leaving Bob suggested I join him and Blanche for drinks after dinner. That was hours ago so I must have refused his invitation, or he never asked and I went to bed early.

009

A YEAR AGO YESTERDAY I removed all the markings from my front door. Then I petitioned the city to unname the street that I live on. They refused. The calendar/clock on the bottom right of my screen is also a problem. I don't like it watching me. This morning I covered it over with a post-it stating the time and date of my choosing, thus erasing all discrepancy between forward and stasis.

Elsewhere the march continues. I'd need a computer with a drone at the end of it to stop that from happening. Sticky notes will do until those machines become affordable. Shouldn't be long now that the Chinese have begun replicating whatever they're making at Lockheed Martin. Soon the good people of Kabul will be looking at us looking at them, drag, click, and then they too will go to McDonalds.

There's no getting off some merry-go-rounds, so feel free to scream or croak if you have to. We're keeping the party going, said Leonard Cohen. People are just numbers, targets in waiting, for the Pentagon mostly and some for Al-Queda, part and parcel of the same algebra.

To recap, Murdoch's redhead is enjoying her London offices and the pine beetle has now reached Ontario. The president's memoirs are a hit everywhere and in Romania, just not in Iraq and Afghanistan, that's how it is when towers go missing. Suffice to say, despite Bob, it was a hell of an evening.

Speaking of New York, Blanche and I lived there in the forties. She was Rita Hayworth and I bore a striking resemblance to Humphrey Bogart. I sold arms to the British, or was it the Germans. Blanche wore a red dress, but I had to say so to see it because it was before RCA laboratories introduced us to technicolor.

I'm a cancer, astrologically speaking, random and therefore unstoppable. When I was a journalist, reportedly, but who am I to say otherwise, I preferred the myth to the scoop, the gist to the story. I simply did not need to know where I was going. Blindly, blindly, is how I still greet the morning. When I'm important or famous – why not both, said Kiki – I'll move to Manhattan so I and the moneyed can be scared together.

008

WHAT BOB DOESN'T KNOW will kill him eventually, a patch of ice or a bus, I'll decide later. He called this morning, suggested we meet over breakfast to talk about his dinner with Blanche. But I could only speak on the phone because I was in Saskatoon, or was it Stockholm, with Kiki.

I could tell by the bounce in his larynx he was elated, downright giddy. Too good to be true, he said. They kissed on a bridge under the stars or a lamppost and then walked in the rain or the moonlight. I wish I could be more specific but Bob's particulars contradict what I will later say happened.

Familiarity will dull those feelings eventually, I assured him … that's not what I want … want has nothing to do with it … I did find some of what she said unsettling … like what

… nothing definite … that's the worst … yet I felt compelled to respond … naturally … converse … obviously … construe … always … deflect … as necessary … humour … careful … amuse … that's better … entertain … there you go.

I chose life right out of the womb, and then smack because I didn't want to be there when it happened. Soon there'll be a dented chair where my spine used to be, in a room full of aged woods and poetry. This house was a pit of old memories. Not mine, not yet, but I did meet the family, the residers before me, soon after they buried their patriarch.

Before moving in I gutted the place, tossed the walls, the floors and the windows, made the space mine, as it were. That's why you don't feel its sadness, said Blanche. What used to be matters, apparently, or whatever it was I threw out with the garbage. Now I have this chair, these books and a son to greet the next occupant.

Mornings are for doings, afternoons are for shopping and at night I talk to my mother when I'm not watching television. That's how I know her death didn't happen. Contrary to Blanche's surmisings, our grief does not reside in old boards and plaster.

Allow me to explain, sound travels at three hundred and forty three meters per second, subject to atmospheric conditions. Our foregoers, and therefore my mother, do not hang in the rafters – I checked – thus all of our talking has by now left the galaxy. Somewhere in the universe she is still hollering.

007

THERE WILL BE A reckoning and it will come from heaven, or what I sometimes call meteorologic conditions. Like god, we too have learned to make hay out of nothing. We have the technology. By then I hope to be on Jupiter or Jupiter adjacent, unless the White House taps me to head the Department of Homeland Security.

It's possible, since I used to be a diplomat in Babylon. I served at the pleasure of a sparrow who reported directly to the Pentagon. Remember, he said, a wink is as good as the body count when briefing the president. What the White House doesn't know is all there is and what you're not hearing is good for the nation. That bird still makes me smile, and then spit.

In the meantime there's work to be done, but that's nothing too, spun out of dry rot and polymers. Whereas other species know to embrace their stupidity, they've learned to make do with matter as given. They have their own brand of industry, my feathered friend explained, excluding, of course, sparrows who work for the government.

That bird was completely coherent, more upright than a Manhattan tower. He went to great lengths to outline the empire's agenda in and out of Nebraska. Hunger, mostly, as inevitable as the next market bubble, followed by the boss's downward trajectory from the corner office. There'll be no absolution, no plumed salvation, not even the reckoning I alluded to earlier, or so said that bird the last time we spoke.

006

I'M GOOD AT SLEEPING, the before and the before after that is the thing I can't manage. You mean being awake, said my analyst. But I'm not familiar with the distinction he's making, from the pisser to the street and on his couch by Tuesday is what I know of therapy.

Going is more important than knowing, said the Buddha approximately. As for the tinkling, check for blood and log the frequency because if you're not on the president's or somebody's hitlist, it's everything else that'll kill you.

Death is so simple when you don't have to cover it up later. I'm a man, a woman or a three-headed chicken. I'm a corpse without a secret. Last night I dreamt the meaning of everything.

I'd happily attest, in detail and without hesitation, but the particulars were all in Hungarian.

I don't speak Hungarian, in case you've forgotten, and the world's unraveling is not reason enough to contradict what I said earlier. Still, I wrote it all down so I wouldn't have to dream it again later, and so I'd know I know everything in another language.

If a tree falls in the forest I'll be on the phone. I keep a map of my head in my head, it looks like France. Imagine the thrill when I wake up in Paris. Tonight I'll be in some jazz club, the sound of a saxophone all up in my nostrils, and by morning I'll have the stories to prove it.

Dreaming is as natural as the weather for us humans, I know for I subscribe to that channel. Turtles dream too, but that can't be corroborated. Dreaming also comes in handy for people in prison, or in line at the minimart.

Climate events are disastrous for poor people and walruses but, for a time, we'll grow more tomatoes. David Suzuki will explain it all after dinner, that's why I always take dessert in the living room. Sometimes I forget so he tells me in my sleep what he said on television. Last night he told me in a few hundred years fish will swim in the cities we drown in, and fluorescent zebras will commandeer the warehouses of Union Carbide.

Everywhere the temperature is rising. Geese were the first to detect this. They trilled and they squawked but, no matter how loud or how often, they couldn't compete with them Rolls Royce jet engines. I couldn't hear them either, nor those aeroplanes, because of my double glazed windows and central air-conditioning.

A blind man sees what he can't forget, he will learn to surmise the rest. There never seems to be enough time to unlearn what I'm seeing, not while I continue to rack up these sentences. That and television is how I beat back what's happened, what my analyst later pulls from my noggin. There's no escaping anything, what we do and don't see is written in our skin, a poet once told me. A Russian and a socialist, may god forgive him. I would, except he was dead when I met him.

I AM THE NOISE my mouth makes, a proponent of the wars that never get fought. I came here to deliver a running commentary of whatever is on television, of the weather primarily since nobody dies on that channel. I take full responsibility for the things I'm not telling you, unlike those journalists tucked safely behind their compatriot armies.

Bob says everything I think is inconsequential. As opposed to what, I wonder. Surely he's not implying there's something beyond our externalities. Such is the sound of two Bobs talking. Three, were I to subscribe to his theory, but I have yet to discern my half of that argument.

I am surviving my anonymity and lately I've taken to charting the earth's rotation, its weightless indifference to our slow moving suicide. It feels more like a gallop, a tortoise once told me, but not the one I spoke about earlier. This one runs the anthropology section at our local library. Thus well versed on the subject of dissipation, our waltz with oblivion. How exhilarating your performance, she said, for all other species.

For a time squirrels will fare better than people, rats too, until we start eating them. By then there'll be no trees and less dirt for rodents to play in. In centuries to come archeologists, descendants of that tortoise perhaps, will chronicle how we made the world better for cars and stilettos. We had to do something with the steel inside those mountains and the hides of all the cows we were eating.

God loves capitalism, why else would he have gone to such lengths to demonstrate his own scorched earth strategies. Blessed our things and services, the invariability of our collective stupidity. Where there's no ice there's no ice to speak of, said Antonio Guterres. Next year in Greenland, from where I will resume my real estate practice, and then I'll sell ocean views to mining executives.

Everybody made out like bandits in the fifties. Congress just couldn't say no to all those white boys returning from the best war ever. A chicken in every pot, a Harley and then a station wagon in the driveway. Look honey, how that old bike kept its value. A baby girl, oh well, another and finally a brother to replace all those exploded people.

America is making war safer for its men and women in uniform. Our troops are the beneficiaries of what engineers set in motion. That's why there are no pilots in the airships they're casting at Lockheed Martin, no cup holders either. In deference, they say, to those heroes who were shot down over Europe and the Pacific. The increased margins from those paired down technologies are wholly incidental, said The Wall Street Journal.

004

My inception is irrefutable, just not the name that came with it. When Blanche and I were together she'd buy me flowers for what she said was my birthday. Pre-Facebook so I cannot now consult my digital other, those gifts can't be authenticated, nor what came after. The point is I have not aged a day since Blanche left for the Rockies.

Bob's in the kitchen again. He's looking for a knife and fork to carve up his half of what I thought was my dinner. Blanche, he says, is on her way over … when … she said something about laundry … be specific … the spin cycle … why don't you go there … where … her place … it's a mess … so … it depresses me … I have somewhere to be … you don't … that's not the point … it is the point … what I do, where I go, who I see, is my prerogative … are you sure … no.

Blanche arrived between the main course and the salad. Dressing on the side, she instructed while hanging up her jacket. As always, I'd decided the seating before her arrival and staked my own place with a half eaten potato. The only chair left was askew from Bob's line of vision. He's oblivious, but Blanche sees the game I'm playing and registers her disapproval by ignoring me completely. She must know by now her contempt would only encourage me.

We're talking about international aid and Blanche's plan to take down big philanthropy. Benefactors are a force for good, I counter, so long as no one fucks with their assets. Or their taxes, says Bob. I praise the government and blame the hippies. Blanche refuses the bait, so I let the line fester while I mull up another. Slowly, as Bob will often do my work for me, by way of a look, a stutter, or the words billowing.

I pretend to focus on the lettuce because the other heads in the room aren't for cutting. I blame the church, or the government. Blanche is acquainted with my maneuverings, as I wait for a crack in their conversation. She walks from the table to the counter and back again, for napkins and such, with just enough swagger to keep the walls moaning. She's helpful like that.

003

I'VE EXPLAINED BLANCHE'S STYLE of walking to my analyst. That's why men have garages, he said … I told you that … did you … I think so … or it's common knowledge … in the air, so to speak … that's right … I hadn't thought of that.

After each session I plunge ears first into the twirling. Organize my days to make sure all of my weekends happen on television, or in New Zealand with Kiki. As the sun sets I make it a point not to look or find anything. Before sleeping I create lists in case I'm called upon to do something different.

I have annihilated my soul to save my skin, learned all I could from the squirrels in my neighbourhood. That's why they think I'm a fool or a hero, but that difference is imperceptible. This is too big for us, they say, too big in general. But I'm not worried, what I don't know I don't know even more after they say that.

In the clear light of day I pretend I'm not mad, but temperance has its price and its limits. I'm doing all I can to stop the world's turning. I'd need a wrecking ball to counter what my friends are saying, and then a dumpster for the things I'm not telling them. But I'll save those conversations for when Blanche is not wielding a fork.

Sometimes I pretend I'm the queen, the president or that Koch brother, the one that's not dead yet. It is they and not the meek who, for a time, will survive the apocalypse. In the beginning the universe was no bigger than my thumb. Kicks from the cradle, screams, cackles and mother, I presumed. It was she who turned me out and into the universe, where I had no choice but to grow my vocabulary.

I began stockpiling words. Finally, something I could use or throw, but I had grown susceptible to her charms and tactics. I couldn't even find my toes while my mother was within hurling distance. There was no defending against her magic key ring, the peaches or freshly cut figs her jangling would conjure. I waited until she left to eat them because I didn't want her to know my vulnerabilities. I must have suspected even then she was an operative, a plant, for love or some other middling orthodoxy.

002

The Aztecs built pyramids to immolate humans, but after the priesthood had a go at the pretty ones. Ecclesiasts did not believe in event planners, of the kind that took pictures. Hence there's no proof of said depravity, apart from its inevitability. That was also true of Jesuits, of clerics, except their arrangements were a little less formal so god and the pope wouldn't have to know about them. Victims were rewarded for their silence, for the truth in their stomachs, and then all they had to do was lie about it.

I must remember to disassociate from the species, from my friends in particular. I put a reminder on the fridge, next to a slate on which are the foods I'll be needing. Following which is a list of Bob's favourites so I know what not to buy in oblivion. Here, on earth, I couldn't stop him from eating.

God will provide, except when he doesn't. Let shopping be my salvation, the excursions, the surprises that are in no way diminished by knowing, by the list in my pocket. I have my staples, dry goods, mostly, some canned legumes. As for tomatoes, some months are better than others, a real crapshoot after November and don't even get me started on blueberries.

Lord, help us to get through this without you. Let soldiers be children again and don't promise them anything. The numbers are more manageable when we kill for no reason. It's true your son's dangling, his rising, is still much admired, and we're doing our best to annihilate his detractors. Perhaps then you too will have had your fill of cadavers.

Give us back our death, our place in line, or at least put it under new management. A scientist this time, of the quantum persuasion, so we can continue to thrive in these absences. Someone who does not differentiate between spirit and carrion, surely by now even you can see how they're similar. If you should see fit to correct your mistakes I agree to take back all I said, and end this thing on a fucking geranium.

001

I WAS BORN ON a day when bananas were peaches, before they acquired their differences.

Acknowledgements

A note of thanks to those early, all important readers, including Francesco Loriggio, Stephen Horne, Andre Jodoin, Ted Goossen and Brenda Sailsman. A further thanks to Brenda Sailsman for her exhaustive proofreading.

Thanks also to Michael Mirolla and the people at Guernica Editions for bringing this work into the public sphere.

Note: Earlier versions / portions of *I'll Be* were published in *Geist Magazine*.

About the Author

Claudio Gaudio is a Toronto-based writer. *Texas*, a novel published by Quattro Books, has been translated, in part, by Francesco Loriggio and included in *A Filo Doppio*, an anthology published by Donzelli Editore, in Calabria, Italy. *Texas* was shortlisted in 2013 for the RELIT Awards, and his work has appeared in ELQ (Exile Literary Quarterly), *Rampike Literary Magazine* and *Geist*, and reviewed in *Descant Magazine*. Selected readings, reviews and videos of his work are available at claudiogaudio.com.